A Love Beyond

Leslie P. García

author of *His Temporary Wife* and *Wildflower Redemption*

CRIMSON ROMANCE

F+W Media, Inc.

Published by
Crimson Romance
an imprint of F+W Media, Inc.
10151 Carver Road, Suite 200
Blue Ash, OH 45242. U.S.A.
www.crimsonromance.com

ISBN 10: 1-4405-8607-1
ISBN 13: 978-1-4405-8607-1
eISBN 10: 1-4405-8608-X
eISBN 13: 978-1-4405-8608-8

Cover art © 123RF/Julia Shepeleva

In memory of my nephew, Marine Corps Major Luke Gaines Parker. Luke died in his small plane on way to Michigan to honor a fallen fellow Marine with a flyover during services.

Because of distance—his mother, my sister Stephanie Parker McKean, never lived near to my growing family—my children and I came to know Luke best as a young adult, then a loving father and husband who inspired us all.

Almost two years after his death, Luke's mother and wife still receive words of tribute, encouragement, and love from all over the world, including correspondence from Luke's friends in Afghanistan and Iraq. A young woman in the army drove up from Georgia to Alabama to meet Stephanie—she said she owed Luke a great deal for helping her when she had difficult times in her work. He accomplished so much and made such an impact on so many that I am truly touched—and more than a little overwhelmed.

Rest in peace, Luke. And because your faith and love of family defined you even throughout your career—God bless you, and all those you loved.

Acknowledgments

Writing a book is easy. Whipping it into what you want it to be isn't. I'm extremely grateful for the dedicated professionals who help me along the way.

Erica P. Salinas—who will shortly become Dr. Salinas!—you know that I'm grateful. I go to you for teaching advice, to whin—I mean vent—and when my Spanish fails me, as it still does—being able to touch base with you at any hour of the night or day provide means more than I can say.

My siblings are all amazing, but Victoria Morgan Potter happens to be a professional editor. Sorry Vicky—terrible job choice when two of your sisters share your love of writing. On *A Love Beyond*, Vicky actually had me trying to slip her questions about plot issues as she came out of anesthesia. (I'm kidding. Sort of.) Seriously, Vicky gets requests from me to take on emergency edits, computer crashes, incompetent use of Word tracking, and issues of paranoia, fear, and anxiety—and she never lets me down! Thanks for going over every manuscript for me with such thoroughness and insight, Vicky!

Finally, I take great pride in being a Crimson Romance author. My short career with Crimson has given me solid footing in what means to have my work accepted, then polished, by an amazing group of editors. Tara Gelsomino, Julie Sturgeon, Jess Verdi, Lauren Spielberg and Jen Safrey—thanks so much!

Chapter One

On the banks of the Rio Grande, Laredo, Texas

The river, black and barely visible, slid silently past. Trees pressed close to the bank, leaving only a narrow strip along the water's edge, and AJ Owens set one foot in front of the other cautiously. She was unafraid of the water, but not eager to be found out, whether by one of the law enforcement agencies screening the river for illegal activity, or by any of the criminal agents plying their trade alongside the fabled Rio Grande. Unconsciously she tightened her hold on the worn leather reins in her hands. Slight rustling in the brush startled her, making her stiffen and stifle a gasp. Alongside her, the chestnut Thoroughbred balked, throwing his head up in alarm. His snort echoed through the still night, sending some unseen smaller animal scurrying off into deeper cover.

"Sssh," she breathed, laying a hand against the horse's face. "Steady, Goof." The gelding's nostrils flared and his head swiveled, dark eyes searching for cause to flee. After a moment, though the big horse sighed heavily and dropped his head, allowing AJ to ease him forward along the riverbank.

His hooves thudded softly on the damp ground, echoing the dull pounding of her heart. Quietly they walked, shapes moving in the darkness, screened against tall reeds and stunted brush. Where the river curved slightly, its bank jutting out into the placid waters, AJ stopped, again laying a comforting hand against the horse's head and stroking him gently.

The river was narrow here, although squinting, she could hardly make out the opposite shore, cloaked in darkness. Due to the severe south Texas drought gripping the area, it was shallow, too. Not a scenic spot along the river, by any means. But she knew what lay on the other side—whose land rose up from the river into the dry, cactus-studded Tamaulipas countryside.

Again the horse's head came up nervously and its huge body tensed as he, too, peered across the water. Far off, a coyote yipped, and dogs, closer by, barked.

A breeze stirred the undergrowth behind her, carrying with it a sound, low and plaintive, like the moan of someone in distress. Someone stricken by grief, or overcome by an agony beyond imagination. Unbidden, the legends of childhood rushed back: *La Llorona*. The spirit of a humble woman, whose husband had abandoned her. A distraught young mother had drowned her three children in these dark waters, only to realize at daybreak what she had done. Now the ghostly figure of this woman strolled the riverbanks, wailing, calling endlessly into the night wind for her children.

AJ shivered. It was lunacy, being here, and she knew it. The legend of *La Llorona*, the wailing woman, was fantasy. Real threats, concealed in the shadows just yards away, might surround her now. Drug and alien smugglers, rabid coyotes—these were the real dangers. But there was no other alternative, no way out. She tightened her grip on the reins, keeping the horse still as he struck a hoof impatiently against the ground. If worse came to worst, she'd jump on him and ride out of harm's way. But hopefully that particular race would wait. Racing a horse headlong over rough footing in the dark could wait. Giving him a final, calming stroke, she turned to lead him away from the riverbank.

• • •

Laredo, Texas

Chance Landin stood in a corner of the large, crowded room, aware that the shadows partially concealed him. As long as he remained still, he doubted anyone would notice him. That provided the perfect opportunity to scan the revelers: dancing, drinking too much, swirling in a tide of evening clothes and jewels around the party's host, clamoring for his attention. He frowned and drained the drink he held in one quick gulp. Affairs like this were evidence of just how ugly his job could be.

A woman in a transparent gown was laughing up at Mike Towers, all willingness and no reluctance. The oil man could take her into any room in this too-big house and do whatever he wanted to her. Chance breathed in deeply, let the air out slowly. The easiness of women wanting money amazed him. And disgusted him. He supposed his boss was as much to blame as anyone; the widower took what he wanted. According to his sources, the man always had. Chance stopped his head mid-shake and stretched it back instead, trying to relax his cramped neck muscles. Being a glorified bodyguard was hardly the career he'd expected, but since he'd accepted it, he'd better quit worrying about the morals—or lack of them—among this international crowd of movers and shakers.

Apparently the middle-aged woman hadn't caught Mike's fancy; he nodded dismissively at her and turned away. Lights glinted in his silver hair, and Chance watched the bright blue eyes, not yet faded by age or excess, sweep the crowd for more enjoyable pursuits. A couple hurried over to claim Mike's attention. Chance recognized them from numerous other gatherings. The man was in oil, his wife from one of the legendary South Texas ranching families. The Cantus owned sizable portions of Webb and LaSalle counties, and rumor was that the oldest Cantu son was being groomed for a gubernatorial campaign—backed by Mike Towers and his millions.

He didn't watch their conversation, instead looking around the room for problems. There were no apparent threats to his boss from these well-dressed, well-known invitees. Urbane men in tailored suits and polished boots and women in body-skimming evening gowns. No reason to expect an attack from any of them.

Still, he continued to watch the room, aware that the most recent threat on his boss's life had been received just days ago. The unsigned letter had been mailed from San Antonio, little more than two hours away. So Chance watched, in spite of the scarce chance of an attack occurring, and straightened abruptly when he saw another woman approach Mike Towers.

He hadn't seen her before. She was tall and slender, her body barely covered in a dark green sheath that displayed long, well-turned legs to perfection. Silver heels glinted as she walked. Everything she wore—or didn't—called attention to her well-tended body. She approached Mike with a slight half-smile, her hand brushing long, loose strands of hair away from her face. Her hair was an entrancing color, somewhere between the darkest shades of blonde and lightest shades of brunette. He doubted the color was natural; in fact, he suspected little about her or anyone else here was particularly natural.

Mike grinned at the newcomer and leaned close as they talked, and Chance could see right away where this was headed. The lady in the transparent black dress hadn't caught his boss's fancy, but this tall, elegant woman had him drooling. Setting his drink down on the glass-topped table in the corner, Chance headed toward the two. Danger didn't always come from disgruntled employees or from male business rivals who had suffered a loss at his boss's hands. Women could do plenty of damage. Mike should have learned that from his last wife, for God's sake. Hell, even without him having money, Chance's own ex had drummed that lesson home.

Mike nodded briefly as he approached, placing a hand on the woman's arm as he turned to Chance. Was it Chance's imagination or did the intimate gesture make the woman flinch?

"Chance, I lost track of you." The older man dropped his hand from the woman's arm and Chance knew he didn't imagine the relief in the dark green eyes she cast in his direction.

"This is AJ," he went on. "AJ, Chance Landin, my assistant."

She held out a slender hand. "AJ Owens," she announced.

He smiled politely and took her hand briefly. "No story to my name, I'm afraid. And I'm also Mr. Towers's head of security." He wasn't sure why he tossed that in. The green eyes assessed him before she turned a bright smile on his boss.

"Head of security, Mr. Towers? In Laredo, for heaven's sake?" The question indicated a knowledge of Laredo, but the accent wasn't local. She shrugged, moving smooth, bare shoulders, her breasts all but exposed under her clingy dress, making him forget her quick, clipped speech altogether.

Mike chuckled, reaching out to clasp her hand. Again, the quick, almost imperceptible distaste.

"You obviously haven't kept up with your hometown, my dear," he chided. He turned to Chance. "She hasn't been here years, you know. Doesn't know how it's changed. AJ's been in—" He stopped, clearly not remembering.

"Philadelphia," AJ supplied easily. "The City of Brotherly Love." The words came out in a sultry breath and she smiled at Mike. "But I'm from here, originally." The fool looked smitten. She wasn't the buxom, petite type he usually went for. Truth be told, he supposed Mike didn't have a "type." Anything with skirts and a smile seemed to work since he'd lost his wife. Even before that, according to rumor.

Pain stabbed through Chance's head, indicating the onset of one of his cursed headaches. He'd taken this job because it provided him the best chance he had to prove Mike, not his uncle, butchered horses for insurance money, but there was little pleasure in it. Some nights were worse than others, and this one looked bad. He'd seen a lot, but when these parties descended into cat fights and orgies and self-important men trying to impress each other—nothing he'd seen struck him as so base and degrading to the people involved. And with Mike's attention clearly centered on AJ—he wondered if she knew and really wanted to be part of it all.

"Laredo used to be safe," Mike went on, his tone self-important. "Still is, I guess, for folks with no money. But in my position …" He shrugged. "I have to be careful now. It's worse across, of course, even though things have calmed down a little."

"Oh, do you have business across, too?" Ah, a local. To Laredoans, Nuevo Laredo, Mexico, was just "across."

"Much of what I do is there," Mike explained, never hesitant to brag. "My place—my real place—is there. Actually, I have quite a bit of real estate there. My house in Colonia Longoria, the ranch, and of course, my forwarding agency and warehouse."

"Colonia Longoria?" Again, a hint of huskiness in her voice. "I remember seeing those houses when I was little. Mansions, really."

Mike basked in the admiration, as if he were responsible for the wealth accumulated from his profitable first wife. He had inherited the holdings years ago, although the titles were all in his stepson's name, circumventing Mexican red tape over border properties. Chance fought off a frown and felt the tightness return to the base of his neck. He reached up to massage the bunched muscles, and saw AJ Owens cast him a quick glance.

"Nice to meet you, AJ," he lied, giving her a quick nod. "So, now that you're here in Laredo, where are you working?"

She sighed and looked away for a moment before giving him a tight smile. "I'm not working. Yet." Although he had asked, she directed her answer at Mike. Not surprisingly. "I'm looking for a job. I'm staying in this horrendous little room in a motel with weekly rates, but I may not be able to stay in Laredo and get reconnected the way I had hoped."

"Well, gosh darn," Mike drawled. "We can't have that, can we? Look, AJ, most of these nice folks are taking the party across tomorrow. I'm gonna show 'em my place, the ones who haven't seen it, have 'em stay overnight and enjoy themselves with a little Mexican hospitality. Now if you don't have any plans, and you're livin' in a rat's nest—come on over."

AJ blinked and drew in a breath. "Well—if you're sure." She shrugged and placed a hand on Mike's arm. "I don't want to be in the way."

"Hmmph. Woman who looks like you is never in the way. It's all settled, AJ. Come stay long as you need to, meet some folks—who knows? Might be useful to us both. I have a reputation of helping out my friends, right, Chance?"

Chance nodded curtly and addressed himself to Mike. "I'm going to take a stroll around now, check on where the dogs are and that the stables are secure."

AJ looked back up at him, her expression one of clear interest. "Stables?" she repeated, and Chance nodded but waited for Mike to answer.

"Sure don't know much about me, do you, girl?" The businessman seemed to find her lack of information amusing, as he chuckled again, too loudly. "Why, I'm breeding Thoroughbreds and quarter horses that can beat the best bloodstock in the country—or will in a year or two. Like horses, do you, AJ?" he asked, looking her over with undisguised interest.

"Yes," she answered, without the breathy tease she'd used moments ago. "I've been around Thoroughbreds all my life. Had to give them up in Philly, though." She gave both men a small smile. Chance wondered how such a slight twitch of her skillfully painted lips could be so attractive. Women he met on the job rarely attracted him, partly because they were usually after Mike. More than one had expressed interest in him after being turned down by his boss, but he'd had little interest in accepting their invitations. So why had his whole body responded to a tiny half smile?

"Could I go?" AJ asked, and Mike and Chance exchanged startled glances.

"Uh—go where?" Mike rubbed a hand over his chin. "You mean, go to the stables?"

The smile she shot Mike this time was sexy, an open appeal to the man to do her bidding. I'd really like to see your horses, Mike. Memories of what I haven't had lately, I guess."

Not "*Mr. Towers*" anymore, Chance noticed grimly.

"You're not really dressed for stable duty," he told her, and Mike nodded.

"Chance is right, my dear. Perhaps another day—"

"I just want to look, not muck stalls," she protested, a frown touching her lips. Then she shrugged again. "But of course, if it's not possible—"

"Hellfire, girl, I didn't say it wasn't possible!" Mike waved a hand at Chance. "Look, get Chance here to show you the horses. I can't leave my guests, but you go ahead."

AJ smiled at Mike, then cast a glance at Chance. "I'm not sure Mr. Landin wants me to go," she murmured. Mike laughed.

"Mr. Landin wants to do anything he's told to," he assured her, then winked at Chance. "Right?"

Chance lifted a shoulder. "You're the boss," he said. "We'll be back in a few minutes." He gestured toward the door. "This way, AJ."

• • •

Walking beside Chance Landin—or a few steps behind, since her heels made keeping up with his long strides difficult on the uneven flagstone walk—AJ could feel his unspoken resentment at being forced to show her around the Towers stable. She glanced speculatively at the broad expanse of his back as he hurried. No matter what Chance thought of her, and she had noticed his gaze sweep over her scantily clad body more than once, he was the head of security for Mike Towers. By definition, then, he was the enemy. She should never have noticed the tiny sparks of flame in his dark brown eyes when they'd been introduced, or the way his light brown hair glinted in the lights from the chandelier. Her lips quirked slightly. Well, so she'd noticed him noticing her. He should have known better, when she'd clearly been coming on to his boss.

She couldn't quite suppress a shudder of revulsion. The brief dress, the artful makeup, and the provocative behavior were not really Alejandra Joanna Owens. She normally had nothing but scorn for these so-called feminine wiles. You didn't need those on a racetrack. Strength and intelligence were all you needed there. But experience was a hard teacher, and she knew exactly what men like Mike Towers wanted. So she showed a little bare skin and turned perfectly innocent words into soft little sounds of sexual interest. And the man responded just as she knew he would. *The bastard*, she thought bitterly. *The lying, cheating bastard*. But she had known how easy it would be to get him. To get her sister's widower.

Another, stronger shudder shook her.

"Cold?" Chance glanced over his shoulder at just the wrong time. With the security lights glaring harshly down, he obviously hadn't missed the shiver. She didn't miss his sarcasm. Even at this late hour, the temperature was above ninety, so she understood his thinly veiled taunt.

She forced a smile and shook her head. Her hair flopped heavily against her neck and she wished she'd put it up. Her whole body burned, more from Landin's scornful glance than from the June heat. "I'm just excited," she retorted sweetly and saw the muscles in his jaw clench. Unlike Mike Towers, Chance Landin seemed more or less immune to provocation. He might have looked, but his attitude said clearly that he wasn't buying.

And that was fine. Staying out of Mike Towers's bed while getting what she wanted would be tricky enough. She knew enough about the man to know that he promised and cajoled, then took what he wanted if he couldn't get it any other way. He'd destroyed her sister Gina's life, so he couldn't hurt AJ more than he already had. But other men could, if she let them. Chance clearly thought she'd stepped off a street corner into his boss's glitzy world. His disgust with her was evident and handy. Looking to the future, she would have to deal with him on a professional level, finding ways to slip under and through whatever security arrangements he oversaw. But she wouldn't have to worry about him wanting her.

They reached the door and Chance paused, this time facing her as he talked.

"If you know Thoroughbreds, you know they tend to be hot-blooded and easily riled," he warned. "Disturbing them this late isn't a good idea, so I hope this visit down memory lane will be quick. And quiet."

She nodded briskly. "Sure. Like I told Mike, I'm not going to muck stalls." She slipped past him into the wide, air-conditioned corridor of the barn. The smell of horses and hay surrounded her, more familiar and comfortable than the expensive perfumes that had eddied around her in sweet, nauseating waves up at the house. Quietly she walked down the row of stalls, pausing to peer into the shadows.

Brass nameplates outside each stall identified the pedigreed royalty inside. Most of the horses were dozing, one or two lying in the straw, the others standing in the backs of their stalls.

The name she was looking for didn't hang from any of the stalls. She hadn't expected to find it, but she had hoped.

"Rose Slew," she murmured, running a finger over the cool brass. "Is she really a Slew mare?"

He shrugged. "I'm head of security, not the trainer."

Fighting her disappointment, AJ nodded. "Sorry. Silly question."

He leaned on the half open door and peered into the stall. The mare nickered and came over, blowing softly on his arm, and he smiled and reached out to scratch the base of her ear.

"Friends?" AJ asked pointedly and he grinned wryly.

"So maybe I have a passing interest in these guys," he admitted, relenting. "Yeah, Mike's really high on her. She goes back to Slew."

AJ didn't say anything, lost for a moment in memories. Way, way back, the famous Thoroughbred Seattle Slew had won the Kentucky Derby, Preakness, and the Belmont Stakes. The Triple Crown. As adolescents, helping their mother with the tiny racing stable she had taken over when her husband died, Gina and she had dreamed of having horses like the immortal Slew. Incredibly, they had come close. So close.

Ruthlessly shoving away the pain, she, too, patted the bay mare, then turned and looked around the corridor. "Nice mares. But does he send them all out for servicing? I thought he probably had stallions, too." Her heart picked up its pace as he considered her question. Pushing him didn't seem wise, but she needed him to show her the stallions. Keeping her face expressionless was an effort, when she wanted to plead. Or demand. After a long sigh and a deliberate glance at his watch, he again waved her toward a door.

Outside the door, more flagstone wound its way across a vast expanse of yard to a duplicate of the first barn, pristine and white under the bright lights. Paddocks, neatly railed in white, took the place of the barbed-wire fences more commonly found on south Texas ranches. Elaborate and expensive, the facilities here were like the best of those in Kentucky or near Ocala, Florida. High upkeep, but she doubted that Mike Towers knew or cared about the time spent keeping those fences up. It didn't matter. Excitement simmered through her as Chance pushed the door open enough to usher her through. She was going to see the stallions.

The stallion barn was designed to give its residents space. There were only four stalls, and each one was separated from the neighboring stall by a short corridor, wide enough to keep restless and territorial stallions away from each other.

The first stall held a magnificent buckskin quarter horse, unbothered by the nighttime intrusion into the stable. Calm and disinterested in their presence, he stayed where he was, even when AJ coaxed him to come closer.

The occupant of the next box raised a ruckus. Hooves clattered on wood even before they approached and AJ stayed well back when a dark, almost black head thrust out, warning them away with gusty bursts of air.

"They tell me this one's bad news," Chance offered, although AJ had already figured that much out. "But some of his colts have done really well, so he's in great demand."

AJ nodded. She'd heard the name. *Incendido*, Spanish for "on fire." One of his colts had won the Kentucky Derby a year ago, driving his value as a sire up. He hadn't been much of a racehorse himself, retiring after never winning a race as a two-year-old. It happened. Besides, she didn't care about him.

The next stall was empty. *Bold Attempt*. She looked at the plate and moved on to the last stall, glancing at the name on the door.

Rebelde Dorado. Golden Rebel. Her heart pounded, and as she stepped up to the door, breathing hurt. The stall was empty. For several long seconds, she couldn't force herself to turn around. When she did, looking at Chance Landin was hard.

I knew this, she reminded herself, angry that she felt overwhelmed by disappointment and loss. *I knew.*

"Just the two stallions?" She made the question light, trying to sound interested as a horsewoman. Or a gold digger. Not as Rebel's legitimate owner.

Landin shrugged. "I haven't worked for Mike long. I think I heard that Bold Attempt had to be put down. He wasn't here when I came."

"That's terrible," AJ said softly, and meant it. "So I guess you don't know about the other horse?" She peered again at the engraved plate, hoping she wasn't overdoing it. "What's the name? *Rebelde Dorado*?"

Chance lifted an eyebrow. "Pretty good Spanish, for a Philadelphia girl."

"Not Philadelphia. I'm a Laredoan, remember? My mom's maiden name was *Rivera*—Spanish was her first language. We've been away forever, that's all." She didn't mention how long she'd been away, though, or that she'd studied Spanish in college to regain her fluency. She had to force herself to ask her next question. "So do you know what happened to this one?"

Just for a moment, she thought he didn't know. Or wouldn't answer. Was that suspicion flickering in his shadowed eyes? Then he glanced at the stall and turned to walk back toward the door they'd come in. She followed him.

"You're awfully interested in Rebel," he said.

"I saw him run." That answer was honest and innocent enough at the same time. Rebel had owned the racing world, if only briefly. "I didn't know who his owner was. But then, I don't follow racing that closely anymore." She smiled at Chance, a real smile, instead of the deliberately coquettish one she'd offered Towers. "He looked beautiful on television."

Chance nodded. "Magnificent animal. I've only seen him a couple of times, though. Mike has him standing at his ranch in Nuevo Laredo this season." He turned back toward the door, waving her ahead of him.

Almost halfway back to the house, a long, plaintive wail sliced through the night air. Unending, a cry of unbearable pain and grief that raised the hair on AJ's arms. She shivered again, hard this time. Beside her, Chance tensed, looking around intently, and from somewhere nearby, large dogs barked threateningly.

"Probably a coyote," Chance murmured, and in spite of his dislike for her, he laid a comforting hand on her shoulder. Warm and heavy, his hand evoked another shudder of an entirely different kind. Whether he realized the difference, she didn't know, but he slowly removed his hand.

"I've heard coyotes," AJ retorted, her head cocked, listening for any other faint sounds in the night around them. "Not recently, of course, but I don't remember them sounding like that. Mountain lion, maybe—but not here. Not in Laredo."

Chance shrugged. "Then?"

AJ looked up at him. "*La Llorona*?" she suggested, teasingly, although the wail could well have come from some poor, deranged soul. From a woman who'd bet everything on love and lost. Like Gina.

She expected him to laugh. Or scoff. Instead, he stared down at her, his face hard, dark, and emotionless.

"Maybe," he said laconically. "There's a world of hurt in the world." For a long moment, he held her riveted there by the intensity of his gaze, his presence. Then he gave another shrug, and turned away from her. "Let's get you back. The dogs are out and you're not safe alone."

"I'm not alone," she said, although she had to hurry to keep up with him. "I've got you," she added breathlessly, partly to annoy and partly because he walked too fast in his hurry to ditch her.

The glance he cast her menaced. Said clearly that he wasn't amused. Or attracted. But he didn't speak. Neither of them spoke until he pulled the side door open to let her back into the crowded ballroom.

"Good night, AJ," he said politely, but his eyes were filled with distaste as, from across the room, Mike Towers waved at them. "I hope you enjoyed your tour."

His dislike and lack of respect hurt, she realized. Silly, since she wanted him to dislike her. To stay away from her. She managed a final, flirty smile. "More than you can imagine," she purred seductively. "I'll tell your boss how good you were to me."

Anger tightened his face and thinned his lips, but he said nothing, just turned and disappeared around the corner of the house. Mike Towers was coming toward her, all smile and swagger. Undoubtedly, he thought she'd be grateful to him for the midnight tour. She couldn't let him know how repulsive she found him. Not yet.

She drew in a deep breath and tilted her chin up in determination. Towers had stolen her horse and her dreams. That was nothing. Gina had taken her life because of him. AJ had no proof, but she knew. And nothing would protect him from her plans for revenge. Not his money, not his power. And certainly not a man like Chance Landin, no matter how diligent he was as head of security.

Far off, so faint she might be imagining it, a high, keening wail echoed in her ears.

"*A world of hurt*," Chance had said.

She had taken the words at face value then. But a sudden, strong awareness told her his words weren't meant to comfort. He was warning her. No. More than that. Threatening her.

Chapter Two

Nuevo Laredo, Mexico

Butterflies were everywhere. Frail, tiny bodies drifted in waves and swirls around the car as it crept down the drive between narrow banks of bougainvillea, blazing in the early afternoon sunlight. The carefully planted bushes soared to impressive heights, a solid bank of fuchsia, hiding the manicured lawns behind them. At least, AJ supposed the lawns were as well kept as the bougainvillea, although on her right side, she knew that the vegetation must eventually dissolve into the tangle of bush and reed that banked the Rio Grande.

Rio Bravo. She corrected herself with a tiny, grim smile. Here on the Mexican side, the name changed from "big river" to "angry river." Given her emotions and intentions, she suspected Rio Bravo was much more appropriate. She braked as a small, drab roadrunner scooted across the drive in front of her. The bird's name in Spanish, *paisano*, meant country man, someone who shared the culture and heritage of the land. Unlike Mike Towers, though he had certainly taken advantage of his first wife's money and real estate holdings.

The interminable road curved more sharply, and at last the bougainvillea walls gave way to great, green expanses, dotted with clumps of pampas grass and occasional plantings of roses. Glancing around, AJ couldn't find any sign of the Dobermans Mike had warned her about.

She supposed that they were in kennels for the moment, since the businessman expected a large contingent of guests to arrive before the poolside dinner scheduled at nine. The drive turned again and the Towers mansion loomed ahead on the left, flaunting the man's wealth and arrogance. Two stories of gleaming white soared into the blue summer sky. Grecian columns supported a broad balcony, and climbing roses spilled onto the porch and scaled elaborate trellises on each end of the wide veranda. A fountain spouted water into the air, creating a million dancing rainbows in the bright sunlight. *Paradise.* AJ exhaled. Had that been her sister's first thought?

Reluctantly she eased the car over to the parking area, and looked around once more for the dogs. They were still not in evidence, and she unbuckled the seat belt and opened the door.

The Dobermans materialized out of thin air, or perhaps just from behind the rose bushes, a pack of huge, silent killers baring shiny white teeth at her, but mercifully, not attacking. She hesitated, unsure whether pulling her leg back into the car would provoke them into lunging at her.

"*Capitan*! *Flaco*! Back, boys! Back!"

AJ recognized the voice without turning from the dogs. Chance Landin appeared out of nowhere and called off his attack dogs. The Dobermans obeyed immediately, falling away from the car and disappearing around the corner of the house like shadows driven by a rising wind. With a small sigh of relief, AJ slid out of the car.

"Talk about being glad to see someone." She smiled, ignoring the irritation that pulled his brows low and tightened his bronzed face. Even angry, he was a compelling man. Authoritative. And she couldn't complain about that. A pack of killer guard dogs probably wouldn't have much respect for some wuss.

Chance nodded curtly. "Hello, AJ. Mike mentioned you were coming. But I assumed you'd be here later. With the rest of the …" He fished for a word. "Crowd."

She raised an eyebrow. "You don't sound happy about your boss inviting a few friends over for some fun."

He shrugged. "His place. But if he's seriously worried about his safety, he shouldn't invite strangers over."

"Surely you're not worried that someone like little ol' me could hurt big ol' Mike Towers?" she cooed, determined to manipulate his contempt and dislike to her advantage. The less he wanted to be around her, the easier her job would be.

He didn't answer immediately, just closed the short distance between them. His body was taut, his obvious physical strength and height were intimidating. "Drop the act," he said tersely.

She blinked at his unexpected response. "Act?"

"Yes, act. You don't like Towers." The smell of his spicy aftershave teased her, mingling with the too-sweet smell of some nearby gardenias. His eyes were dark brown daggers, spearing her, refusing to let her turn away. "All that come-on stuff, all that panting—"

"Panting?" AJ stared at him in outrage.

Chance smiled, and dimples teased his cheeks. "That's better. I bet that high, squeaky voice is a lot more normal than the one you use on Mike Towers. And on me."

The devil. If he read her that easily, she was in trouble. AJ turned to close the open car door, calculating how to deal with Towers's head of security. *Head of security*, she reminded herself. The man who could bring it all down—if Towers didn't. Turning back, she offered a half-shrug and a smile.

"Experience is a hard teacher," she ventured truthfully. "Men don't like their women to—what did you say? Squeak?"

Humor lightened his expression, but only briefly, as he thought over what she'd said. "Their women?" he probed. "As in … Towers's women?"

She sighed. "None of your business, Mr. Landin. He very kindly invited me to stay—as long as I want to—while I figure out where my life's going. I accepted. And just for the record, I don't despise Mike Towers."

"No?" He shook his head, moving away a little and looking around the elegantly kept lawns, then back at her. "Look, keeping Towers safe is my business. My job." He paused. "I'm good at my job." Again, a warning note couched in the matter-of-fact words.

"How much harm can I do?" AJ demanded, frustrated by his perceptiveness.

"Maybe none. Maybe a lot." Chance frowned, hesitated, before adding, "His last wife did a bang-up job in the damage department. Redefined the word *harmed*."

AJ had taken a tentative step toward the house, but his words froze her in her tracks. Gina? Gina had harmed Mike Towers? Her hands clenched momentarily, before she remembered how much was at stake here. He couldn't know how upset, how outraged, she was. Opening her hands, she glanced over her shoulder at him. "How like a man to blame a woman," she offered. "If there was harm, I doubt it was one-sided." Then she managed a faint smile. "But Mike's marriages are no concern of mine. At least, not any previous marriages."

He didn't answer, just waved a hand at the house. "Go on in," he suggested, "before you get sunstroke. Mike had to run an errand, but the house staff will take good care of you."

AJ shook her head slightly and frowned. "Look, Chance, let's make a deal. I won't coo at you—and you don't patronize me, okay?"

He looked at her blankly. "Patronize? I—"

"I don't need your protection from the sun and I don't need a house staff to wait on me."

"Prickly, aren't you?" he asked, and she shrugged, but didn't answer.

He was silent briefly, watching her before he matched her shrug with one of his own. "You did almost get torn to bits by the dogs," he said, a little smugly. "You probably can't fend for yourself nearly as well as you think you can."

He left the car and walked toward her, a towering, menacing man. Not a spare inch of meat on him, but all breadth and muscle and height. He probably pumped iron, she thought. Beefed up for the job. Whatever, he was impressive—and the enemy's right-hand man, she reminded herself for the thousandth time since they first met. He thought she couldn't fend for herself? Satisfaction tugged her lips into a quick, secret smile. Let him think that until the day he found Rebel's stall empty and she and the stallion long gone.

"Amused by the idea of guard dogs attacking?" he asked, with consternation.

"Not at all," she assured him, her grin widening. "Just thinking." She trailed her eyes slowly downward over his body. "And now, if you'll excuse me?" She nodded at him as she turned back toward the house. "I'd hate to get sunstroke."

• • •

Chance glanced at his watch. Eight thirty. He walked over to his window and glanced down into the huge patio behind the house, still almost empty. Not surprising, really; here, dinner at nine meant dinner at eleven or twelve. Traditions were to come late, eat late, stay late. Towers had invited quite a few of his friends. He often did, although his summer get-togethers weren't as common as the ones he held every fall for his hunting buddies.

Chance smiled grimly. He'd learned a lot about Towers. Someone might think he'd worked here for ten or fifteen years, instead of just two. Two years. Had time ever moved more slowly? He moved away from his bedroom window, crossing the elegantly tiled floor to the dresser, and slowly pulled out the top drawer, rummaging under his personal items until he found the small metal case.

He really should hide it, he supposed. But Towers trusted him, the fool, and who else would look? If they did, who would recognize the photo of the laughing, middle-aged man inside the case? Even Mike Towers wouldn't recognize his former trainer, the man whose life he had destroyed so meticulously, with such calculation. That man, Robert Newhouse, looked nothing like the man agonizing in a cell in Arizona, incarcerated for insurance fraud and the gruesome slaughter of three of the world's highest-priced horses—horses Mike Towers had given him shares in. Nothing like the man who loved Chance like a son; who had taken care of him and Chance's mother when her husband was killed overseas.

Before Robert Newsome went to work for Mike, he had been a respected trainer, able to work miracles with any horse that stepped onto a track or into a show ring. His reputation of kindness and insight into a horse's psyche was legendary. Now, he was loathed when remembered, but largely forgotten.

His wife Emily remembered. She lived in Laredo now, clinging to Chance's generosity and the hope of one day finding proof of her husband's innocence. She believed in his abilities to clear Robert, more than he himself did. He'd thought once he managed to secure a job with Mike that the rest would be easy, and sometimes thought that Emily expected too much. Four years—two finding out who the real culprit was, then these last two getting within striking distance of Mike—seemed interminable. What if Emily gave up before he could accomplish anything?

There was so little hope, so little time. Too much had happened already. He thought with piercing sadness of the baby Emily lost during Robert's trial; Emily almost lost her mind. She was still seeing a therapist, after a failed suicide attempt nearly ended her own life. What if Chance let her down? Saved neither her nor his uncle?

Robert would have never killed a horse. His uncle's kindness ran deep. His tenacity in finding cures for injured horses was well known. But character wasn't proof, and he had no proof. His uncle didn't have an alibi. Mike had invited Emily to join

María, his housekeeper, and Ella, his secretary at the time, for an overnight shopping trip to Dallas. He'd arranged for their flight, their ground transportation, and insisted on paying. Mike called it a bonus. To Chance—and in hindsight, to his uncle—it was the lead card in framing an innocent man. And so for these four years, Chance had been pursuing the truth, without success.

Initially, he'd been hopeful. Some of the grooms who helped Robert off and on had given Chance a lead: someone named Bone. *El Hueso*, in Spanish. The grooms claimed to have seen Bone talking to Mike Towers on several occasions, even visiting the stable and looking at the horses. Unfortunately, Chance's optimism faded quickly. The man might better have been named "Ghost." He had yet to materialize along any of the paths Chance had pursued, and time and hope were running out.

As essential as Bone might be to his investigation, though, the nugget of information one of the grooms had given him kept his hopes alive. The man's name was Eli, and he was one of Mike's newer grooms—a timid young man with three children.

"You can't tell anyone I met with you," he whispered to Chance after agreeing to meet him at the horse show in Tucson. "If Towers or Bone find out—"

"Find out what?"

"There was a picture," Eli said so quietly Chance had to strain to hear. "I don't think anyone but me knows. Bone is—he's evil. I told the police Robert wasn't guilty. That he couldn't hurt a horse."

Eli hadn't been able to meet Chance's eyes as he continued. "That night, someone knocked at my door. Late. My wife and kids were asleep. I opened the door and Bone held out this—this horrible picture of one of the horses." He stopped and swallowed hard.

"He told me Mike would always know where to find me. That if Mike wanted him to—God, Chance—Bone said he could do the same thing to my family as the horses." Eli stopped and sniffed, looked away again, then turned back to Chance, distraught. "I couldn't go to the police. They hadn't believed me and I didn't have the picture anyway. I—I couldn't."

He'd been furious at first that Eli lacked the courage to approach the police, but as he learned more about both Mike Towers and the power he wielded, he couldn't fault him. Who could risk their own children, given the horror of those poor horses' fate?

When the path in Arizona ended abruptly with the disappearance of Mike Towers's probable henchman, but the promise of other physical evidence came to light, Chance forged ahead along the only path that seemed open. He had a master's degree in criminal justice, along with certification as a peace officer in Texas. He'd studied martial arts during and after his time in college. He'd even worked in security for a Dallas firm with wealthy clients around the world, and the firm's recommendation got him a job with Mike Towers when he returned to Texas, his home state.

Chance snapped the case shut and returned it to the drawer, then walked back to the window. Maids bustled around arranging food on a buffet table, while men in white *guayaberas,* pleats gleaming neatly, carried trays of drinks to the few guests who had arrived already. Chance looked down upon the blue expanse of pool, with its ostentatious waterfall at one end, and clenched his fists.

Towers had destroyed his uncle's life in the blink of an eye. And Chance would return the favor—at any cost. Towers would fall. Die. The cold, hard word stabbed through his mind. He didn't know if he could kill. But Towers—

A sudden rap on his door startled him and he jerked guiltily, almost as if the person outside could have fathomed his thoughts.

"Yes?"

"*Señor* Chance?"

Relief flooded through him and he hurried over to pull the door open. "Rosita, come in," he invited, reaching out to relieve the young woman of the baby she carried. She did, smiling up at him provocatively. She pursued him, but he avoided her advances and valued her friendship. And he cherished the time she let him spend with the little guy, too.

The baby cooed and patted his cheeks with pudgy little fists, laughing when Chance threw his head back, pretending to dodge the insistent blows to his face. "Easy, there, Gordito," he grinned, using the baby's pet name. No one called the baby by his given name—would be surprised, in fact, that he knew the given name. He hugged the baby close and thought about his unborn nephew. Had Emily not lost the child, he would be almost four now.

"¿*Que pasa*?" he asked, gently removing the child's fingers from a too-intimate exploration of his nose.

Rosa grinned. "The little one adores you," she announced. "And your nose!"

"I have no idea what the fascination is," he said.

She shrugged, an exaggerated movement meant to call attention to the low-cut knit top she wore. He determinedly ignored the display and kissed the baby's cheek.

"You're wanted downstairs," she told him curtly, and he smiled at her.

"*Ayy*, Rosita," he scolded, the affectionate form of her name taking the sting out of his words. "Give it up. I'm not worth your time or trouble." He handed the baby back to her reluctantly, then leaned over to kiss her forehead. "Friends, okay?"

She nodded slowly. "*Bueno*. Friends. But you could be much more—we could be."

"Who wanted me?" he asked, briskly, discouraging any more personal conversation. "Towers?"

"Yes. He's in his study. He hasn't gone out yet." Her tone filled with disdain, as it always did when she spoke of the man. She'd never confided the reasons, but Chance suspected she, too, had an agenda for staying here. He doubted she was here for the money.

In fact, Towers paid only certain members of his staff well. Yet in spite of her contempt and dislike of the man, he knew she'd followed him here from Arizona, as had the housekeeper María and several of his other staff members.

She turned away, carrying the baby down the hall, calling over her shoulder. "Go quickly. He's in an awful state, even for him."

"Any idea why?" Chance asked, and she shook her head.

"No. But I'm taking *mi angelito* away right now!" She hugged the baby and hurried on toward the nursery. Towers spent little time or attention on the baby, but given his temper, it seemed well advised to keep the child away from the man. Poor Rosa. He didn't envy her position at all, for whatever reason she stayed. Maybe his plans for Towers would affect her in some positive way. What was that Spanish saying: "*Muerto el perro, se acaba la rabia*"? The logic held in English. Kill a rabid dog, stop the disease. Sighing, he headed down the curved staircase to the first floor.

"In trouble, Landin?" Jaime Bustos asked as Chance reached the bottom step. Jaime, a large, beefy man, held the same position he did, without the title, and the two of them didn't like each other. Chance didn't bother replying, just ignored him as he usually did when they crossed paths. (As requested—to include more on Jaime)

The chandeliers were all on and light glinted off the gold-framed mirrors and decorative hangings in the hall that lead to the study. He knocked and pushed the door open when Towers ordered him in.

"What's up, Mike?" he asked. While he usually used the more formal "Mr. Towers" around guests, the millionaire had always insisted on being addressed informally in private. He seemed to view Chance as one of his cronies rather than an employee. Usually. When something upset him, he treated Chance like anyone else in his employ: as a not-quite intelligent piece of furniture to be kicked and pushed around, or discarded completely. He was upset, his face livid, as he waved a paper in Chance's direction.

"Did you see this?" he demanded, agitated, and Chance shook his head.

"What is it?"

"A threat! A threat on my life, and you're nowhere to be found! What the f—what the hell am I paying you for?"

"May I see that?" Chance kept his own tone businesslike, calm. Upsetting Mike further served no purpose.

The page Towers handed him was nondescript copy paper. The single sentence of type said, "You're a dead man." The line was at the top of the page—nothing unusual about the spacing, the spelling, nothing unusual at all as far as he could see, except maybe that it was in English instead of Spanish. Here, on the Nuevo Laredo side, one might have suspected an attack from Towers's Mexican enemies, rather than those from the U.S. side.

If, of course, there were anything at all to this. He looked at the letter one last time, then at his boss, who was pacing back and forth across the large, carpeted study in agitation.

"How did you get this?" he asked, and Mike turned and came back over to the desk, letting himself collapse into his leather chair.

"A little boy came up to the truck while I was in the bank," he said with disgust. "Jaime saw him walk right up. When the kid stepped up on the bumper, he yelled and the kid ran. But when Jaime checked, he found the letter inside the bed. The kid dropped it in."

Chance considered the information, rubbing his chin thoughtfully. Jaime again. Mike trusted him. But Chance always thought his behavior was off in some way he couldn't identify. In fact, many of the recent incidents of implied or direct threats had reached Mike when Jaime was watching over him. "You should have taken me instead of Jaime," he muttered after a moment, and

Towers banged a hand on the top of the polished desk, rattling the framed pictures and gold pen stand.

"Never mind Jaime! He's been with me since before you were, and I trust him absolutely! We've been over this before! What I want to know is—can you keep me safe or can't you?"

"No." Chance clipped the word, meeting Towers's incredulous gaze implacably. "No, I can't—if you insist on ignoring my advice and doing whatever you want. You travel with those armed guards of yours—all of whom had records when I checked them out— and you make needless trips without even telling me. Here, I can protect you. Out there—you've seen the carnage." He shrugged. "I hope Jaime is as trustworthy as you think he is."

Mike worried his lip with his teeth while he fiddled with a spotless notepad on his desk. "Look," he said finally, in a conciliatory tone, "you have to understand. Things aren't the same here and back in the States. That's why I usually don't have you over here. I hired you mostly to watch the Laredo place, and didn't think I'd need you over here in Nuevo Laredo. You're more useful on the other side in some ways. You can carry over there, but since you're American, you can't legally carry a gun on this side. Wouldn't worry me if you carried without telling anyone out in public, but if you got caught, keeping you out of prison wouldn't be worth the time or money I'd have to pay to fix it."

Chance paced over to glance out the window, thinking. "I can head on over to Laredo," he offered. "I came because you told me, to, but—" He held his breath, hoping that Mike wouldn't take the suggestion. He'd pretty much exhausted his search for anything related to his uncle's case when he'd been on the Texas side. Mike might be the devil in amiable disguise, but he attended civil functions and donated to a lot of good causes, so he had been away from the house a lot. If the pattern held true here—

"Hell, boy, if I'd wanted you there, I'd have left you there." Mike snorted. "I decided I wanted you here where there's more going on. Kidnappings, theft, and the cartels fighting in the street—you're good to have around. No one cares if you carry a gun on these grounds, so you're worth plenty to me here on the ranch. But out on the streets, you'd just call attention to me. And Jaime and the others may have records, but they're loyal—because no one can pay them more than I can, and they know that. They're big here, because of me—and they know that, too. Yeah, I've seen the carnage. And the bodies hanging from bridges. No way in hell am I going to end up like that. My men are from here. You're not. They don't call attention to themselves like you do. I don't have to worry about them. Trust me on that. Whoever wrote that threat isn't from this side, I'm almost sure. The warning is in English."

Chance waved the paper, which he still held, impatiently in the air. "Damn it, Mike, what does that prove? It's not difficult to translate one sentence from Spanish to English."

Towers colored and scowled, but didn't contradict him. "So … do you think it's from this side? And for real?"

Chance put the letter back on the desk, tightening and relaxing his shoulders to relieve tension. He couldn't afford to upset Mike enough that he lost his job, and his boss didn't like being confronted. He had to keep his job, while keeping the man alive until he had the proof he needed. Some days he could barely keep from just walking away. He couldn't. Robert and Emily needed him, and he owed them. "Real, yes," he agreed. "We'd be stupid not to think that. But I'm actually inclined to agree that it's not from this side."

"Why?"

"Don't you watch the news?" Chance supposed he was being rude to his boss, but the man's ignorance annoyed him. "Things may have been quiet recently, but if you've made enemies—here you would have been gunned down in your car, not warned so that you could defend yourself."

Towers nodded. "True." He gave a heavy sigh of relief. "You know, I'm not going to worry. Not tonight." He forced a smile and ran a hand through his gray hair. "That's your job. And I have a party."

"Just don't leave it without telling me, okay?"

"Sure." Towers grinned at Chance, his anger and worry fading away. "Unless of course—but never mind. You're not interested in my little encounters."

"You know, even a woman can pull a trigger," Chance muttered, but Mike just laughed.

"Some of 'em sure do pull my trigger," he said. "Got some fine ones coming out tonight, too. Party time!"

Chance didn't answer, thinking abruptly, unwillingly, of AJ perched on the car seat, one long, shapely leg dangled in front of him. Temptation. But she was here to party with the big man, and he couldn't let himself be tempted. He had to keep Mike from harm, until he could prove his uncle's innocence. Then—his eyes hardened. Then he would become Towers's worst enemy.

"Course," Mike went on, lewdly, "the little filly I plan on riding isn't too well broke just yet, but she'll come around."

Chance didn't ask, but his boss filled in the blanks anyway. "You remember her," he added. "That AJ girl—what was her last name?"

"Owens," Chance answered shortly, and Mike chuckled.

"Yeah, that's her. Put on airs when I invited her. Said she just broke off an engagement and isn't sure they won't patch things up." He stood and straightened his sleeves with fleshy hands. His diamond ring glinted in the study's soft light. The grin he shot at Chance was malevolent. Full of evil. "Oh, yeah, she'll come around. I'll just play her game for a day or two and then—" He snapped his fingers as if calling a dog. Chance wanted to slug him. Instead he turned toward the door, carefully keeping his face expressionless.

"Time for me to make the rounds," he said.

"Don't be a stranger around the pool," Mike called after him. "I might be attacked. By girls in little bikinis." The man's raucous laughter followed him out into the heat of the summer night. "Or better—buck naked.

Chapter Three

AJ leaned against the wall in the hall and made herself breathe deeply, trying to ease the pounding in her head and the queasiness threatening to become full-blown nausea. She hadn't stayed very long at the first of Mike's parties—just long enough that once he'd asked her a second time to come across "for a few days" she felt comfortable telling him she'd go home and make arrangements to leave her room for the time being. In the time she'd been there, the guests partied, but more decorously than they were doing here. She sighed. She hadn't lived a sheltered life; her mother Betty and father AR barely made ends meet raising Thoroughbreds. They had raised their two daughters in some rough-and-tumble places, safe but not always decorous. She'd seen a lot. But to turn a corner and find groups of guests indulging in very public sex, to be offered a steady stream of invitations to join in and a variety of drugs she didn't even recognize, appalled her.

Was this what had happened to her sister? Had Gina seen her husband at parties like this, surrounded by women who wanted his money—and made no bones about what they'd do to get it? Did they behave differently out of respect for Gina when she was alive? Somehow AJ doubted it.

A woman passed her on her way to one of the bathrooms, just down the hall. Gloria Whitehall was wealthy and well known in Texas social circles. AJ had heard her name often since she had moved back to Laredo. The woman's blond hair was a mess and her lipstick was smeared. She shot a brief, dismissive glance at AJ as she passed. Fortunately, though, she didn't speak. AJ had nothing to say to her. Or to any of these people.

With some effort, she pushed herself off the wall and debated which direction to take. Sooner or later, she'd have to return poolside. If she didn't, Mike might look for her. He'd been drinking all evening, and even though finding Rebel was at stake, she really didn't want to deal with him tonight.

Tomorrow, she would deal with him. She'd put on her sexiest outfits and she'd pretend she wanted to be his next plaything. But she wouldn't lower herself to sleeping with that bastard— the man who had stolen her horse and destroyed her sister. She wouldn't prostitute herself. At first, she'd refused to accept Mike's invitation. Then, when he wheedled, she'd made up an imaginary fiancé. They had broken up recently, she lied, but she had hopes that things would work out, and she wanted to remain faithful to him until she decided whether or not she could return to him.

"You have to understand something very clearly," she'd told him, feigning sincerity. "While you're a very attractive man, I just don't think I'm interested in anyone right now. I can't take a chance on ruining everything with my fiancé. I—I planned on marrying him, and that was everything to me. So until I know for sure that it's over—I won't get involved with someone else. If it doesn't work"—she looked directly at him—"then I cut my losses and move on. "He'd insisted that his invitation was innocent and friendly, and that her stay could be open ended. That she was attractive and good company, and that he just enjoyed having company. He pointed out that many if not all of his guests would stay overnight, and some might stay longer than that. He assured her that she was safe, that he wouldn't demand a sexual relationship. They both knew he was lying. He'd expect her to sleep with him, sooner or later. And until she could find Rebel and put her plan into motion, she had to string the man along. She whispered a silent prayer for success, knowing her plan was shaky at best. Knowing, too, there weren't any other options.

She had hoped fervently to find Rebel on the Laredo side, because proving ownership would be simple. She and her mother had Rebel's papers and could go to court; Mike Towers's money wouldn't matter when there would be overwhelming evidence that he belonged to them.

Not so here, though, with a different legal system and where money often dictated justice. She couldn't take a chance on finding honest lawyers and judges in Nuevo Laredo. Towers was simply too powerful to take on here.

She felt cornered, even though at the moment she was alone. With no other place to go, she decided to retreat to the small but luxurious room she'd been given upstairs. She could also slip in a quick call to her mother, letting her know that she was fine. There was no chance that the festivities around the pool would end any time soon, and she'd go back out later, make some excuse to keep Mike at bay, and then call it a night. Tomorrow would be busy. She'd have to finagle a trip to his stables.

Would he send her with Chance again, she wondered? Probably not. She sighed. Chance had appeared and disappeared throughout the evening, rarely doing more than glancing around or exchanging brief words with the guests. Dark and good looking, the man had clear appeal even if he wasn't the biggest fish in the Towers's tank. She'd seen more than one of the women in attendance approach him, most in brief, wet swimwear. He expressed no interest in any of them, although she saw him look at her on several occasions. His gaze was intense—brooding, almost. He'd spoken to her only once, early on, wishing her a brief, "Good evening, AJ." Formal, and as always, disapproving.

She'd smiled and turned away, afraid that she might throw herself at him only to fend off advances from other men. When one of the guests had been too insistent that she share a slow dance with him, she'd looked around and spotted Chance almost immediately.

How he'd realized her problem still mystified her, but he'd come across the patio, holding out a bronzed hand. "Excuse us,

Carlos, won't you?" he'd said easily. "Miss Owens promised this dance to me."

Carlos, drunk and belligerent, muttered something about the hired help. Chance lifted an eyebrow at him. "Mr. Towers specifically asked me to see to Miss Owens's welfare." He eased AJ away from the man, then glared down at him. "Do you really want to push issues with Mr. Towers, Carlos? I don't think so."

Carlos gave both AJ and Chance a venomous last glance, muttered a profanity, and headed toward the poolside bar.

Chance turned to AJ. "Maybe we should really dance," he suggested. "That man's ego is notorious, but he'll probably find someone else by the time the song's over."

AJ grinned wryly. "The most romantic offer I've ever had," she murmured, and let Chance sweep her into his arms. His body, warm and strong, shielded her. Protected her. The sensation was novel. She hadn't let a man hold her in so long—

"This isn't about romance," Chance growled near her ear. "Don't think that for a moment. This is just protection."

"Part of your job?"

"Yes," he said, harshly, but the feel of his body against hers lulled her into indifference to the words. Better just to feel, not think.

• • •

AJ reached the landing at the top of the stairs and glanced down. No one watched her. She thrust the memory of Chance away. So she'd allowed herself five minutes of luxury, of pretended normalcy. Dancing with an attractive man, feeling safe and feminine in someone's arms—he'd served his purpose. Time to put him aside. Resolutely, she walked toward her room, which was near the end of the long hall. The lights were mostly turned off; soft night lights glowed from sconces, but the dimness separated the host's private quarters from the downstairs, still ablaze from the light of the chandelier.

As she pushed the door open, there was a slight movement, something large and white moving near the foot of her bed. She gasped and flicked the light on, her heart racing, sure that she'd seen someone's pet, or—or—

A baby. A baby sat there, one chubby hand clutching the bedspread, looking at her with round blue eyes. She supposed he was just under a year, clearly able to sit and crawl, but apparently not walking. His presence here, however, was a mystery. She hadn't seen any of the guests bring a child, and somehow she doubted anyone would bring a baby to a Mike Towers's affair.

"¿Gordito?" A woman's plaintive voice carried softly from some other room. "¿Gordito? ¿*Donde estas*? Where are you?"

Relief flooded through AJ. The darling little boy must belong to one of the staff.

"Hey, little guy," she murmured gently, going over and bending down. She held out her arms. "Will you let me take you to your mom?"

The baby considered her gravely for a moment, then smiled and thrust his little arms out. She swept him up and kissed his cheek impulsively. "You're one cute dude," she crooned, and he laughed and grabbed her nose, twisting it playfully. "Not nice, but cute," AJ muttered, and he giggled again.

Holding him carefully, she walked out in the hall just as a young woman came out from a room several doors down.

"You found him!" she cried softly, running toward AJ. "He's never gotten out of the nursery before!" Her English was excellent, virtually without an accent, and she was stunningly beautiful. Dark hair tumbled around her pale shoulders, her dark eyes full of relief as she took the baby from AJ. "My bad, bad Gordito!" she scolded. "You scared me!" The baby merely smiled at her and made a grab at her nose, too. She obviously knew the little hand was coming, and she caught it and placed a kiss on his palm, making the baby laugh merrily.

AJ smiled at the young mother. "What a beautiful baby," she said sincerely. For the briefest of seconds, she thought about commenting on the baby's light hair and blue eyes, but stopped, horrified at how rude she'd almost been.

"Thank you," the woman said, shifting the baby to hold out a slender hand. "I'm Rosa. I work here, for Mr. Towers." The slight hesitation in the soft voice spoke volumes.

"I didn't see the little guy earlier," AJ mentioned, reaching over to pat the soft cheek one last time. "Does he stay upstairs most of the time?"

"Always." Rosa turned away abruptly. "You must excuse me. *El Gordito* should be asleep."

Watching Rosa hurry back to her room, AJ understood with sudden clarity. Mike Towers's baby. Undoubtedly, the baby was his. Her eyes narrowed. Towers hadn't wasted much time after Gina's death, had he? Gina had been gone just over seven months. Anger flared briefly, anger at the beautiful young woman who must have shared Towers's bed—during her sister's marriage.

But the rage faded away, replaced with unbearable sadness. Nothing could hurt Gina now. Not even the loss of the baby she'd wanted so desperately, but had miscarried a few months before her death.

"AJ?" Chance's voice from the top of the stairwell startled her, making her jump.

"Sorry," he apologized, coming down the hall toward her. "Didn't mean to give you a heart attack."

"My nerves are on edge," she admitted, trying to hide the weariness in her voice. She seldom stayed up this late; years of rising before dawn to care for Thoroughbreds made going to bed early critical. "What can I do for you?"

His eyes swept over her. Given the skimpy cream short set she was wearing, she wouldn't have been surprised at some off-color suggestion. Lord knew she'd heard a few of those already tonight.

"Nothing. I actually came to do something for you," he said, after a minute.

"Really?" She arched an eyebrow at him. "And that would be?"

He seemed a little abashed. "I may be totally out of line," he said slowly, watching her. "But you looked a little uncomfortable out there."

She should be concerned, she knew. He was reading her inexperience, wasn't too far away from the conclusion that she wasn't here as Mike Towers's next sexual adventure. But all she could do was smile with gratitude. And relief. He knew, and he seemed concerned. "A little," she agreed.

"Do yourself a favor," he murmured, glancing around to be sure he wasn't overheard. "It's gotten ugly out there. Don't go back out tonight."

She sighed. "Mike might look for me."

She hadn't meant it the way it sounded, but the disapproval returned to his eyes immediately.

"Look," she amended, running a hand through her hair, trying to come up with an explanation that wouldn't give too much away. "What I'm afraid of is that Mike's been drinking. We had an agreement about my visit, but I'd just as soon not have to deal with him tonight. Not alone. So I thought I'd go back down where there were people."

"Don't." She puzzled him; she could see that, as he regarded her more with confusion than condemnation. "If you don't want to go, you'll be safe here. I'll handle Mike."

She smiled, sincere and temporarily unworried about letting her gratitude show. "Thanks, Chance." At her door, though, she paused, turning to look back. He still stood there, watching her with those dark, unreadable eyes.

"Why are you doing this, Chance?" she asked.

He shrugged. "Call it moonlight madness," he said. "But, AJ—"

"Yes?"

"All bets are off from tomorrow on, okay? You bought into Mike's game, and I can't protect you. Not when I'm paid to protect him."

The hardness was back in his voice, but she nodded slowly. What he said was true enough. And she had her own job to do.

"Good night, then, Chance," she murmured, and pulled the door shut behind her.

• • •

The soft gurgle of a baby's laughter woke AJ at six thirty. She sat up in bed, blinking, and looking around the shadowy room with gritty eyes. Had it been a dream? The cute little boy from last night was nowhere to be seen. She shuddered slightly as she remembered the wail that she had heard on Towers's ranch on the Laredo side of the river. *La Llorona*, she had dubbed it. She knew that the myths and legends of her childhood were no more true—or untrue—than the Boogeyman or any other tale of terror.

Being here, in the house where Gina had lived so recently, was harder than she had expected. She almost expected her sister to open the door and rush in on a burst of sunny, excited innocence. Gina's naiveté charmed everyone who knew her. Her sister hadn't been shallow, and her belief in everyone around her was sincere and flattering. But in the end, how dearly it had cost her and those who loved her.

A tear rolled down her cheek and AJ brushed it away with such force that her face stung. There would be no tears for Gina now. Just vengeance. She would get Rebel home to her mother, somehow. *Or die trying*. The cliché repeated itself in her mind like a litany. Death was a distinct possibility. For her. For the stallion. But she wouldn't think about that. She couldn't.

No wonder she'd woken to the imagined gurgle of laughter. Babies were so full of innocence, of hope and love. She smiled again, imagining the baby's round little face. The dim light wouldn't have done him justice. She'd have to look in on him today. Surely no one would mind. She wondered if his eyes had been as brilliantly blue as she remembered. Towers had blue eyes, of course, but not nearly that vibrant. She couldn't think of anyone with those sapphire eyes except Gina.

The pain threatened again. She fought the urge to pummel the wall, or to sink to the floor and scream. Gina. Gina, with the brilliant blue eyes. Gina, who would have cherished the baby she'd miscarried, just as Rosa cherished her son—would the pain never stop?

No wonder *La Llorona* still haunted the riverbanks, wailing her agony. How could you lose your own—destroy your own—and bear the anguish?

An abrupt knock at the door startled her, and she snatched up a robe, wrapping it tightly around her. "*¿Quien es?*" she asked, hoping that it was merely one of the maids, checking to see if she needed something. It was much too early to deal with anything major like Mike Towers. Or Chance.

But it was Chance's voice on the other side of the door.

"AJ, it's me." He paused before adding, "Chance."

She cracked the door open and peeked out. For a man who couldn't have slept much, he looked amazingly alert. He hadn't shaved, but the dark growth shadowing his chin just added to his appeal. His hair was tousled, and she wondered momentarily whose hands had mussed those dark locks, but pushed the insane thought from her mind. It was none of her business, and she didn't care anyway.

"What's wrong?" she asked, not opening the door any wider even though he stepped closer.

"Just checking to see if everything's okay," he said. "I thought you might be up already."

"Why did you think that?" she asked, curiously. "I hadn't planned on being awake this early, as a matter of fact."

He shrugged. "You said you used to be around horses. From what I know of the business, it involves long hours."

She laughed softly. "You're right about that," she agreed. "I'm not up, really. And I'm not dressed, either. But I'm fine. So you can go away now."

He nodded. "Remember you sent me away, though," he warned. "You might miss me at lunch, when you have to face that crowd from last night again."

"I can't expect you to spare me from them forever," she chided. "Don't worry about me. I—"

"Can fend for yourself," he finished, nodding. "I remember. See you later, then." He turned to go, just as a rotund little form scooted toward him.

"*Mi Gordito!*" he exclaimed, scooping the baby up. "There you are! I thought I had lost you!" The baby burst into laughter and wound his tiny hands into Chance's hair, pulling with abandon.

"No wonder your hair's a mess," AJ said wryly, and Chance sent a wounded look her way.

"My hair is never a mess," he informed her.

"Chance—" Rosa's voice on the stairs held a quiet note of concern and Chance turned immediately and walked toward her, holding the baby out. "Good morning, Miss AJ," Rosa called, before whispering something to Chance. He bent his head close and they conversed briefly, then he shook his head and watched as the mother and baby disappeared into their room.

Strange, AJ, thought. For just a moment she wondered if Chance and Rosa were involved, but tossed the thought aside.

The baby didn't appear to be theirs, with all that blond hair and those laser blue eyes, and if Towers wanted him hidden away—

Again she wondered what her sister had lived through. Time to get on with her work. Time to quit thinking so much about Chance and his relationships. With Towers, with Rosa, with the baby—none of that could matter.

Somewhere on this property was a horse worth millions of dollars—a horse that had been stolen from her. Resolutely, she pushed the door shut and locked it, then headed for the bathroom. She wouldn't wait to strike out on her own. Because she might only have days before Mike demanded payment for his hospitality. Or before he remembered that once, several years ago, he had met Gina's sister, Joanie. No one called her anything else at home, and he probably hadn't heard her married name, so there wasn't a lot of danger that 'AJ' would jog his memory in the few days she planned to be here.

Names aside, she shared some of Gina's mannerisms, as well as a faint resemblance. Saving Rebel would be hard enough with an unsuspecting Mike Towers pursuing her. With an aware Mike Towers—a man with money, weapons, bodyguards, and trained attack dogs—there would be no way out.

She thought of Chance Landin, warning her away from the pool last night. As kind as he had been, he would stop her if his suspicions were raised. He would keep her from taking the horse and fleeing; he'd told her he was good at his job, and she believed him.

She needed to go downstairs and start figuring out how to move on her plans. Before that, though, she needed to make a quick call. She dug for her cell phone; she hadn't hidden it, exactly, but given Mike's invitation to stay and her vague memory of how lengthy visits here on the border worked, she didn't want to generate a lot of curiosity about whom she knew or didn't.

The fewer conversations anyone overheard, the better. Especially, she thought with a slight grin as she poked numbers, this one.

Randy answered on the third ring. "You? Talk about unexpected calls—"

"Are you busy, Randy?" she interrupted, knowing if her ex-husband had a chance to go on forever, he would.

"If you mean do I have my naked fiancée lying here beside me, no, Joanie. How are you, girl?"

"Good. Look, Randy, I can't talk long. Remember that paper you wrote?"

"The one you grilled me over when you thought I was lying? You were an English tutor. You should have just corrected my grammar—"

"Seriously, Randy. Please. Just listen. You said you used two horses—the one you ferried the stolen horse—"

"We called them commissioned, but yeah. We would lead one horse across from another. Why?"

"I brought Goof with me from Ocala."

Dead silence before Randy drawled, "Should that mean something?"

"Yes. Goof is my second horse—you said I needed a horse to get my horse back, remember? You would ride one and lead one when you crossed."

"I remember. Vaguely."

Randy didn't mention that he'd been more or less stoned when he coached her on how he and a buddy made a living stealing and crossing livestock from one country to another when they lived in Laredo.

"Hey, Randy—could you come? I don't have much time. You've done this—"

"Sorry, babe. No way. Can't get away, and things are too dicey now on the border. Look, let the horse go. Nothing's worth your life, Joanie."

"Rebel—"

"Is a nice horse, but let it go. See you, Babe." The phone went dead as Randy hung up.

"Like hell I'll let Rebel go," AJ muttered. Throwing off her clothing, she stepped into the shower and turned the water on full blast. Chance Landin wouldn't be able to stop her any more than Mike Towers could. There was too much at stake. She closed her eyes and let the water pound her. Vengeance would come to Mike Towers. Nothing would stop her.

Chapter Four

Gold-plated utensils gleamed under the chandelier light and the polished wood table stretched out forever under its assortment of fine china and gleaming tableware. Crystal bowls sparkled with bright colored jellies, and a huge tray of Mexican sweetbread, traditionally served cold, competed with floral arrangements for attention. There were, however, no other diners.

AJ looked at the table indecisively. Had other partygoers eaten and gone about their activities already, or was she the first one down? Could she wander about on her own without being attacked by guard dogs, or interrogated by Chance?

"AJ, my dear! How wonderful to see you!" Mike Towers walked into the room, surprisingly silent for someone of his stature—with a hangover to boot, she suspected. The man looked a bit rumpled, a bit weary—but just a bit. Clearly his all-nighters were routine enough that they no longer fazed him.

AJ accepted a peck-on-the-cheek kiss without flinching, although she drew away when he laid a hand on her arm. If he minded, he was as adroit at hiding his real feelings as she was. He just gave her a wide smile and waved at the table.

"Guess the others are still out of it," he said. "So join me for a bite to eat, okay?" He gave her a wink. "Since your *company* is all I'm getting."

She flushed, and frowned. "Mike—"

He held up one soft hand and shook his head. "My fault. I know. The fiancé." Contempt colored his tone briefly, but he continued to grin at her affably. "Sorry, girl. Old habits and all that. Have a seat, and I'll be a good boy."

AJ pulled out the chair next to his, but didn't immediately sit down. "Mike, this probably isn't a good idea," she murmured.

Gauging how much wiggle room he'd allow the situation would be crucial to getting out of this with her self-respect and dignity intact. "You've been more than kind, but ..." She purred, deliberately, and he lapped it up.

"Now, now!" He placed one of his meaty hands over hers, still on the chair back, and patted her comfortingly. The words and gesture were patently false; she sensed that he was considering every word, every gesture that he offered.

"Sit down, girl," he insisted, pulling out his own chair and sitting, then smiling again broadly when she did. "Look, I know— no strings. You're welcome here, AJ. I told you that. You don't have a place to stay, and I've got enough room for an army. Most of my guests will be gone later today. You'll be doing me a favor, staying. Keep an eye on my staff, though María's been with me a long time. You can keep an old man company when I'm here— but I'm always getting called off on some deal or another." He waved a hand in the air, and a maid hurried in with a basket of steaming tortillas, while another carried in plates of food—*huevos rancheros*, hash browns, eggs and bacon, a spicy bowl of *menudo*— more food than any two people could possibly eat.

"As long as you're sure ..." She spooned eggs onto her plate, deliberately keeping her eyes down, hoping he'd think her demure and unsure of herself. Hate bubbled through her, threatening to spill out. She wanted to fling the steaming bowl of *menudo* at him, cover him in cow tripe and burning broth—to snatch the paring knife lying on the fruit platter and sink it into his chest.

The violence of her emotion startled her. Retrieving Rebel was one thing. Entertaining thoughts of murder was another.

Mike had heaped his own plate with most of the offerings, and waved a spoon of spicy food in front of her. "Damn, girl, eat a little!" he ordered, looking at the scant portions on her plate.

"I'm fine," she protested, shaking her head at him. "Really."

He shrugged and lifted some eggs to his mouth. "Suit yourself," he said. He ate for a few minutes without further comment.

"So tell me, AJ … what did you do? You know, job wise?"

She finished chewing. "Before I left Philadelphia, I worked for a tour company. Historic Hour. Do you know it?"

"Nope. Not a history buff, myself. The here and now." He grinned boorishly. "Dead guys don't make you rich, AJ. Not unless you kill 'em yourself!"

He hooted at his own wit and slammed a fist into the polished wood. "Just playin' around there, girl! Don't you worry about me," he said, when he quit laughing and noticed her expression. He swallowed some coffee and waved his fork around again.

"So did they pay you enough so you could afford not to work now?"

AJ smiled. This question she'd prepared for. It was a logical one. "Nope. They paid minimum, but I like dead guys. You'd be surprised how many tourists tipped."

She picked up her glass of juice and sipped it, then finished her carefully programmed answer. "I saved a little—some college monies I didn't use. My grandmother left me a small amount when she passed away. But I'll have to get back to work pretty quickly."

"Shouldn't be hard to do," Towers offered. "Smart girl, pretty like you … you'll find a job in no time."

"I'm sure I'll find something," she agreed.

Silence fell around them again briefly, broken when a tall, hefty man came into the room, his dark eyes glancing around, his manner one of nervous impatience. His gaze flicked over AJ with contempt, but he merely nodded at her, coming over and whispering something to Mike.

"Ah, *si*?" Whatever the man told him obviously pleased Towers. He wiped his mouth with a flourish and stood up. "AJ, my darling, I hate to leave, but business calls." He tossed the napkin onto the uneaten food and reached out to pat her arm. "Do me a favor, would you, honey? Find Chance and tell him I had to leave. Tell him just to keep his eyes on things here—Jaime'll take care of me elsewhere. Oh, and if I don't catch María on my way out, look for her—she'll want to meet you anyway. Tell her I had to go and to be sure none of my friends help themselves to more than breakfast." He gave her another grin. "I'm a generous man, but I don't like to be played for a fool, AJ."

AJ nodded without comment, glad that Jaime had come to lure his boss away. It was much, much easier to snoop without him around.

Mike and Jaime headed for the door, when the older man stopped, and tossed her a glance over his shoulder. "María already knows you're staying. Don't forget to check in with her, though. She takes her job real serious.(as per introducing María earlier) Get Chance to show you the grounds while you're at it," he suggested and gave her his leering grin again. "Just don't go forgettin' that fine fiancé of yours. I'd hate you to be the one mistake a good man like Landin makes!"

Mike offered the advice lightly, but the warning spoke for itself.

Before she could answer, the two men were out the door. Idly, she wondered what kind of business could be that demanding. From what she'd heard all her life, negotiations on this side of the river were conducted in a leisurely manner. And later than nine in the morning, for that matter. She pushed her plate away with sudden impatience and stood up.

Mike wanted her to "check in" with the housekeeper. She frowned. She knew from older family members and friends that when you stayed with someone, you were expected to pretty much stay. At least, those had been the rules years ago. Apparently Mike didn't want her roaming around, if she had to report to a staff member. Too bad. Once she knew a few essential details about Rebel's location and how closely he was watched, she'd be gone and Mike wouldn't see her again.

She walked through the dining room to the kitchen, where a number of women were preparing dishes and cutting more fruit.

One of them, a heavyset woman with suspicious features, looked at her as she hesitated in the doorway.

"Yes?"

"I'm—"

"I know who you are. You are the *gringa* that Mr. Towers told me would stay over." She shook her head. "He never learns, *Don* Mike. I will do what he ordered, and you can ask me for anything you need. But I won't pretend you should be here. *Debes a ir*—you should leave—with the others." The woman paused and stirred a sauce simmering on the stove, then wiped her hands on an apron and squinted at AJ. "You look like the dead *señora*," she added.

AJ's heart thudded hard and her breath caught in her throat.

María lifted a spoon full of the sauce, sniffed it, and returned it to the pot, but pointed at her. "*Si, otra gringa rubia*—another blond *gringa*. All of you look alike." She sniffed. "And all money-hungry *perras*."

A couple of the other women sent AJ sympathetic—or maybe just curious—glances, but no one spoke. Clearly, María ruled the house with an unpleasant iron hand.

Relief replaced the momentary panic AJ experienced when she thought María recognized her as Gina's sister. The woman had called her a bitch? She'd been called that before. Often. No reply really seemed appropriate, so AJ just turned and walked out, considering her next step.

She'd been ordered to find Chance—and not to fall for him. Mike couldn't possibly have known that Chance sent tiny prickles of awareness skittering through her body with his dark, brooding glances.

A slight, grim smile tugged at her lips. Well, so much for Towers's orders. And his warnings. Because Chance was a hell of a lot more attractive than Mike was. And whether or not she'd ever let anyone know—the man sparked something inside her she hardly needed sparked at the moment. Too bad he was on her worst-enemy list, along with his boss. She glanced at her watch and headed for the door. She didn't care where Chance was. But she was sure the stables wouldn't be hard to find.

* * *

Chance cursed under his breath, low and with feeling. He moved slightly, pushing the itchy branches of the carefully nurtured bushes aside. The hedge framed the path to the stable, and in spite of the nature of his job, he didn't usually skulk here in hiding, one hand holding a dog's collar to keep the nerviest of the Dobermans quiet and controlled. He didn't curse the awkward position, though, just the damnable tightening in his groin when AJ Owens walked blithely past, unaware of his presence.

Last night's shorts were replaced by jeans that clung to her slender hips and long legs, and the sleeveless top was a concession to the sun, already blazing down. She walked with considerable purpose toward the barn, apparently unconcerned about the possible presence of guard dogs. Or guards. The idea that she didn't remember his existence, let alone worry about his position as head of security, annoyed the hell out of him.

He watched her implacable march toward the stable for several moments before hissing "stay!" at the Doberman and following her. The young woman had a keen interest in Mike Towers's horses. Too keen, even if she had been raised around Thoroughbreds. There were other, more accessible stables other places for her to visit. Stables she didn't have to barter her body to visit. His lips twisted with disgust. The idea was impossible to understand, let alone accept.

The stable doors were wide open, but most of the activity was over for the moment. Horses had been exercised, fed, and watered.

Grooms had mucked the stalls and brushed those glossy coats worth hundreds of thousands of dollars. Some heads appeared instantly in stall doors as AJ drifted down the row, stopping occasionally to croon or pet one of the inhabitants. She was oblivious to him; if she turned, she'd see him trailing after her, but she had eyes only for the horses.

He studied her expert progress down the corridor. She upset none of the flighty animals, spoke in calming murmurs and avoided the ones displaying open distrust. Obviously she was comfortable around horses. Yet just as clearly, none of the horses here were of any special interest to her. Interesting. She reached the far end of the corridor, still without a backward glance, and went out.

He had a fairly good idea she where she was headed next—the stallion barn. Her interest in Towers's stallions was evident on her visit to his Laredo digs. Too much interest. Something felt wrong. Frowning, he eased himself out the door, still not bothering to hide himself. She seemed so intent on her destination that nothing would deter her. Or maybe she just figured she already had Mike wrapped around her little finger. If she looked over her shoulder and saw him, he'd confront her directly.

Still, though, she seemed unconcerned about being seen, just walked across the expanse of lawn to the roomy white barn and disappeared inside. She moved with silent grace. Like a cat. Or a wraith. Unbidden, he remembered her mention *La Llorona*, the accursed young wife who drowned her own children to try to hang onto a philandering husband. Frowning, he eased into the shadowy stallion barn, not wanting her to get too far in front of him.

He watched as she stepped near the middle stall, peering at the brass name. That Thoroughbred, a particularly rambunctious animal, not much in demand at the moment, had been turned out; he'd noticed him grazing on the far side of his private paddock earlier. AJ stepped back, then stood motionless. She suddenly seemed apprehensive; he saw her hands clench and unclench. Then she moved to the next stall.

The top half of the stall door was partially closed, protecting against a harsh beam of sun angling in from one of the skylights. He saw her glance at the door, looking for a name plate, but the box hadn't been marked. Hesitantly, she stepped closer and pushed the top of the door inward.

Even with the dulled noises of horses shuffling and birds chirping around him, he heard her sharp, indrawn breath. He watched incredulously as she unlatched the door and stepped in, shutting it behind her. He heard unmistakably her quiet, triumphant, "Rebel!"

Chance approached the stall cautiously, not able to move as quietly as she had. One of the stallions across the way threw his head up and snorted thunderously, annoyed by his presence in the barn. Immediately, he heard Rebel's hooves strike the wall of his stall, and flinched, hoping he hadn't endangered AJ. He probably should have stayed back.

"Quiet, boy. *Quieto!*" Her soft reassurances worked. The stall grew quiet again. Almost immediately, she opened the door and emerged, looking a little abashed. And infinitely content about something—smug, almost. He thought about demanding to know how she knew the stallion. Discarding that idea, he decided instead to string her along. If AJ had an agenda involving Mike Towers's horses, he needed to know.

"Hi," she murmured as she finally noticed him.

"'Hi'?" He parroted her intonation, and she blushed slightly, but met his gaze evenly. "'Hi'? What the hell were you were doing in a stallion's stall on Mike Towers's private property?"

"Doing?" She shrugged, a gesture entirely too appealing, although she wasn't being deliberately sexy. He was pretty sure she wasn't. She just couldn't help herself. He glowered more ferociously, angered that the self-control he prided himself on seemed to slip whenever she approached him.

"I wanted to pet Rebel," she offered as explanation. Her tone labeled him a fool and deepened his frown. "You must have seen me in there, petting him."

Chance hesitated, wanting to call her bluff, but again, resisting. "But you know horses," he pointed out reasonably. "Strangers shouldn't just walk into a stallion's stall like that."

She shrugged again. "Impulse," she said matter-of-factly. "I told you before—I saw him run. How could I resist?" She seemed to sense his doubt, because she smiled slightly. "As you said," she reminded him, "I know horses."

She jerked a hand toward the box down the corridor, where a stallion was still watching them with distrust and occasional, angry puffs. "I didn't walk into *his* stall."

She watched as Chance considered her answer, holding her breath. Hoping that he'd accept her explanation—and that he hadn't heard her call the horse's name. Because even though she might have recognized the animal, she'd greeted him with relief—and with love. Two emotions she wouldn't have showered on a strange horse, even one that she'd seen perform. And Chance Landin, damn him, was undoubtedly sharp enough to realize that.

After a moment, and a glance at the annoyed stallion down the aisle, Chance nodded slowly. "Good choice, then, I guess," he muttered. He walked close and looked into Rebel's stall.

The horse came over to them immediately, his regal head lowering as he reached out to nuzzle AJ's cheek. In spite of her concern over Chance, she smiled and reached to scratch the burnished forehead, then trailed a finger across his brilliant white star. Chance, too, put an arm out, stroking the horse's shiny neck. The horse jerked his head back, turned to look at Chance, then refocused his attention on AJ.

Chance arched an eyebrow at AJ. "You're a fast worker," he murmured, and she frowned.

"I'm not sure I like how that sounds," she retorted. "But yes … I have a way with horses. Always have."

"And men?" Chance pressed, but the smile he sent her took most of the insult away.

She shook her head slightly, thinking momentarily of her two-month marriage. "No. Not men." She couldn't quite bite back a sigh. Reluctantly, she turned from the stall. "I'm supposed to find you," she remembered. "Mike's orders."

"Really? And here I found you." He, too, turned from the stall. "Does he want to see me?"

"No." AJ shook her head, cast a final glance at Rebel, and took a few steps away from the stall. "He left. Didn't say where, just to let you know. Jaime—I think that's the name—went with him."

"Okay." He started a slow trek back toward the open door of the barn.

"He told me to ask you for a tour of his place." Demanding the tour made sense, she realized abruptly, even though it would force her into an unwelcome alliance with Chance. But to make good on her plans, she needed to know the layout of the ranch as exactly as possible.

She watched the familiar, involuntary tightening of Chance's facial muscles, annoyance threatening to make her incautious. His dislike was much too apparent and she wasn't sure that he believed her story about Rebel, either. She chewed on her lip, weighing her options if he objected to following Mike's orders.

Chance sighed slightly, glanced around, and then turned his attention back to her. "I should be there at the house," he said, after a moment. "Keeping an eye on things. Usually, we have a rider or two out checking the fence lines to make sure there aren't any trespassers, so I don't go out often." Then a casual lift of one shoulder, and a wave of his hand. "But orders are orders. What do you want to see?"

Adrenaline surged through her as he agreed. She could get a picture of escape routes. Maybe Mike wouldn't come back before she could move. She grinned at Chance. "Everything."

Chapter Five

The horses picked their way carefully down the slope that would lead eventually to the riverbank. The sun beat down, pummeling them, but AJ seemed oblivious to the onslaught of heat. She rode easily, paying Chance scant attention, but looking around with clear interest at her surroundings. He narrowed his eyes slightly.

The personal tour of Mike Towers's property allowed him a thorough appraisal of the woman riding ahead of him, and he found himself more puzzled—and intrigued—than ever. He had expected that she, like so many other women finagling visits to the Towers estate, had eyes for a potential monetary windfall. Part of the lore about his boss was that he opened his heart—and his purse—without restraint when tempted to do so. Perhaps Chance was short-sighted to have believed so readily that she was just another brazen gold digger. Well, okay. If he'd been far-sighted, he wouldn't have a failed marriage to his credit.

In fairness, he fully intended, just a few short years ago, to dedicate himself to the world of Thoroughbred racehorses. Learn from his uncle, forget his ex, salvage his life and think only about track surfaces, nutritional supplements, and short, talented men who could ride fast. Becoming Towers's bodyguard wasn't part of his original plan.

The irony of his thoughts made him laugh, short and harshly, and he saw AJ look over her shoulder as if he'd lost his mind. Sun glinted in her oddly colored hair and he could see the vibrant emerald eyes stare at him. At least, he imagined he could, although the brim of her visor did a fair job of shading her face. Grinning a little, he nudged his horse into a quicker trot,

catching up. Yes, her eyes were like some molten, precious gemstone, all sparkle and pleasure, in spite of the relentless afternoon heat.

"My riding skills amuse you?" she suggested, not with irritation.

"No." He tightened the reins slightly, shortening his mount's stride to stay abreast of AJ. "No, to be honest … I was thinking of jockeys." Better to admit that than that he found her extraordinarily attractive and would like nothing better than to lean over and—

A sudden dry-leaf rustle from nearby startled them. AJ's horse danced nervously, but Chance's big blue roan reared and shied violently, sending Chance sprawling onto the path.

"Sh—" Chance bit off an oath. AJ looked down from her horse, drawing in a sharp breath at the sight of the rattler, its thick body coiled, just feet away.

"Ideas?" she hissed at Chance, fighting the urge simply to kick her horse into full throttle and flee. The chestnut danced, his hooves beating a tattoo on the ground, irritating the snake even more.

"Can you shoot?" Chance hissed back.

She blinked. "Yes," she said.

Chance nodded almost imperceptibly. "The pistol. Saddlebag. All Towers's hands carry them … in case of snakes."

Keeping one eye on the snake, and trying to find the saddlebag with the other, AJ finally extracted a .22 from the leather pouch, keeping one hand on the reins, and aimed at the reptile. The snake showed no sign that he'd simply slither away. In fact, he seemed to be coiling himself even more tightly, ready to strike.

"Shoot!" Chance demanded hoarsely, and he saw her hand straighten and still, and her finger move slightly on the trigger.

The snake sprang forward in a blur, AJ's horse shied away, and AJ's shrill little "iiig!" of alarm raised the hair on his arms. Not "eek," not a real scream at all, just a shrill, plaintive *iiig*!" He'd heard that before, only once, but couldn't dwell on the source. The rattlesnake slithered off, unharmed. The chestnut bolted and AJ fell. Right on top of his sprawled body. Reflexively, his arms closed around her, steadying her. Clasping her. Instinctively, too, his body reacted to her, hardening with need.

Emerald eyes stared into his own, surprised. Unwary. And very inviting. Lips, slightly puckered, exhaled, the warm, soft kiss of air as erotic as its physical counterpart might have been. And then, just as he decided he'd reach up and kiss those parted lips, her head fell forward. Clunked, really, onto his shoulder, and she shuddered all over.

"I hate snakes," she murmured against his neck.

"Yeah," he agreed. *Just don't shudder anymore, okay?* His hands moved slightly over her back, comforting her. Keeping her from putting any sunlight between her body and his.

He knew when she sensed his arousal. She shuddered again, then stiffened and moved slightly away. He half expected anger or indignation. Instead, she sighed, then carefully pushed herself to her knees beside him.

"So … " she said, eventually. "Is this your usual tour when someone asks 'to see everything'?"

He laughed. "No, AJ. I can assure you … snakes at close range and um … the pebbles and native grasses are only for special gue— visitors." The word seemed less offensive to him than "guests." Right now he didn't want to think about Mike's interest in AJ.

Reluctantly, he, too, pushed himself up, and began brushing debris from his clothes. AJ watched him briefly before following suit, glancing around as she ran her hands over her arms and swiped at her hips and legs.

"If you're looking for the horses, I wouldn't," he told her wryly. "They're probably almost back to that air-conditioned stable of theirs."

"Great!" she muttered. "Now what? I don't have anything to shoot snakes with!"

He stared at her, open-mouthed, before hooting a derisive, "Thank God for that!"

He turned up the path the horses had taken, but she stopped him with a hand on his arm.

"What's up?"

"Aren't we near the river now?" she asked, and he glanced off toward the curtain of scrub trees and grasses that lined the path down.

"Well, yes, but we're on foot. Our transportation high-tailed it home."

She made a face. "Can't walk a few more—what? Miles? Parts of a mile?"

"Yards. But you've seen rivers before—even this river."

"We were on our way when you fell off your horse," she pointed out. "Why don't we just walk the—yards, you said? And see the river from Mike's side. I've mostly seen it from the other."

He tilted his head back a little, thinking. He'd never met a gold digger so interested in things like horses and nondescript river banks. Still, his boss had said to show her everything. She might have to crawl back by the time they finished her tour. He waved a hand at the tangle of vegetation.

"Plow right on in," he invited. "River's maybe a thousand yards straight ahead."

She glanced back and forth from the vegetation to him, then gave him a slight smile.

"Perfect," she said sweetly. Then she did an about face and plowed right on in.

• • •

Curtains of weeds, stunted bushes, and carrizo reeds weren't nearly as impenetrable as they looked. AJ wanted to shout out her relief. Rebel could be ridden through here. With any luck, she could just trot him through. She would run him if she had to, but—why worry about worst-case scenarios? He might suffer a few scratches, but unless he tripped and fell, he should be fine. She glanced down to see a tiny trickle of blood on her arm. Not anything to worry about. Rebel had thicker skin than her.

"You're enjoying this?" Chance's question conveyed his dislike of the circumstances and she kicked herself mentally for letting her glee show too clearly. She'd just have to convince him she was full of quirks. Shouldn't be too hard.

"Yes." She smiled. "Sun on my shoulders, fresh air"—she sniffed before continuing—"touched with the smell of trash burning somewhere, and all this glorious space. I'm loving it."

He didn't look convinced, but she forged on ahead, stifling a small gasp of triumph when they burst out onto a clear bank, sloping easily down to the water's edge.

Rebel can do this. We can do this. She walked all the way down, noticing the relatively clear path and the lack of rocks and roots that could trip a horse.

The Rio Grande stretched out in a placid band here, wide but calm. She could see the rocks under the surface a few feet out from the bank. Those would be the danger. She'd done research and been surprised how deep the river could run. But here, now, with drought conditions and no rain—excitement bubbled through her. Rebel loved water. Her mother used water conditioning with all her runners, and Rebel had hydrotherapy when he strained his left foreleg.

"If you're thinking about throwing off your boots and bouncing in, I wouldn't," Chance said behind her. "Low as the river is here, and slow as it's running right now, there might be an issue with contaminants."

"Wasn't planning on going in alone," AJ retorted, then realized her mistake.

"No?" Chance stepped up beside her. "Mike Towers isn't here, AJ. So if you don't plan on swimming alone—"

She didn't realize quite how close he was until she turned to him, her breasts brushing against him and his arms closing around her for the second time in less than an hour.

"Who are you going in with?" he finished, his breath caressing her from the slight space between them.

She looked away, refusing to answer.

"Mike's not here," he said again, then lifted a hand and laid it against her cheek. His calloused fingers moved slightly against her skin, the friction of rough against smooth sparking need.

Swallowing hard, she raised her own hands and spread them against his chest. Under her fingers, under the soft cotton of his worn shirt, she could feel his heart beating. "Back off," she warned, forcing herself to remember Rebel. And Gina. "I'm Mike's guest, not yours."

He did, but the contempt colored his eyes again and she saw his mouth tighten. "Afraid I can't afford you?"

His words were insulting, but perfect. She wanted him to keep away. Not to tempt her with that burning gaze or unyielding touch.

But behind the contempt, she thought she heard disappointment rather than dislike. Maybe even concern. That was scary, if she wasn't overanalyzing his words. She couldn't afford softness. On his part or hers.

She tilted her chin and spoke truthfully. "I can't afford *you*, Chance."

He looked at her a moment longer, then fished a phone out of his pocket.

"I don't have time to walk you home," he muttered.

She knew the less time she spent with Chance, the safer her secrets were, and the sooner she could ditch Mike Towers forever.

But she wished they had a little longer anyway.

Chapter Six

A bolt of lightning electrified the night sky, sizzling neon blue against the windowpane. AJ shivered and stepped back. She'd never been a fan of thunderstorms. Almost immediately, she thought of Rebel—the high-strung horse hated storms. He'd cut his fetlock badly as a foal, kicking out in terror at his stall walls during one violent summer storm. AJ's lips quirked slightly at the memory. She had nursed the colt back to health, while Gina had hung around, crooning at Rebel one minute and at her crush of the moment the next. They were little alike, she and Gina, except in their love of horses.

Another vicious flare rattled the windows, and she shuddered. The violent, impulsive movement brought back the memory of Chance's body beneath her own, stiffening with surprise, then with desire. Gina might have had a world of suitors and a slightly longer marriage, but AJ wasn't an innocent herself. Chance had wanted her. And she had wanted him. Memory of her head falling weakly to his shoulder, the warmth and smell of him, teased her. Made her own body react impulsively, but she refused to listen to its clamoring. Instead, she went to the closet and fished for anything to use as a shield against the downpour. She'd come too far to let Rebel hurt himself while she trembled with fear. Or need.

•••

The rain slashed down ferociously. AJ gained half the distance to the stallions' barn before she even thought of the chance of happening on one of the guard dogs. Would those snarling beasts be out in this mess? And if so, would they attack her? Chance had taken her by the kennels, but warned her not to think that the dogs, docile enough when he barked commands at them, would greet her with wagging tails when on duty.

The dogs weren't her only concern, though. Blue fire zigzagged through the sky again, startling her, and making her race faster. No point in being a conduit for the next electrical strike. Her legs were wobbling from the exertion and nerves by the time she reached the barn door. She reached out for the handles, her hands wet from the rain, praying that the doors weren't locked at night. Since grooms—and security, perhaps Chance himself— were likely to check on the horses overnight, hopefully they didn't bolt the animals inside. Drawing a few, steadying gulps of air, she tugged on one of the ornate brass handles. Silent and precise, the door slid sideways, allowing her to step inside.

Thank God. I won't have to wait for doors to be unlocked in the morning when I take him out.

Soft lights glowed warmly on the sawdust-sand mixture that matted the barn floor. Immediately she heard the sounds of restless horses—hooves rustling bedding, nervous snorts, the occasional thud of a hoof striking a wooden panel. AJ paused, listening. Surprisingly, barn sounds were more evident than the continued onslaught of the storm, testifying to the building's careful construction. Relieved at the thought that Rebel probably wasn't unduly alarmed, AJ made her way down the corridor, more cautious now of calling attention to herself. Midway down the stall, she paused, hearing a slight sound from the office set off in the corner.

A light flickered and moved, darting around like a flashlight. Silently, she watched, skin tingling with awareness that something was wrong. When no one came out, she padded toward the door, careful not to move suddenly. The office door had a single functional window. Scarcely breathing, she stooped beneath the glass and crept across to the other side, pressed against the wall, and peered inside.

The pale light from a lantern lay on the desk, focused on the filing cabinet. Chance hunched over an open drawer, ruffling papers, pulling files out, perusing them briefly with a second, smaller flashlight, and then returning the documents with care. Her heart hammered in her chest. Head of security or not, Chance's actions made no sense. What in the name of heaven was this man—the man who said he had no interest in horses—doing examining files? Surely nothing in those documents had anything to do with Mike Towers's safety.

Chilled by the combination of suspicion and the air-conditioned cool against her wet skin, AJ ducked across the door and hurried back to the main corridor. Chance had not yet come out of the office, so she continued on to Rebel's stall. He snorted softly and came to the door, and she gave him a quick pat and murmur of encouragement. Then, unwilling to confront Chance—in this place where neither one of them should be—she slipped out the door, closed it, and bolted for the house.

...

Chance walked noiselessly up the stairs, wet and dispirited. He had waited so long for Towers to be gone; his boss had called earlier to say that he'd decided to fly to Acapulco with a business acquaintance. Chance was to secure the homestead. Mike considered Jaime and his small cadre of bodyguards qualified enough to take care of him.

"Try not to let my little filly escape," Towers had said, and Chance could almost see the man's face twisted in his usual leer. "I told her there's nothing for her on the other side and plenty at the ranch. Don't want to worry about losing her if I don't hurry back. She'll keep. Business down here can be fun, if you hit the right places." Towers had laughed and given a few routine instructions until he returned. Soon, he'd assured, but he didn't know when.

Opportunity had filled Chance with hope, but those hopes hadn't come to anything. Why had he expected proof, some shred of evidence of insurance fraud, to be filed neatly away waiting for him? Clearly the photos he'd been assured existed weren't in the filing cabinet. Going into Towers's suite of rooms at the house would be risky if María happened on him. She cleaned his room personally. But if the pictures weren't there, his only real chance was to track down the mysterious man named *Hueso*—Bone. And Bone would have no reason to be around, unless Mike decided to use his services again. If he'd known the man since Arizona, maybe he had an ongoing relationship. Someone as intimidating as Bone might be a valuable tool for a criminal who wanted to keep his hands clean, like Mike.

How long would he have to wait just to see if Towers moved against the stallions he now offered at stud, and called Bone in to kill one or more of them? The thought sickened him, and he wasn't sure he could afford to stop Towers if he made an attempt. If another incident occurred here, he could show that other stallions belonging to Towers died while his uncle was in prison, hundreds of miles away. That in itself wouldn't prove anything, but it would raise suspicions. If authorities looked at Towers in Texas—or even here in Nuevo Laredo—that might help a good attorney or a good cop look at the case in Arizona again. Eli might be ready to talk, if he thought Mike Towers and Bone couldn't hurt him from across such a distance.(to strengthen argument about why Chance needed an attempt on the stallions.)

Letting a horse die would make him as bad as Towers. But what would letting his uncle die do to him? His uncle wouldn't be up for parole for almost ten years. What if he didn't survive his ordeal? What if parole were denied? There'd been an enormous outcry from animal lovers over the story, and they accepted what the legal system said—Robert Newsome had butchered three trusting, much loved horses in their stalls. For money.

He sighed. Towers had played his cards so well. The one objection anyone raised about his uncle's guilt was that he only held partial interest in the horses. In truth, Towers hadn't paid his uncle what he was worth in salary, convincing him that ownership over the years would be a far bigger asset. Thirty percent of the insurance money would have been motive enough, the courts decided, to do the dastardly deed. Especially when Towers claimed that he'd planned to fire Newsome over mistreatment of the animals.

He hated to think so, but he sometimes thought Towers's money had helped as much in Arizona as it did here in Nuevo Laredo, Mexico. He wouldn't go as far as to say justice had been bought, but the system found it easier to listen to Mike Towers than his uncle. Other men had profited from killing horses for insurance money. Could greed tempt Mike Towers to act again, or would he simply pursue other means of increasing his wealth?

Sighing and massaging the back of his neck, he paused briefly on the landing. Most of the lights were out, and no one moved up or down the hall. Fortunately, Rosa must have turned in for the night—he didn't want to fend off her determined overtures. The idea of fending off advances of any kind brought AJ clearly, electrically, to mind. Her body against his, the surprise in her eyes as, for the briefest of moments, their physical awareness sparked and flared—

Memory brought another sigh and he narrowed his eyes a little.

AJ. What was it with her? Women constantly pursued Towers, had done so even during his marriage. His uncle claimed that the women had been there all along, even when Towers first began accumulating wealth and power. But something about AJ's interest in the man disturbed him. She clearly wasn't experienced at pursuit, yet she seemed hell bent on hooking Mike for some reason. Why? She seemed ill at ease—perhaps even repulsed—by the man's obvious interest. And still she was here, taking advantage of an invitation that implied that at some point, she would be expected to go to bed with Towers.

The image of her greeting Rebel—with love and excitement—stormed back, along with sudden awareness. Mike Towers had nothing to do with AJ's visit here. Her interest was the multimillion-dollar stud out in the stallion barn. But why?

With a soft oath over the senselessness of his revelation, he stalked toward his room. No unusual sounds from behind any doors, lights off. Gordito's door was ajar, and the room was dark. Frowning, he pushed the door open, knowing the baby didn't like the darkness.

The guardian angel nightlight on the side table was dark; a quick check showed the problem was a disconnected cord. But the crib was empty. Chance rubbed his neck again, not really alarmed. Since the little guy was adept at crawling out of his crib he was missing in action more often than not. The important thing was to find him and be sure he was safe, even if that meant venturing into Rosa's boudoir next door. But if Gordito wasn't there—just the possibility of the child tumbling downstairs made his skin crawl. With a renewed sense of urgency he moved toward Rosa's room.

The muted sound of laughter behind AJ's door down the hall stopped him.

"You, sir, are too much!" AJ scolded, her tone gentle and full of amusement. Momentary anger needled him, assuaged immediately by a different burst of laughter—Gordito's gleeful chortle of mischief. He pushed the door open without knocking.

AJ held the baby, who sported a pair of print shorts on his round little head. He had a diaper on—sort of—and somehow had dragged his teddy bear into the room with him. The teddy bear wore another pair of printed shorts on its head, obscuring all but its floppy brown legs. Completely unaware of Chance, she grinned at the baby, who tugged off the shorts and tried futilely to put them on her head.

He smiled, torn between announcing his presence and retreating, finding Gordito in such capable hands. But just then the two turned toward the door. Gordito laughed and clapped, and AJ drew in a quick, audible breath of surprise—almost the little "iiig" she'd mouthed as she shot at the rattlesnake. And abruptly he knew where he'd heard that same unusual gasp of surprise. Suspicion and alarm knifed through him. Why the hell hadn't he seen the resemblance before? The tall, slender woman watching him with those liquid eyes could only be Gina Towers's sister.

Chapter Seven

AJ glanced in her rearview mirror, shaking her head. Of course there were cars behind her—*duh*. Laredo's traffic problems grew on a daily basis. Did she really expect an empty street behind her?

She didn't know why she'd been so on edge all day; this excursion back to the U.S. side of the bridge was a lark, since Mike Towers was still away. She snorted softly to herself. He'd called her in the morning, apologizing for being detained and asking her to stay. Pointing out she didn't need to spend a penny and no one would bother her. With him gone. He'd laughed when he said that. She flexed her hands slightly on the wheel, relieved when the traffic finally thinned as she headed toward the little piece of property west of Laredo that she'd managed to lease. She braked the sedan as she turned onto the bumpy drive and headed toward the farthest of three ramshackle trailers and the squat barn that sat beyond that.

The neighbors' dogs barked briefly then went back to their own unmarked yards. AJ pulled up close to the trailer, cut the engine, and slipped out of the car. She waved at one of the children, and headed for the barn at a trot.

"Hi, Miss Joanie." Her neighbor Ed appeared from somewhere behind the small building, nodding. "Goof is fine. Fed and watered, just like you asked."

"Thanks, Ed. You got your money okay?"

"Yes ma'am. No problem at all. You still need me to keep an eye out for the horse?"

"Yes." She smiled. "Just for a few more days. I'll be back for good then." He nodded and shuffled off, a kind old man eager to have a job. She waited until he was gone, then walked into the barn.

There was only one stall. Inside, the occupant lifted a regal head and regarded her approach with interest. The bronzed chestnut coat, the majestic head, the deep chest, and perfect conformation were identical to those of a horse standing in a luxurious barn across the river.

AJ smiled at the soft nicker and walked into the stall, rubbing the big head affectionately. "Hi, Goof," she murmured. He *whooshed* another welcome and rubbed his forehead against her chest, also reminiscent of Rebel. Only a keen horseperson would notice the small differences—the strip of white, slightly broader, sliding off to one side just slightly higher up than Rebel's. The very slight difference in height; Rebel stood an inch taller at the withers. And, of course, Goof was a gelding.

AJ sighed and pressed an absent kiss against the horse's broad forehead, knowing that any astute handler would remark immediately on the most damning difference—Rebel's eyes burned. With spirit, animation—a will to win. Trainers pursued horses like Rebel for a lifetime. The gentle beast standing next to her was Rebel's half-brother but looked every bit a full sibling. But the fire, the determination—the speed—were absent. And that was why he was here. She blinked hard. The idea of risking Goof for Rebel hurt. But by God, she'd find a way to reclaim Rebel. Gina had never intended Towers to have him. She leaned against the door frame, biting her lip. She'd brought Goof while she still wasn't sure where Rebel was or what a rescue would entail. When she'd read Randy's essay about his horse-rustling experiences, she'd been captivated. Not good, she supposed, because she'd wound up married and divorced in record speed. But the details in his paper provided her the inkling of a plan. Maybe she could swim Goof across from this side, and leave him near the river. Rebel would follow his half-brother the way he had all those lead ponies—and if nobody knew, she could take the river carefully. Her lips twisted in a smile. Truth be told, she'd considered switching the horses, so no one would look for Rebel until she got him out of Laredo. That seemed a little difficult now. She needed to think it out more clearly. Anyone seeing Goof's head through a stall window might be fooled into thinking Rebel was there. And even if someone noticed the switch, surely no one would hurt the gelding.

"Ready to be a hero, my friend?" she asked, and Goof's head came up sharply, his ears pricking.

"Hey, what's the deal, guy?" AJ chided, patting him. "You haven't been this spooked since we heard the old wailing lady." When Goof's attention stayed fixed on the door behind her, she turned, expecting to see Ed. Or the children from next door.

What she saw instead was Chance Landin. Arms crossed. Not smiling. And blocking any avenue of escape.

Briefly, words wouldn't come. From the expression on his face, though, it didn't matter; she didn't think words would soothe him. Ease his suspicions. Help her. So when she did speak, she attacked.

"Well! So do you follow all your boss's guests, Chance? I don't believe I invited you to come home with me."

He didn't answer for a moment, then glanced briefly around the small, poorly kept barn, and the weathered trailers outside. "Home?"

AJ shrugged, pushing past the horse and coming out of the stall. Chance didn't move and his physical nearness intimidated her. She turned and locked the outside of the stall before turning back to face Chance, his arms crossed and features drawn into something like a frown. Or a snarl.

"A girl's gotta live somewhere," she cooed. Maybe she could go back to Plan A and make him believe she wanted Mike Towers's money. She'd find a way to explain Goof somehow. She just needed a minute or two to think.

Chance's jaws clenched. Clearly, he found her breathy falsetto annoying. *Good, good*, she thought. *Just give me a minute—*

"Not quite as comfortable as Mike's digs across, I'll admit." He looked at the horse in the stall. Then back at her. "Family's funny," he said slowly, after another long silence.

AJ shifted slightly, unsure where he was going. He waved a hand at Goof. "Brother, I'm guessing. At least half."

She didn't answer.

He stepped even closer and she frowned, reflexively taking a step back. The rough wood of the stall prevented further retreat.

He reached out again, this time tapping her shoulder once, pointedly, with his index finger. "There's nowhere to go, AJ. You're sure as hell not going back to Mike's place. So tell me—why is Gina Towers's sister here with a horse that looks just like the one Gina gave her husband as a wedding gift?"

For a brief second, the unpainted walls wavered and swirled, and tiny specks of light exploded around her. No hope, she knew, that he hadn't seen her reaction to his accusation. She supposed she could be glad that Towers hadn't found her out sooner. And he didn't know what she planned to do—how she planned to rescue Rebel.

"Don't ever poke me again," she said coldly, pushing away the offending hand and sidestepping him. He stood watching her until she reached the barn door, and she stopped and looked back at him.

"If you want an explanation, you can come with me," she added, making it more a demand than a request.

He looked at Goof again, shook his head as if still in disbelief, and followed her.

She walked over to the nearest trailer, opening the door and letting him into the small, neatly kept interior. Again, his bigness and nearness were inescapable, as were his anger and suspicion. She couldn't blame him for that; she had only herself to blame for not thinking more broadly and recognizing possible threats. For not devising a simpler, more effective plan. "Have a seat."

She nodded at the clutter of sofas and chairs left by the previous owners. "I'll get tea."

He stood, glowering, not accepting her invitation. "Don't jerk me around with some tea party crap," he said between gritted teeth. "I want answers, AJ."

She ignored his demands until she broke ice out of a brittle tray and filled two glasses, then poured tea from a pitcher, looking at the brown liquid a little dubiously.

"Does tea spoil?" She carried the glasses over, handed him one, and settled herself on the couch, immediately putting her drink down on the low end table. She folded her arms across her chest and smiled slightly, determined to keep him off balance. He frowned at the glass, then at her again, but finally walked over to sit on the far end of the sofa, putting his own drink down and turning to face her.

"So?"

She dragged in a deep breath, lifted a hand and idly turned her birthstone ring around her finger. The ring had been a present to her from Gina shortly before she married Mike. The last gift, in fact, her sister had given her.

"What do you want to know?"

"Who you are. Why you lied. What the deal is with Towers."

His questions rapped out with machine-gun staccato. She didn't look at him, just considered the ring. "Well, as you said in the barn, I am Gina's sister." She looked up at him then, unwilling to deny the bonds of blood and love. "Her older sister."

"So why doesn't Mike know?"

She stood up and walked over to the window, then to the counter that separated the small kitchen area from the living area. "He never bothered much with us ... my mother and me. He met me once, briefly, but everyone at home calls me Joanie." She shrugged. "I don't look a lot like Gina. At the time I had dark hair, and I was just this tall, gawky, not particularly pretty stranger. He didn't pay attention to me."

"But the wedding—"

"He insisted on having the wedding here in Laredo. Mom went … Gina and I quarreled. I didn't come."

"Okay." He rubbed a hand over his face, then tapped a forefinger on his forehead thoughtfully. "So … Mike didn't know you. Yet I'd never met you—and I saw the resemblance."

"How?" she asked, mystified. She had been wondering that since he dropped his bombshell in the barn.

"That silly little noise you make when you're startled. I never heard anyone else make it. And then, when I looked carefully, the two of you are similar. Not identical, certainly. But there are similarities."

Which she hoped Towers hadn't picked up on—if Chance didn't give her away now. What if he threatened to reveal her true identity? She leaned against the counter, pain shooting through her head. Breathing was hard.

"Why are you here?"

The severity of his tone hadn't lessened. She had an answer for that, though.

"We were always very close … before we fought. When I knew she was gone … it hurt." In spite of herself, a tear slipped from the corner of one eye and she dashed it away. God, it still hurt. "I … I don't know exactly why, but I felt that I'd find … closure. Some kind of comfort, if I visited her home."

He shook his head. Once, with decision.

"No." The one word response brokered no softening, no belief in her story. "Because if that were the real reason—you wouldn't be out to bed Towers." He, too, stood up, closed the door between them, and leaned on the opposite side of the counter. "I mean, for God's sake—you're trying to sleep with a man who was your sister's husband just a couple of months ago. Just how much did

Towers mean to your family, AJ, that you and your sister would both go after him? Is it just about money?"

Anger at his disbelief, at his accusations, seared her nerves and straightened her. Irrational anger, because her ploy to pass as a gold digger had worked. But how dare he accuse her of not honoring her sister's memory?

"Think what you want," she said. "I went to Mike because I had to." She turned away.

Almost immediately, she felt his hand on her shoulder. Warm steel, gripping her, again preventing escape. But carefully, not hurting her.

"Okay. We'll come back to that." The fingers lightened slightly and she reluctantly turned back to face him. He dropped the hand away and propped his elbows against the ceramic tile of the counter. "So tell me just one more thing now—and AJ?"

"Yes?"

"I want the truth. As plain and as raw as you can tell it. Just what the hell's the deal with Rebel?"

Her fingers drummed the counter in agitation. How much to tell? Could she salvage any hope of recovering the horse that meant her mother's future—and her own, perhaps?

"Rebel belonged to my mother. Not Gina." She paused, but Chance said nothing, just watched her with that unreadable stare. "Gina begged my mom and me to let her loan him to Mike Towers. For just one breeding season. He'd had that leg injured and just been retired. We weren't sure if he could race again. Mom and I didn't agree on whether to stand him, or wait and race him in a few of the classics for older horses the following year. But Gina pleaded the case for letting Mike borrow him and—Gina usually got what she wanted from Mom." She turned away from his scrutiny and walked over to one of the small dust-covered windows, glancing out absently. Finally she came back to the counter.

"He never came back." She shrugged. "I love the horse, Chance. We raised him. I just needed to see him again."

Chance jerked a hand through his hair, stared at her a minute more, then stalked over to retrieve his tea and bring it over to the counter. Instead of drinking it, he merely twirled the glass around, sloshing the dark liquid inside, and then set the beverage down again.

"I could believe that," he said slowly, "if there weren't a dead ringer out in the stall. Why have you burdened yourself with a second Thoroughbred—one who looks like Rebel—if all you wanted was to see your horse?"

Goof?" The question was dumb; there was no other horse around. But she didn't know how to allay his suspicions. How to turn this around.

He looked disconcerted. "Goof?" he echoed, frowning. "What kind of a name is that?"

In spite of the knotted muscles tightening her neck and making her head pound, AJ smiled slightly. "A false name. A descriptive word that can be used in polite company. His registered name is Rebel's Answer. But unlike his brother—he had no desire to run." She stretched her shoulders, moved them a little. She couldn't help but notice the slight change in Chance's expression.

But she would not play on whatever physical attraction the man felt. "He's an overgrown puppy dog."

Chance nodded. "Okay. If I buy that, there's another question I'm a little curious about—why is he here?"

"Mom had to stay with her horses. She didn't want me to come alone."

He lifted an eyebrow. "She sent a horse to take care of you?" he asked, the sarcasm clear.

"You'd have to know my mother," AJ countered matter-of-factly. "Goof wasn't working—one less body for her to feed and worry about. There's no other reason."

"No?" The terseness of the clipped word startled her. "Sorry, AJ. I don't buy it. Personally, I'm banking on insurance fraud."

AJ's breath caught in her throat and she couldn't speak for a painful second or two. When she did, she spoke with indignation. With outrage. "Insurance fraud?"

He faced her, relentless and accusing. "Happens all the time. Rebel won't run forever, even if someone put him back on a track. If he makes it as a stud, you can get a pretty penny through syndication. If he bombs …" He shrugged and leaned farther over the counter that separated them. "If he bombs, you'll have nothing. You probably thought you'd find him here in Laredo, right? You bring a horse you think you can fool everyone with for a while—just long enough to get him out of sight. Then there's an accident, you collect insurance—"

"That's just insane," AJ whispered.

"Look what happened to Alydar, and he was huge. Too many horses to name. A big policy, an unfortunate accident, money. Fast, easy, and only a little distasteful."

"Insurance fraud, legs broken with iron pipes, stomachs slashed open, a 'little' distasteful? Just what kind of woman do you think could do that, Chance?" she hissed.

He didn't answer for a long while. When he did, his eyes and voice were equally cold and cutting.

"A woman who could sleep with a man to get what she wanted," he said. "A woman with an agenda. You."

Chapter Eight

His accusation hurt her. She took a faltering half-step back, hand going up slightly as if to ward off his accusations. Or slap him silly. He gave his head one hard, angry shake. What did she expect? Maybe Towers hadn't had her yet, but she'd known that was the plan when she accepted his invitation.

Her sister's husband, for Christ's sake.

Her wounded green eyes, her silence, the way her body trembled—he just didn't get it.

He thought for a moment he might take it back, say something to lessen her hurt, even if he had to lie about his suspicions. But then her body stiffened and stilled. Her chin tilted slightly. He hadn't known Gina well, but he remembered seeing that very same gesture. Not often. Twice, maybe. Gina hadn't defended herself, usually. Her sister glared at him from her side of the counter.

"You filthy bastard," she whispered.

The rawness and controlled fury of her tone struck him like a sucker punch to the gut. She sounded sincere. Didn't sound like she had an agenda. And she looked like a woman in pain. He wanted to step forward and wrap his arms around her. But he couldn't. Because no matter how true her words rang, they made no sense. And she could be a huge thorn in his side. If Mike found out that this was Gina's sister, he might start looking at everyone around him a little more closely.

The chances were increasingly good that the photos Eli told him about no longer existed. He needed a little longer to search the Nuevo Laredo estate before he could be sure that he couldn't turn up something. If Towers became suspicious, then he could block any further searches, just by watching everyone more carefully. Chance wouldn't be able to seek evidence to exonerate his uncle.

Very possibly to save his aunt's life. Evidence that Mike Towers, not Robert Newsome, had slaughtered horses for insurance money.

But Lord, he wanted to hold her.

The irritating beep of his cell phone interrupted them. He fished it out of his pocket and glanced at the name on the display. Mike. AJ turned away and walked over to the window, silently ignoring him.

"Yeah?" Maybe not the most professional way to greet Towers, but it was the best he could do given his agitated state.

Towers's voice, too loud and demanding, hammered him. "I called the house first. You weren't there."

"No."

"María said that AJ left just before you did." An accusation, not a question. Towers's voice must have carried, because AJ turned from the window and watched him from across the small space of the trailer.

"She shouldn't have left?"

Towers snorted. "Well, I didn't have her tied to the bed, much as I might have wanted to. But I wish she hadn't." He paused. "And I damn sure wish you hadn't gone with her."

"I didn't." Chance kept his voice level. Reviewed every bit of evidence he could to be sure he hadn't been followed. He didn't think Towers suspected him of being anything more than a glorified bodyguard. Didn't think Towers could know he was standing here a few feet away from AJ.

"Well, you may not have left in the same car. But I got the idea from María that your leaving looked mighty damn suspicious."

He allowed himself his own snort. "María's suspicious of anything that has legs and walks," he retorted. "We both know that."

"Yeah, but—"

"Look, Mike, you pay me to watch your backside. The truth is, I followed AJ into Laredo—just to be sure everything was on the up and up. Thought you'd want to know if she had decided to leave or if she saw anyone."

He could see AJ's expression change, although he couldn't decide whether she was apprehensive or relieved.

"Well, yeah, but … where did she go?"

"Drugstore. Hamburger joint."

"Hamburgers?" That seemed to tick Mike off more than anything else. "She didn't have to leave the ranch for a damn burger!"

"Yeah, sure, but you know these kids." Her eyebrows threatened to disappear right off her forehead, but he couldn't resist the slight dig at Mike's age. "She's not as mature as you are. Still into junk food."

Towers was silent on the other end.

"So … are you on your way back?" Chance prompted, not wanting to cause too much more friction. He couldn't afford too many little jabs right now, no matter how much he loathed the man.

"I'll be back when I'm back," Towers answered and the words sounded vaguely like a warning. In the background, muffled voices clamored for his attention. "Gotta go," he said, abruptly. "Chance?"

"Yeah?"

"Keep your nose clean, my friend." There was nothing jocular about the voice. And no doubt that it was a warning as he added, in a slightly lower tone, "And your pants on, Chance. AJ's mine. And remind her that unless she's really going back to the unknown boyfriend for good—we have our traditions. She accepted an invitation to stay at my place. Just remind her of that."

Towers clicked off and Chance shoved the phone back in his pocket.

"Bastard," AJ said again.

"You've already called me that once," Chance reminded, and she shook her head impatiently.

"Him. Not you." She came over and looked up at him. "Why do you work for him?" She crossed her arms over her chest as if chilled.

"You're asking that? As indignant as you got a minute ago, AJ, what are you doing accepting his invitation to stay at his home? You had to know—"

"And if I didn't, I do now, don't I?" She sighed. "Look, I can't help what you think. I need … time. I don't have any other way to get it." She held up a warning finger when he started to speak. "And you know perfectly well that I've no intention of selling my body to Towers. Not for time. Or money."

She hadn't meant to say that, Chance knew. Her eyes widened slightly, and her whole body tensed. "As if you have a choice!" Chance scoffed. "You're not used to men like Mike, AJ. You said you came to see Rebel. You saw him. Give it up!"

"Not yet."

He reached out, caught her arms, shook her gently. "Then when, AJ? When?"

"When I'm ready."

He sighed, released her arms, and dragged a hand through his hair. "I don't want you back across," he said. "Look, go back to your fiancé. Go back home—"

"What?" Disbelief sharpened the single word. "You don't get an opinion, Chance. You don't get to dictate what I do or don't do. There is no fiancé, and I can't go home without—"

"It's not in Mike's best interest to have you there."

She stared at him as if he'd sprouted horns and turned red. Or smelled of sulfur and brimstone. "Not in Mike's interest?"

He shrugged slightly. "I'm head of security for a very rich man. You're there under false pretenses, and I know you have some agenda with Rebel. I can't let you go back."

He saw stubbornness shade her eyes. There was something else there, too—a fleeting look of desperation. That disappeared almost immediately.

"Fine," she said. "I'll call Mike and explain that you don't want me there." She paused, then added coldly, "and I'll mention that you sneak into his stables at night and go through filing cabinets that I'm sure aren't any of your business."

He stared. She smiled.

"A few days," she murmured. "I'll be ready to make my peace with Gina's death in a few days. But you've got to let me go back."

He blew out a breath. She'd spied on him? He hadn't heard anyone the night he'd gone through the papers. Hadn't thought he needed to be particularly careful. But she couldn't be bluffing; she obviously had seen him.

"You can go back," he said finally. *As if he had a choice.* "But I'll be watching every move you make, AJ."

He expected matter-of-fact acceptance since she'd forced his hand. Instead, her eyes teared up and she laid a hand on his chest. The touch did more to burn than comfort. "Thanks," she whispered, full of relief. And she stepped past him and headed for the door. After a bemused moment, he turned and followed her.

• • •

Chance stood in the corner of his room and peered out the window, ignoring the throbbing headache that had plagued him for hours. Towers's absence troubled him; the man seldom was away for so long at a time. Since his intended conquest was here, it was surprising as hell that he hadn't returned. Much of his business was conducted by phone or computer anyway, and Chance couldn't ignore the nagging sensation that Towers was up to something.

Lights shone on the manicured lawn. Everything seemed quiet. Serene. Just as he started to drop the sheer curtain panel, a shape appeared, heading across the lawn toward the barn.

AJ. Dressed in white, moving wraith-like through the night. Unbidden, he thought of her comments about the wailing woman, *La Llorona*. The legend was as much a part of his childhood as hers. A woman who had sacrificed herself for love. Or greed and jealousy. The story cut either way, and how you looked at the woman probably said a lot of psycho gobbledy-gook. Did you trust women and their motives, or suspect them?

He hadn't known much about his own mother. She'd brought him into the world, then left him. No father. No mother. Briefly, he'd had a wife who decided she wanted better than a stable bum. But he'd had his uncle, and when the gruff trainer married, his aunt. That had been enough. Both his mother and ex, if either were cast as *La Llorona*, would have done away with their kids for personal gain. Hard not to be a little suspicious of women and their motives. Look at Towers's wife. She'd had it all and thrown it away.

At least that's what he'd been told by Mike and by María. Rosa had always defended Gina. Now, though, the question was moot, and he didn't need one more worry fueling his frequent headaches.

He frowned as AJ reached the stables and disappeared. No woman had intrigued him as she did—not good. He couldn't afford distraction. Couldn't afford discovery. His uncle's fate depended on him hanging close to Towers until he found something, anything, to prove that Towers, not his uncle, had been behind the insurance fraud. Desire, lust—heck, whatever it was that had jolted through him from head to foot with a light touch of AJ's hand, there was no place for that here. Now.

The soft knock at his door startled him. He turned as Rosa pushed the door open and came in.

"What's up?" he asked, and she gave him a subdued smile and brief headshake.

"*Nada*," she said, coming over to where he stood. She glanced out the window. "Problems?"

"No," he lied. "Just doing my job."

"As I am," she murmured.

He turned away from the window, letting the drapes fall to cover the window. He didn't want her to see AJ slipping around outside. He knew that Rosa worked for Towers out of need. At least, Rosa told him that shortly after he met her. At first, she said, the salary allowed her to support her ailing mother while attending college at odd hours. He understood that part. But Rosa had finished four years of college. Sadly, she lost her mother along the way. She didn't have to be here. And that made him suspect that she, too, had an agenda. But what she could be seeking remained a puzzle. Before her death, he supposed Gina's friendship had played a part. The two women had been good friends from the time they met. Another mystery. Why would Rosa defend Gina, who had apparently done so much harm to the small circle of people around her? Anyone who maligned Gina— and from María to Mike to jealous women attending functions at the Towers's properties, people spoke ill of her—received scathing rebukes from Rosa. Now, with Gina gone, Rosa lived for Gordito, to the extent that strangers might think the child was hers. But was the baby the only reason she stayed here, working as a maid, when she could have taken better positions elsewhere?

Too many puzzles. He sighed. "What's up?" he repeated.

"You like her," Rosa said with certainty. "AJ."

"Yes." He grinned at her, reached out to touch her cheek. "I like you, too, Rosa. But—"

She waggled a finger at him. "Never mind! I don't want to hear again about all your good reasons for us not to be lovers. But Chance, you know that you can't have her either. The boss—"

"Yeah." He nodded. "Not to worry. I'm smarter than I look." She giggled at that and went over to sit on the bed. He knew something was on her mind, because she made no effort at all to attract him. To seduce him.

"So are you going to tell me what's bothering you?" he asked gently, sitting beside her, but not too close.

"It's Gordito," she admitted, her voice full of concern.

"He's sick?" Chance hoped not; the little guy was a joy to be around. All chubby innocence and laughter.

"No." She turned troubled brown eyes on him. "He lives like a prisoner. You know how the boss is about him. I worry that if he ever wanders downstairs …" Her voice trailed off.

"Come on, Rosa. You don't really think Mike would hurt his own son, do you?"

Rosa's tone was derisive. "His own son? You know that he doesn't even acknowledge that."

Chance considered her answer for a moment. "Tell me," he said, finally, "what do you think?"

She stood up, paced around the room with some agitation. "*No se*," she admitted, finally. "But he's Gina's son and that's enough for me. I don't trust *el patron*. He doesn't like children."

"But do you think Towers is his father?" Chance pressed.

Rosa didn't immediately answer. Finally she sighed softly. "If so, I pity *mi chiquito*," she murmured. "Gina was not a tramp, Chance. She, like me, like many of us, was a desperate woman—not a bad one. She told me that she never slept with anyone except her husband."

"Yet she died in another man's car. A man Towers claimed was her lover. And I saw them together, sometimes. Not intimately, no. But … together."

"Would you blame someone—anyone—for trying to escape Mike Towers, even for a bit? She should never have had the baby here. On the U.S. side, divorce would have been possible. Here, she lost her power to fight, Chance. She was not some demented woman who could risk her child for her own well-being." She stopped in front of him and caught his hand. "You will help me, yes? You will help keep Towers away from *mi Gordito*?"

Her little one. The words reminded Chance once again of the *Llorona* legend. Women and children—bonds that gave life. Or destroyed it. What would happen to Rosa if she ever lost Gordito? Now that he knew who AJ really was, Rosa would have to give the little boy up. Mike Towers denied being Gordito's father. But AJ—AJ was the boy's aunt, and sooner rather than later, Rosa would lose any right to keep the baby.

• • •

Rebel moved restlessly around the stall, snorting and pawing. AJ crooned soothing words, but something had spooked the stallion. Big time. She hadn't seen him so edgy since the last time she'd watched him enter a starting gate. He never started well, not liking the cramped metal quarters and the chaos around him. But he should have listened to her here, in this roomy, well-padded box.

"Honestly, boy, you'd think you'd seen a ghost!" she scolded, easing out of the stall and latching the gate. No matter how well she knew Rebel, an agitated stallion posed safety risks. No good would come of being trampled under his quick hooves.

She took a deep breath, then released it slowly, watching as Rebel continued to snort and pace nervously. The stall was carefully enough constructed that he couldn't hurt himself, as far as she could see, so she gently closed the upper half of the door, hoping that screening him from any further distraction would calm him. Idly, she looked around the barn. No noise came from any of the other stalls; only Rebel seemed upset and edgy. If there were a ghost, only he must have seen it.

Gina's ghost? She shivered in suddenly chill air around her. *Stupid.* There is no ghost. No *Llorona*. Nothing but the memories of a vibrant young woman no longer alive. No longer there with that smile that dazzled and that wink that made the world smile back. Blinded by tears, she turned from the stall door and took a few unsure steps.

"*Hola, señorita.*" The soft, jeering Spanish stopped her in her tracks. She blinked hard, clearing her eyes, and looked up at the man standing in front of her. He was tall and lean, with an untrimmed mustache, a recent scar across one bronzed cheek, and cold, hard eyes. She hadn't seen him before, although his disreputable appearance made her think of Jaime, Towers's other bodyguard.

She nodded coolly. "*Señor.*" Her heart thudded in her chest, but she managed to maintain her composure, even as she wondered how this man had breached security to be here. *Dammit!* Where was Chance when she needed him? The man stood there, leering, apparently not afraid to be seen.

"May I help you?" she asked, pointedly. He laughed and chills ran up and down her arms. Towers was oily evil; this man was blatantly evil. "*Mira, señor—*"

"No, Miss, *you* look," he interrupted, mockingly, in heavily accented but clearly understood English. "You need not worry." His eyes swept over her body insultingly. "I'm not here for a woman—not *la mujer de mi patron.*"

The man's vulgar contempt infuriated her. And frightened her, but might be her only protection. He looked vicious—capable of anything. And he had gotten past the dogs and night watchman. He had gotten past Chance.

A shiver shook her again. How could he have gotten past Chance? Very little did. She thought of Chance rummaging in the file cabinet. Insurance fraud. He'd mentioned that. Why? Her chest tightened and breathing normally took effort. Was this man in cahoots with Chance? Could Chance possibly intend to do something to Towers's horses? To Rebel?

No. He had nothing to gain. After all, the insurance policies couldn't be in Chance's name. Surely Towers wouldn't kill stallions for the insurance money. He didn't need money.

She took a few steps forward, refusing to be cowed. "Unless you have business, you should leave," she warned. "I'm calling security."

He laughed again. "You call," he invited, with a threatening smile that bared stained, yellow teeth. She headed on toward the door, keeping from hurrying her steps. As she reached the door, she glanced over her shoulder. The man was gone.

Nearby, she saw the night watchman, patrolling with one of the Dobermans. She started to call out, but quickly changed her mind. The man might have dodged into the corridor to the office, but she didn't think so. He'd escaped into the night somehow. Telling the night watchman would just call unwelcome attention to herself. When she saw him turn her way, she raised a hand in his direction, and after peering toward her, he nodded and waved back.

Chance. She didn't know him. Couldn't trust him. But there was no one else she could tell. With a final glance around, she hurried toward the house.

• • •

Rain spattered against the windowpane and lightning turned the sky blue. AJ couldn't sleep. She stood by the glass, looking out, annoyed at herself. Lord knows, she'd seen worse storms. Summers in Florida were a nightmare. She even knew of horses struck in pastures, unable to escape nature's fury. But she also remembered how seldom it stormed in the border area and how quickly the flat ground flooded. After the day's chaotic events, she would have liked nothing better than a quiet night sky to lull her into sleep. Besides, too much rain would ruin Rebel's rescue. Even tonight's rain might stir up debris, increasing the risk to a Thoroughbred's fragile legs. Would it be wrong to pray for the drought to continue just a few days longer?

She didn't hear the slight knock at her door at first, not over the relentless drum of rain punctuated by loud thunder claps. When the sound came again, with renewed insistence, she turned, slightly startled, then walked over and pulled the door open.

"I heard you were looking for me," Chance said, stepping into the room without an invitation. Drops of water glinted in his dark hair and his shirt clung to him. He apparently noticed her appraisal, because he smiled wryly. "Duty called. I stepped out to have a look around."

"Without an umbrella? Or a raincoat?"

His half-smile broadened into a grin. "Umbrellas attract lightning and raincoats are for wimps and city boys." The grin faded. "But you shouldn't lecture me on foolish endeavors, my dear. AJ, you're pushing your luck wandering around this place alone. Especially at night. The dogs—"

"Forget the dogs!" She brushed past him and closed the door. He quirked an eyebrow in her direction, but she ignored that. "Look, Chance, I don't know whether or not to tell you this, but there was a man in the barn. A strange man."

"What?" He seemed genuinely surprised. "Not a hired hand, someone you just hadn't seen there before?"

"No. I'm sure he shouldn't have been there. He was—" AJ gestured helplessly with her hands, seeking the right word. "Evil. Up to no good."

"Why didn't you call someone?" Chance demanded, agitated. He took a step closer, and his nearness unsettled her. He smelled of clean, damp rain. Of some subtle hint of aftershave or cologne that the rain hadn't washed away. Tantalizing. She frowned at him.

"I saw the guard. But when I looked back, the man was gone. So I decided to tell you instead."

"What did he look like, this ghost of yours?" Chance prodded, and AJ closed her eyes, concentrating on her answer. "Tall—not quite as tall as you. Very thin—but a strong thin. An old tank top. Muscled. A tattoo of a bloody knife on his left shoulder. He had a scar on his right cheek and a scraggly mustache. And he had ugly yellow teeth."

"Sounds like you could identify the man if you saw him again," Chance said.

For just a moment, AJ got the impression that he knew exactly who she had described. She watched as he ran a hand over his jaw, and then brushed at his hair.

"Well," he said finally.

"Well, what?" she demanded impatiently.

He winked. "I'm glad I floss."

She frowned. "Darn it, Chance, the man scared me—"

"Hey, calm down." He stepped closer, and reached out tentatively to place a gentle hand on her cheek. The caress reassured her. 'I'll check into it. But if he got in and out so quickly and quietly, he must be long gone. Or maybe he was an ex-employee—neither of us has been here very long. I usually stay at Mike's U.S. properties, not here."

She didn't want him to take his hand away. She thought, for the briefest of seconds, that she should turn her head. Place a kiss on that large, work-roughened palm—the thought shocked her. She felt color rising in her cheeks and realized that she was blushing. Well, there was no way he would know why. She took a step back from him, but her foot caught on the boots she'd pulled off and left by the bed. With a small, startled sound of surprise, she fell backward, winding up on the edge of the bed.

In his effort to catch her, he tangled his own feet somehow and came thudding down beside her, an arm digging into her chest, a muscular thigh pressed along the length of her thigh. Heat spiraled through her, and need. She hadn't wanted a man in so long, hadn't felt this growing, breathless ache. He turned to look at her. Leaned toward her. She couldn't breathe, didn't want to. Wanted to feel his lips on hers, to hear him whisper her name.

Instead, Rosa's surprised "*Caramba*!" exploded behind them.

AJ struggled to her feet, her face burning. Chance straightened and regarded Rosa with annoyance.

"We didn't hear you knock," he said, ignoring the irritated look AJ turned on him.

"Better you didn't hear me knock than *el jefe*," she retorted grimly. "And he's on his way in from the airport."

AJ heard him suck in a deep breath, and nodded at Rosa. "Thanks," she murmured, dismissively, and after a moment the young woman shrugged and went out, closing the door behind her.

Chance sighed. "I'd better go," he said, after a moment. "I need to meet Mike."

She followed his lead and ignored any thought about what might have happened. "Will you tell him about the man I saw?"

He shook his head. "I'm not sure. The man already worries about his safety—more than he has to, probably. But I'll take care of the situation. I'll tell him if I think I need to."

She didn't believe him. But she didn't say anything. She still had one last, desperate plan to save Rebel. She wouldn't do anything to further jeopardize her opportunity to save the stallion. She liked Chance. Wanted him, in spite of herself. But she wouldn't trust him. And she wouldn't lose Rebel. Not for anything in the world.

"Good night, AJ," he said, as he stepped into the hall.

"Good night, Chance," she whispered, but not until the door swung shut between them.

Chapter Nine

Chance sat in a corner of the study and stared holes into Mike Towers's back. The man hadn't been home half an hour and was already on the phone. While he waited for Mike's briefing on everything that had happened in his absence, he turned AJ's information over and over in his head. Not smart, really, to replay her graphic description of the man in the barn, because if Mike turned and saw his face, he might notice the anger and disgust threatening to boil over. To explode.

Had AJ noticed the way he'd reacted when she told him about the man with the scar? The woman was sharp; she might have guessed he knew him if she'd been paying attention. Damn! That wasn't good. Towers would find out soon enough—he must have called for him, in fact. But Chance damn sure wouldn't mention the man's arrival. Besides, he didn't want Mike to know that AJ had developed a habit of visiting Rebel day and night. In spite of her denials, she obviously had some interest in the horse besides old family ties. If the horse had been loaned to Gina, and not sold, she probably hoped to get him back—and returned to the U.S. side where she could conduct a legal fight. On this side, she had to know she didn't have a chance.

Then again, with Bone back, Rebel might be in mortal danger. He couldn't tell AJ that, though. He'd blow his own cover. Worse, he might put her in danger. That thought stopped him for a moment. When had he been concerned about someone else being in danger? Not in a while, and the last errant effort to help someone had ended in tragedy. And in death. Gina and he hadn't known each other well. His loyalties should have been to Mike. The accident that had taken her life—

He refocused on Bone's sudden reappearance. He'd pursued his chosen course of action for so long now, closing his eyes to the most repugnant aspects, that he was surprised to feel fear coursing through his body—fear for AJ. He doubted she'd appreciate it. He smiled a tight, grim smile. What a pair they were, AJ and him. Both here under false pretenses. Both with agendas.

Mike's voice rose angrily and Chance forced himself to listen to the conversation instead of dwelling on more intriguing thoughts. Like hidden agendas. And undeniable attraction.

"Three million … no, of course not!" Towers slammed a heavy hand on the polished wood, then cursed into the receiver. "I'm not an endless well … of course. Yes. Of course. Okay. Call me back." The receiver slammed back into its cradle, and for several seconds, Towers just sat, shoulders hunched, turned away from Chance.

Finally he swiveled slowly around to face Chance, scowling. "Damn parasites," he muttered. "A man has money, everyone wants it."

Chance didn't know what to say to that, so he just waited for Towers to make his point.

"Never mind, my boy," he said finally. "Anything out of place happen here?"

"Nope. Everything's fine," he lied easily.

"Hmmm." Mike's eyes speared him. "So AJ didn't see anyone on her little trip into town?"

"Nope."

"You followed her the whole time?" Towers persisted, and Chance shook his head.

"No. Not the whole time. You gave me the impression she was free to come and go," he said. "Buying a hamburger and whatever she got from a drugstore didn't seem particularly suspicious to me."

"No, of course not." He rocked a little in the chair, filling the room with annoying squeaks.

"You know, it came to me when I was in D.F.—she reminds me of someone. Just can't think who," he said, more to himself than Chance.

Chance shrugged nonchalantly, though he felt his pulse quicken. "Beats me. Doesn't remind me of anyone I've ever seen."

"Check her out, Landin."

The use of his last name sounded a clear warning: he was the employee, not the buddy. And Towers had some little niggle of doubt about AJ. That could be dangerous. For both of them.

Chance stood. "You're the boss," he returned easily and gave the man a quick grin. "What do you want to know?"

"Just be sure she's who she says she is," he elaborated. "That she's from Philly. That she has a fiancé she's trying to get back with." His look hardened. "That she's not out to screw me," he finished.

She's definitely not out to do that. Chance bit back the sarcastic rejoinder. The info his boss wanted was fairly general. Maybe he could cover for AJ and still protect his own interests. For damn sure he wouldn't expose her. He wouldn't hurt her. Already plotting how to protect AJ and himself, he nodded at Mike and left the study.

• • •

AJ knocked lightly on Rosa's door, straining to hear the sleepy "*Pase*," that invited her in. Rosa sat up in bed, blinking, not nearly as annoyed at being awakened as AJ might have expected. The young woman worked hard, and AJ doubted she got much rest.

"Yes?"

AJ fumbled for words, not willing to alienate Rosa. The young woman obviously wanted Chance, and AJ couldn't allow herself the luxury of competing for a man. Not with Rebel's future at stake.

"Listen, Rosa, about Chance—"

She snorted derisively and held up a slender hand. "No, Senorita AJ." She shook her head, dark curls dancing around her face and shoulders. "You are going to tell me not to worry, that you are not interested in Chance. No?"

"Well ... yes."

"Don't bother." Rosa slipped out of bed, reached for her robe and pulled it on, then hugged her arms across her chest as if she were cold. "Look, AJ, truth always speaks. Not always loudly, but always it speaks." She rubbed her arm absently. "You and Chance ... a fool could see that the *chispitas*, the sparks, are there—no?"

Lying would be safer. But AJ couldn't. "Yes, At least for me, there are sparks. But that doesn't matter. I'm just visiting. I won't be here for more than a few more days. And besides, Chance and I ... well, we have different lives. I can't ... I'm not going to stay in Laredo. I don't want to encourage him."

"*Mentirosa!*" Rosa taunted, but without malice. "You are not a good liar, *mi amiga*. And I *am* your friend. If I had not interrupted, Mike Towers might have."

"But you—"

Rosa sighed heavily, turned away briefly, then faced AJ with resignation. "Chance will never be mine," she said quietly. "We are friends. I would be more. But he—" She shrugged. "Who can say why these things happen? He will not let me love him. He does not love me."

"I'm sorry," AJ whispered.

"Again I say—you are a liar. *Una mentirosa.*" The words were more teasing than accusing, and Rosa smiled. "You are more than a little in love with Chance."

AJ didn't answer. In love with Chance? Ridiculous. He'd saved her from one of Towers's wild parties and he hadn't exposed her lies. He'd comforted her and made her feel attractive over the handful of days they'd shared. None of that constituted love. She wasn't sure she knew what love was, though. Her two-month marriage? Gina's tormented time at Mike Towers's side? Gina had believed in love at first sight. She certainly hadn't found it.

"You have secrets," Rosa said darkly. "Like Chance." She waved a hand at the door. "Secrets apart, and secrets together. Go. No one will know secrets from me. In fact, I myself might have secrets of my own. But AJ—"

"Yes?"

"Be very careful." Rosa's warning snaked through the dark room. "Do not play with Mike Towers. Sometimes he plays a fool just to trap those around him in lies. Don't let him trick you. You can only be hurt."

"Sorry I woke you, Rosa," AJ murmured. She walked out of the room, filled with a strange dread. Chance had secrets? She knew that Rosa was right. She had seen Chance in the office that night. Knew, too, that Chance lied about the man she had seen. But could those secrets hurt her? She wouldn't believe that. She might have to trust someone to save Rebel. She was running out of time and options. Maybe Chance would be her salvation. Anything else would have to wait. And *chispitas* be damned!

• • •

Chance frowned as the helicopter beat its way up into the air, rotors stirring up noise and blasting the tranquil surroundings. Towers traveled a lot, but usually he didn't come and go with such frequency. And secrecy. The fact that Jaime was accompanying the man everywhere felt wrong, too. Not that Chance wanted to leave the ranch, but he didn't like the feeling of impending doom that haunted him, cropping up entirely too often.

"I hate helicopters," AJ offered, startling him. He started and heard her soft laugh behind him.

"Some head of security," she teased. "I sneaked right up."

"There was a helicopter taking off," he protested.

"Excuses," she retorted, her eyes dancing. He wasn't sure why she was in such a good mood—maybe because Towers's helicopter had already disappeared—but just looking at her made him smile. And wish he could pull her into his arms and kiss her. Sun glinted in her hair, created interesting golden patches on her bare skin. The white eyelet top and turquoise shorts were designed to cool scorching summer temperatures, but seemed to have the opposite effect on him. She looked hot and sexy, and he guessed his temperature was headed up, not down.

"You seem happy," he said, and she nodded.

"I just came from upstairs."

He swatted at a gnat and frowned at her. "Upstairs? What could possibly be upstairs that made you so happy?"

"I was playing with Gordito," she explained. "He's such a sweet little boy. You know, I don't remember being around little kids very much. But when I hold that kid—" She shrugged. "I sound like some goofy old woman going gaga over a baby, don't I?"

He laughed. "No. You sound like a woman who likes kids. Nothing wrong with that."

"Walk with me to the barn?" she invited and he glanced around, then nodded.

"Sure. Although you usually don't ask."

She didn't say anything, just walked toward the barn, and Chance followed.

"You know," she went on, as they walked, "it's funny about Gordito."

"What's funny?" he asked.

He didn't see it coming. "He feels—I don't know. Like someone I know. Like someone I could love."

Her words hit him with the force of a sledgehammer. Again, a blade of guilt sliced through him. He said nothing though, couldn't, just walked beside her and let her talk.

"I guess it's just that he's so cute," she decided, eventually.

"Could be," he agreed, hoping that he didn't sound as uncomfortable as he felt.

Tell her, you bastard. She stopped, smiling up at him, and his chest tightened. When he hadn't known who she was, everything had been easier. Now, he knew that she deserved the truth about the child upstairs. But what if she couldn't handle the truth? What if she gave herself away to Mike Towers? What if Towers lost it when he found out he'd been lied to? His head started to throb dully. *Decisions. Why did they all have to seem so impossible?*

"You'd make a good dad," she said lightly. "I've seen the two of you together."

"My nose would never survive."

She laughed, the sound soft and sexy in the mounting morning heat. "That would be a pity," she conceded. "Losing a nose like that."

"Yeah," he agreed, impulsively taking her arm. "Now, if we're walking, let's walk. I'm on duty, remember?"

He escorted her into the cool barn, glancing around as he always did, noticing details. The first stall was empty, the stallion turned out in the paddock outside. The sounds of horses, the smells—everything seemed normal. But Bone had been here. And that spoke worlds.

AJ walked down the corridor, speaking as always to all the horses, but greeting Rebel with love. The horse was hers; he could see that. Her story must have been true. He thought about Mike's reaction when he'd reported that yes, AJ was just who she said she was. A young woman recovering from a broken engagement. A woman from Philadelphia with an interest in history and horses. He just hadn't mentioned that AJ's main interest was in the multimillion-dollar chestnut stallion standing at stud in his boss's own barn.

Towers seemed relieved. Reassured. Still, Chance worried. AJ might be under more pressure to sleep with the man—he had a reputation for impatience, and AJ had delayed him for days already.

"You know what's funny?" she asked, coming out of Rebel's stall and closing the door with a bemused expression.

"My nose?" he asked, wanting her to laugh again.

"Besides that," she said, grinning fleetingly before looking around the barn in consideration.

"What, then?"

"Well … with four stallions—very well-known, very expensive stallions—standing at stud, wouldn't you expect to see mares being brought here to be bred? I haven't been here long, but I haven't seen a single mare here that doesn't belong to Towers. You don't make your money just breeding your own mares. And when I looked at the appointment calendar in the office—"

"Yes?" he prodded.

"There were names. But not enough. And I didn't recognize any of them. With the stature of the studs, I should have."

His blood froze. For a moment he didn't breathe. No mares. Bone. She didn't know what her words had just done. Given him hope. Filled him with fear. And desperation. Mike's conversation about money came back to him. Stock market losses, people who wanted money, the payoffs that Mike's shady business dealings probably entailed—a man who needed money. Again.

Stud fees would bring in money. But the cost of caring for mares, guaranteeing live foals—maybe Towers thought he could pull off insurance fraud one more time and collect millions instead of thousands. If so, he'd need a fall guy. He didn't have a trainer onsite here. So, who?

He looked at AJ and peered slowly around the barn at the horses. If Towers moved again, if Bone slaughtered one or more of these animals, he might be able to prove his uncle's innocence. If the method of attack were the same, or if he could videotape Bone's actions—witnesses might place Bone at his uncle's barn, even all those years ago.

He swallowed hard, remembering the way the other horses had been destroyed. He couldn't stand by and let that happen. Approaching Bone, making an offer—could that work? If he could get the man to talk, he wouldn't have to let him act. Did killers like Bone brag about their past work to provide a sort of gruesome reference? Otherwise, Chance would have to wait until Bone acted, and horses could die—even AJ's horse.

"Chance?" AJ put a hand on his arm, concerned. "What in the world are you thinking?"

I'm thinking that I might destroy the two things that could matter the most to you, and that if I don't, there's no escape for my uncle. He sighed and gave her hand a slight squeeze. "I'm thinking you shouldn't have been going through Mike's books," he said. "But since you did, why don't you show me?"

The office, as usual, was empty; no one seemed to pay much attention to the coming and going of the grooms outside in the corridor. Still, Chance made sure that they slipped into the room unobserved, realizing that just his being here with AJ might anger Towers. She seemed unaware of any possible problems, though, going to the desk and extracting a large, leather appointment book.

"Look." She beckoned for him to come closer, and he bent over to see. "All the stallions were booked. Then, suddenly—the appointments stop."

"But wouldn't that make sense?" he argued, already knowing that it didn't. "Breeding season is over—"

"But farms book months, sometimes years ahead," she countered. "If Towers were only going to stand Rebel on this side for a year, as you said, then it makes even less sense that he wouldn't book as many mares as he could. And not one of the stallions has any future bookings."

"Hmmm." He took the book from her, flipped through the pages, then handed it back with a frown. "Strange," he muttered.

"I don't understand it." She put the book in the desk, then sank down in the chair and leaned back, looking over his shoulder at something beyond him. Her concern hurt. He wanted to reassure her, tell her not to worry. But he couldn't. Nor could he tell her about his suspicions as to why Towers hadn't accepted bookings. He couldn't tell her his real motivation for putting up with Towers; she might confront the man in an effort to save Rebel. Thinking of Bone, though, he realized abruptly there was an even more desperate reason to keep the truth from her: if she knew Bone had killed horses before, that knowledge might endanger her.

"So … anything else in the desk you want to tell me about?" he asked lightly, and she pulled her gaze away from the wall and refocused on him.

"I'm not as big a snoop as all that," she protested, and leaned forward to pull open a desk drawer. "I only wanted to see what bookings Rebel had. Mom always chooses so carefully when she has a mare bred. That's one reason I thought we should wait a year with Rebel—it would take her that long to find just the right mares."

He watched her rifle through the contents of the desk, thinking she'd never make it as a private eye; she tumbled and moved things with complete disregard for their original order.

She looked up once, and caught him smiling at the image of her as some kind of secret operative.

"What?"

"Never go into espionage." His smile broadened. "They wouldn't need concealed video to track you." He kneeled down to pick up a scrap of paper that had fallen under the desk. Unfortunately, being on his knees next to those long, bare legs of hers was disconcerting. Too damn disconcerting. Too damn tempting. His body tightened with desire. He could lean over, place a kiss against her thigh—

"This is Gina's handwriting," she murmured in a choked voice.

She looked as if she'd been punched, holding the small piece of paper with a trembling hand. "It's a name," she said. "And part of a phone number, I think. Numbers." Her lips pursed. "And hearts. I don't think Gina ever wrote a word on a notepad or piece of paper she didn't doodle on."

He didn't look at the paper, didn't need to, and she slipped it in her pocket. He knew the name. *Lenny.* Her lover. The man she'd cheated on her husband with. The man who died with her when she fled the ranch. He hoped AJ wouldn't ask, but he wasn't surprised when she held the note out to him.

"Do you know this Lenny? Some friend of Mike's, I guess?"

He hated lying. "Yeah, I think so. I don't really remember." He shrugged, propped a hip on the edge of the desk. "I spent very little time here when Gina was alive." That was true, at least. He saw no reason to tell her what he had learned from Mike. And María. And several others who had been paid to keep tabs on Gina Towers. Even after Towers brought her to this side of the river, she'd apparently been eager for company—male company. Towers had been infuriated to find that his wife was cheating on him with one of his accountants.

"I miss her," AJ murmured.

He made a noncommittal sound that he hoped bordered on sympathetic. "We'd better get out of here." He glanced around the area around the desk, checking that she hadn't dropped any other bits of evidence on the floor. "I should be making my rounds, AJ."

"Sure." She stood up, still teary-eyed. Her sadness tore at his heart. Without thinking, he stepped forward and pulled her into his arms. Held her close, offering comfort. She sighed slightly and leaned against him for a moment. The feel of her against him was—good. She felt good. After a second, she sighed again, more deeply, worked her hands up between them, and gently pushed away from his embrace.

"Get to work," she ordered, making an obvious attempt at levity. "No point in upsetting any old apple carts."

He nodded in agreement and turned to leave, but she stopped him.

"Chance?"

He glanced over his shoulder. "Yeah?"

"Thanks."

He nodded and walked out, wondering how long before he had to hurt her. He knew a large part of the truth about Gina. About Gordito. About Rebel and the absence of bookings. And like that weary old saying, the truth did hurt. Always. Especially since he'd played a part in Gina's death.

• • •

AJ watched him go, the scrap with Gina's handwriting still fresh in her mind. She patted her pocket. Once Gina had married, she and AJ had become strangers. Any crumb of information, even something as insignificant as a name written in her unique way, seemed a connection to the woman her sister had become before she died.

Had Gina realized that the gift she had given Mike Towers—the loan of Rebel for a year—had turned into the outright theft of the stallion? If so, it would have tortured her.

She had written AJ for only the third time during her marriage, and the tone of the letter hinted at unhappiness but not desperation. At the time, AJ assumed that Gina was merely down over being so far away, and the miscarriage she'd mentioned in passing in the letter. Now she wondered. But now—there could be no answers.

She looked around. Chance wasn't here. Mike Towers wasn't here. Her breath quickened. Chance didn't seem to have predictable duties. In fact, he seemed more often than not to be watching her, but since he'd just walked off—

The tack room. She didn't know where the horses' bridles and saddles were kept. She'd seen a couple of youngsters working out on the small training track early in the morning. No one seemed to exercise the stallions, a crime in itself. Rebel would be jumpy and hard to control, but if she needed him to go—no horse would catch him.

Tiny beads of sweat broke out on her forehead. *Please don't let Chance come back. Don't let anyone see me.*

She didn't find tack stored in the stallion barn. As quickly as possible, she crossed over into the mares' barn, ignoring the nickers directed her way until she saw a groom taking out a wheelbarrow of soiled hay. She lifted a hand in his direction and approached the nearest stall, crooning at its occupant and hoping her penchant for visiting the horses was well known enough that the groom wouldn't approach her. Or call Chance.

When he disappeared out the door, she hurried down the stall. The office was near the center of the barn. She pushed the door, finding it open, and went in, looking around.

Bingo. A second door inside the office opened into a pantry-like room. Bridles hung on hooks, along with a few exercise saddles, blankets, and miscellaneous grooming and medical supplies.

None of the bridles was labeled. She chose a headstall that should slip over Rebel's head quickly and debated the use of a saddle. Riding a Thoroughbred like Rebel full out and bareback was a fool's errand. The driving muscles, the sweat he'd work up almost immediately in the hundred-degree heat—the saddle made sense, and throwing it on would be quick work. But Chance or anyone else could appear in seconds.

She picked one up anyway. Chance knew he'd left her in the stallions' stable. He clearly hadn't worried about that. Surely his rounds would take him away long enough for her to get enough of a head start.

Her arms shook slightly as she slipped out of the tack room. She clutched the tack close to her chest and made herself walk normally toward the exit. If anyone saw her, maybe it would help if she pretended she had every right to be there.

Rebel snorted and pawed the bedding in his stall when she slipped in carrying the tack. He'd never been good about the bridle.

"*Quieto*, Rebel," she muttered, nudging the corner of his mouth until he opened his mouth and took the bit. With a sigh of relief she moved to his side and placed the saddle. She hadn't picked up a blanket. There hadn't been time. Hopefully the saddle wouldn't rub him enough to make him try to throw it, and her.

She pulled the girth tight and heard a noise outside the stall.

Damn.

Jaime stood outside the stall, one of the dog handlers beside him, a cell phone in his hand. And two of the Dobermans sitting silently inches from the door.

"*Hola*, Ms. Owens. Where are you off to?" He smiled. "Mr. Towers is nobody's fool. Sometimes he runs … shall we say, security checks. On the security personnel?"

AJ gaped a little. She hadn't seen who was in the helicopter, but surely Mike didn't leave without protection. Chance wouldn't have had any reason to tell her that Jaime hadn't gone.

"I called Landin. I don't believe anyone's allowed to ride these horses. Did he give you permission, Ms. Owens?"

Best to play dumb—at least until Chance arrived.

"Who is Mr. Landin to give me permission? Sorry, Jaime, but Mr. Towers told me to make myself at home." She smiled at the sour-faced man. "This is the prettiest of the horses, and I know how to ride—I figured it would be fine."

"He's a racehorse, ma'am. Or he was. I've never seen anyone ride any of the stallions."

"What's up, Jaime?" Chance asked, coming up behind the guard. He took in the bridle and saddle. "You can go," he added to the dog handler, then addressed Jaime. "When I told Ms. Owens she could ride, she didn't take my suggestion as to which horse. You can go. I'll handle this."

"Might want to be careful, Landin," Jaime said darkly, then shrugged. "Just saying." He stalked off toward the house.

"What the hell are you doing?" Chance demanded furiously as soon as Jaime left.

AJ shrugged. "No one exercises Rebel. There's a training track a few yards from here. What do you think I was going to do?" She let the exasperation over being caught creep into her tone. "Do you think I have a trailer hidden somewhere along the drive and thought I could just ride him off, load him up, and be gone?"

"How stupid can you be, AJ? You're about to blow this for me."

She knew he realized what he said when his face tightened and his shoulders tensed. Fear stormed back at his unexpected words and reaction. What was she about to blow for him? Had he just admitted that he had plans involving Rebel?

"Have you even ridden him before?" he asked, when she didn't say anything.

"Of course. You don't get it, do you, Chance? Rebel is my horse."

"You let Mike know you think that, AJ, and—" He broke off the sentence, then shook his head. "He won't just hand him over. Everyone here believes Rebel is Mike's horse—a wedding gift from Gina and your mother.

"Your ride probably should wait," he said, after a short silence. "Mike's on his way back." Without a backward look, he stalked away. (This is the suggested early attempt to get Rebel back.)

She turned and unsaddled Rebel without comment, knowing he was right, then removed the bridle, rubbing a hand over his head. "Bet you wanted to run, huh?" she whispered. "Well, don't you worry—next time. Next time we get out of here."

She grabbed the bridle and saddle and went to put it up.

Chapter Ten

AJ couldn't sleep. Again. She tossed the covers aside and walked over to the window, looked down at the well-tended lawn. The grass must drink half the Rio Grande; vegetation on surrounding properties had burned in the searing summer sun.

As she watched, Chance crossed the lawn, striding purposefully, flashing a light at the house, the carefully planted bushes and hedges, down toward the stable.

Chance. She smiled. Such an intriguing man. Such a sexy man. More than once this afternoon she'd remembered him crouching inches away from her legs, remembered the feel of his breath on her skin. She'd scripted a whole erotic scene over what might have happened if he'd stayed in that position much longer. Just the memory of some of the things he'd done to her—at least in her decidedly lustful imagination—heated her all over again.

But then she'd found the paper from Gina. She walked over to her dresser and picked it up. Lenny. She wondered who he was. Had he grieved for Gina, too? Or had he been some casual friend of Towers, coming over for dinner, maybe bringing a bottle of wine or flowers for the hostess?

She pulled out the brocade-covered vanity chair and sat down, idly picking her brush up and dragging it through her hair. Over and over, with the mindless concentration that always relieved stress. Gina always scolded her, claiming that she wouldn't have a hair left by the time she hit thirty. Well, she'd been wrong. But she wasn't here to take the words back. AJ took a deep breath and threw the brush down. She would *not* cry.

Outside, somewhere far off, a bloodcurdling wail seeped in the window. High and keening, the sound rose and fell, muffled, but chilling. Inescapable.

La Llorona. AJ swallowed hard. The sound undoubtedly belonged to some predator, though it didn't sound like a coyote. She'd heard that the occasional mountain lion still wandered up from deep in the interior of Mexico, and only a few years ago, the Laredo papers reported the story of a lost bear cub startling people at Lake Casa Blanca. Well, logic was well and fine. Somehow she knew the sound had nothing to do with four-legged animals, and everything to do with a woman's grief.

AJ stood up, agitated. She couldn't face these memories and this sense of loss much longer. There were so many complications—Towers, who had come back from wherever just before dinner. His suggestions were becoming clearer and more demanding. She couldn't be sure he wouldn't simply attack her. She'd spent a lifetime moving bales of hay and buckets of feed, as well as manhandling horses that weighed more than a thousand pounds each. She'd studied martial arts briefly and without real dedication. But Towers wouldn't be an easy match. Even hatred might not protect her.

Then there was Chance. She didn't really trust him—couldn't—in spite of her fantasies. She couldn't help feeling that he'd hedged on her question about Gina's friend earlier this morning. He hadn't explained what he'd been doing in the barn that night, either, come to think of it. Even though he knew she'd caught him, he hadn't even offered an excuse.

She thought about that, mulled over the little she knew about him. He was built like the hottest of actors or bodybuilders. He worked for a despicable man who had destroyed her sister's life. He had followed her across an international bridge—doing his job. He'd stopped her attempt to take Rebel and run—doing his job when someone called him to check her out. She frowned. Jaime might have told Towers. If Mike asked, she would use the excuse about choosing the wrong horse. And pray. Would Chance have tried to explain her actions away to Jaime? To protect her, and maybe his own lack of watchfulness? She needed to remember his job. And most infuriatingly, that he'd accused her of insurance fraud.

Insurance fraud. Her breath caught in her throat, and she stopped in her tracks. Of course. Only a man with some knowledge of horses—or crime—could know that insurance fraud was a huge problem in the blood horse industry. Thoroughbreds, pricy show horses—too often owners destroyed the animals to collect huge sums of insurance money. Stable fires were hideous enough, but she'd heard of some other horrible tactics. Inhuman.

Why would the idea of insurance fraud come so easily to Chance—unless he knew something about the practice? He couldn't collect insurance money himself, of course, but he worked for a scheming, conniving beast. Could Mike Towers not have booked his multimillion-dollar stallions because he had another plan for profiting from them?

Not Chance. She didn't want to believe he was capable of such horrendous acts. He doted on Gordito, treating the baby much like a son. He had protected her from Mike Towers, and let her return undiscovered to the ranch. He hugged her when Gina's loss threatened to overwhelm her. *He hugged her.*

A computer. She needed access to a computer. She'd left her own desktop hidden at the trailer in Laredo, not wanting Mike Towers to get the idea that she was moving in. She also knew that Internet access wasn't always secure, didn't want to use her computer to contact anyone back home. So that was out. So was Mike Towers's study; as Chance had said, she wasn't spy material. Not quiet enough. Too likely to disturb something and not notice that she'd left traces of her presence.

So how? She wondered briefly if Rosa had one, but dismissed the idea. The young woman seemed well educated and somewhat friendly, but she was a servant in this lavish home. Somehow she doubted that Mike Towers allowed his help to have Internet access.

Chance! She glanced at the ornate wall clock. Not quite midnight. Chance seemed to be a night owl, always out and around after dark. He wouldn't be happy to catch her snooping in his room, even if he'd turned a blind eye to her investigations of the stud book. Still, there was little choice. She snatched up her robe and pulled it on over her nightgown. She didn't bother looking for her slippers; bare feet made less noise. With her pulse racing, she slipped out of her room and down the hall.

Quietly she pushed open his door. The room was dark and empty, as she expected. She eased the door shut, but didn't lock it. Someone passing along the hall who happened to check knobs, as she'd seen Rosa do, might question a locked door—if they knew Chance hadn't yet turned in for the night. And Rosa kept close tabs on Chance, despite her insistence that she'd given up on seducing him.

Excitement and relief coursed through AJ when she spotted his computer sitting on a neat, uncluttered desk on the far side of the room. The desk was slanted away from the wall; perhaps Chance never stopped watching for possible problems and wanted to keep an eye on the door as he worked. Whatever the reason for the somewhat awkward placement, it suited her perfectly. Hopefully she would see or hear if anyone started to open the door. And hopefully he wasn't worried about unauthorized users and didn't lock the machine.

She looked around the room dubiously. Nowhere to hide, though. Except under the bed, of course. She bit back a nervous giggle at the idea of rolling under the massive bed, and walked over to click the computer on. Amazingly, the computer was unprotected. As long as she finished before he came in for the night, he should never know she'd been here. Then she thought of Mike and frowned. If Mike were paranoid enough to have a head of security and guard dogs, would he monitor computer usage? She didn't know much about cyber tracking, but knew it could be done. Anxiously, she slanted the screen toward her, wishing it weren't so bright, and glancing frequently at the door as she called up a search engine.

After a moment's hesitation she typed "Thoroughbred insurance fraud." Too broad. She erased it, thought for a moment, and then typed Mike Towers's name and 'horses.' Hit the search key. There weren't many returns; he had said the stable was new. Scanning the information, she didn't even find a stable name; apparently the horses simply ran under his name. A few of his horses with stakes wins turned up, as did his purchase of the stallion, Infierno. (reworded to answer AU question about stable name)

She went to the next page. Scanned down a few entries. Her hands froze on the keys. "Towers's Olympic Candidate Dies." She clicked on the hyperlink and read an account of how three show jumpers—two Hanoverians and a thoroughbred, two World Cup horses and a successful graded stakes winner—had been found in their stalls. Two were dead—broken legs. Axe blows to the heads. Tears streamed down her cheeks, scalding her. The third had been put down. The trainer, a man whose name she didn't recognize, had been arrested, accused of arranging the slaughter. He was, apparently, part owner of the horses. The motive, according to police sources, was financial gain—his share of the insurance money would have been more than his share of any purses the horses might have won.

Plus, the reporter claimed, there were personal issues involved; the man apparently had serious disagreements with Mike Towers over selling the jumpers to move into racing.

So. She didn't doubt that Mike Towers arranged for the deaths of the horses. He'd found someone to take the fall. Had he hired Chance for a new attack? Towers must have been cleared in the last incident. Would he risk his reputation with another attack? She knew he would. Horses as valuable as his were undoubtedly covered by insurance that would pay on damages that occurred anywhere in the world. Here in Nuevo Laredo, where the Towers fortune employed hundreds and likely could buy the silence of hundreds of others, he faced little risk.

She drummed her fingers on the desk. Okay. Knowledge was power. She'd come here with a plan—not a good plan, she knew, but the only one that occurred to her. Well, half of the plan would never have worked anyway. Since Randy, her inspiration for stealing Rebel back, had written about using two horses, she'd brought the gelding with an idea that she could ride him across the river and lead Rebel back to the U. S. side. Failing that, she'd thought she might be able to manage a switch—the two horses looked so alike if you didn't know them. But she could never leave Goof now that she knew what kind of man Mike Towers was— and maybe, what kind of man Chance was. She'd simply start the plan on this side of the river. That would be easier anyway—she would wait for the clearest shot she could get and ride him to the river and across. Once Rebel set foot on U. S. soil, she could fight for him the right way.

She drew a deep breath, glanced around the room again, then typed in a new search. *Rebelde Dorado.*

There were details of his races, announcement of the injury that had ended his career. There was the initial bulletin that he would stand at stud for one season only at Towers's Laredo residence. Nothing after that. Again she wondered if Gina understood fully what had happened once her husband gained control of Rebel. AJ sighed heavily. She hoped not. She knew that speculation around Florida tracks and among Gina's friends centered on Towers's money. Gina married for love, though, not money. She'd gambled and lost. AJ shook her head grimly. Why hadn't she just come home? Surely she could have escaped, even if it meant leaving Rebel here.

She logged off the computer, staring at the screen as it went through the familiar shutdown process. Thought about love.

About dying for love. She didn't hear the door open and close. But the soft sound of a bolt clicking into place jerked her rudely back into awareness. Chance leaned against the door, face taut and arms crossed.

She couldn't think of anything to say, so she didn't speak. He didn't either, just watched her with those dark, probing eyes. Finally he pushed off the door and came across the small space of open floor toward her.

"I thought if anyone came in, I'd hide under the bed," AJ ventured. The truth seemed as harmless as anything else she could think of—at least, part of the truth. She wouldn't tell him the whole truth.

"What were you researching, AJ?"

"None of your business." Hardly true, since she was in his room, on his computer, but oh well.

He sighed. "Did you erase the history?"

"Damn!" she muttered.

"You're putting us both in a bind," he continued, not following up on her lack of stealth. He'd made his point: if she wouldn't tell him, he could just check.

She raised an eyebrow, and stood slowly, careful that her robe didn't snag on the chair and pull open. She felt exposed enough already.

"Do you have any idea how Towers will react if he finds us here together at one in the morning?"

She hadn't thought of that, as a matter of fact—at least, not recently. Her main concern had been Chance. With reason. She went to step past him, but he didn't let her.

"You haven't told me why you were here."

"You'll look anyway." she muttered. "Won't you?"

"Yes."

She shook her head. "Then it really doesn't matter. But if you're worried about us being found together—move!"

He reached out. Traced the contour of her cheek with one gentle finger. "It might be worth it, though," he said softly.

She didn't like the note of huskiness in his voice, or the shiver of excitement as his finger massaged a slow path towards her lip.

"Worth it?"

"Being caught with you. No matter who caught us."

"No." Her denial whispered out. "No, being caught here with you would be stupid. Just stupid. And we're not stupid, Chance."

He sighed and stepped away. "Sometimes I'm not too sure about that, AJ." He walked over to the computer, looked at it, and then turned back to her. "I wish you'd make it easy on me. What were you doing on my computer?"

Making it easy on him was so tempting. If this man weren't obligated to protect Mike Towers's interests, telling him might make sense. If she were sure he wasn't helping Towers plan to kill horses, telling him might make sense. But she didn't trust him and she couldn't expose herself to any more risk. Once she began that final race to safety, she'd never see this man again—this man she wanted so much to touch, to know. She couldn't remember the last time a man had captivated her—enticed her.

"You look ... different," he murmured, leaving the computer to come back over to her. "Are you thinking about giving in?"

Yes. Just not to telling you what I was doing. You should have asked the right question.

"If you think I've changed in a few minutes, Chance, you have a vivid imagination," she chided.

He smiled and winked. "You don't know the half of it." His tone dropped, deepened. "For example, I imagine how it would feel to do this ..." He leaned forward and touched his lips to hers. Softly. Teasing. Inviting her to change fantasy to something more real.

She stepped forward and slid her arms around him. His kiss turned demanding, his hand sliding behind her head to support it while his other arm caught her even closer.

Time stopped for a few frantic seconds. Then he gently eased her out of his embrace and stepped away, his breathing rapid, his arousal clearly evident.

"We can't do this," he muttered. "Towers would go ballistic if someone told him … "

"I know." AJ inhaled deeply, blinked to clear her vision. It didn't help. She still wanted to tear her clothes off. And his. But for what? A few scalding minutes of sex? The idea invited, but she dismissed it. She didn't trust him. And vice versa. But Lord, he made her want him. And want trust. Along with the scalding sex.

"If I told you what I was looking for—" she ventured, her breathing almost normal.

He seemed to understand why she was asking. "I don't know." He considered the question. "I can't make promises that might compromise Mike." He sighed. "And I know that's not the answer you wanted."

Actually, it was, in a sense. It was an honest answer. An answer that spoke of a man who did his job, who cared about loyalty. She could accept that. She just couldn't let desire and need lead her into a trap with no way out. She sighed, a bare breath of air that held a world of frustration. "It's an honest answer," she conceded, after a moment, and smiled. "Which might be a first for us. Good night, Chance."

He didn't answer right away, walked to the door instead and opened it, looking up and down the hall before waving at her. "No one's there. Go ahead."

Just before she stepped into the hall, he caught her arm. "AJ?"

"Yes?"

Again his lips brushed hers in a brief, tempting caress. "Good night." And then he stepped away from her, closing the door between them.

Chapter Eleven

The shadows were deep, dark, and silent. Undergrowth along the river rustled slightly, teased, perhaps, by a breeze. The keening of a coyote, far off, rose and fell, then faded into darkness. Nearer, something large moved through tangled mesquite going away from the river, though, not coming close.

Clouds blanketing the moon drew back abruptly, illuminating a ghostly figure wandering brokenly along the dark, still waters of the river. Damp mud, mold, and the smell of decay made breathing difficult, but still, she watched as the woman on the riverbanks weaved back and forth, flailing thin, pale arms, hair streaming out behind her in pale clouds.

Suddenly the woman paused, throwing her head back, her mouth opening in a silent, unheard wail. And though there was no human sound at all, chills shook her as she realized that the woman was calling for her children, children that she herself had sacrificed to the river's waters. For love. A man's love.

Sweating, AJ jerked upright in bed, throwing her feet over the edge and gripping the edges of the mattress on either side of her to regain some sense of reality. She shivered as the frigid air-conditioned breeze evaporated the moisture on her forehead and arms. A dream! She knew it had been a dream. But Lord, the fear, the smell of the river, the desperation of the woman, were all still so real. *La Llorona.*

Gina. The woman on the riverbanks, wailing her guilt, her anguish, looked like Gina.

That made sense, of course. Grief over losing her sister, the stress of the situation here. Heck, even the growing fascination she felt for Chance could all be underlying causes for giving a mythical woman—a ghost, no less—her sister's familiar face.

AJ frowned and stood up, walking over to stare out into the darkness, trying to push the grimness—and her early morning fantasies—into some kind of manageable perspective. Love had, in a sense, killed *La Llorona*, according to the story. Just as it had killed Gina. Although a car accident might have been the tool of death, desperation and unhappiness must have driven her sister to that nighttime drive. Had she given up, at last, on her marriage? Had she tried to flee, to come home? Worse, could Gina have set out to kill herself? She'd believed since she heard Gina was dead that her sister had snapped and taken her own life, though it had only been a gut feeling.

Tears slid down her cheeks. How many nights had she woken, sobbing, mourning the life stolen from her sister? How long had Gina suffered alone before those few letters had bridged the chasm between them and started to hint at her fear and isolation?

Sudden, muffled crying from another room startled her. For a moment, she couldn't separate her own grief from the new sounds of distress. Abruptly, though, she realized that the weeping must be coming from Gordito's room. Even as she wondered if Rosa would hear, she hurried toward the baby's room. The sobs became louder and clearer nearer his room. Rosa obviously adored the child, but she worked long, exhausting hours and must not have heard him crying.

She pushed open the door, flipping on the light. Gordito was standing up, holding on to the rail of the crib, his stout body shaken with sobs, his face frightened. As she came in, he pressed against the crib rails for balance and waved clenched fists in her direction.

"Shhh!" She picked the baby up, patting and crooning to him. He hiccupped another few sobs, then gradually quieted, laying his head on her shoulder and holding onto her with strong little fingers.

"Hey, you're making me good at this," she murmured, feeling strangely warm and contented by the feel of the child resting so comfortably against her. "I've dealt a little more with racehorses than babies, kid."

He made a gurgling sound against her shoulder, not really moving, and she walked around the room once or twice, hoping to quiet whatever fears confronted him. Gordito didn't react until she went to put him back in the crib. His face screwed up and his little lips puckered.

"Oh, all right. A minute more!" He was heavy, so she walked over to the rocking chair and sat down by the window, then slowly pushed herself back and forth. "I'd sing, but we'd both regret that," she told him, pressing her lips to the back of his head. His silky hair, dampened by his exertions, was a nondescript color—not dark brown, not quite blond. Again, she wondered briefly about the baby's parentage. Surely Mike Towers couldn't despise his own flesh and blood so much that he kept him locked away, even if his mom was just a maid.

His breath quieted, grew more even. At last! Moving cautiously, she stood, trying not to jostle the sleeping baby. She'd put him down, then get a few more hours of sleep herself.

From far off, but still distinct, the eerie, high-pitched wail that had startled her before penetrated the room. A woman's wail of anguish, of desperation.

Gordito jerked spasmodically and cried out, drowning the sound. This time, she couldn't quiet him. He trembled violently, his cries tormented.

The door swung open, and Rosa came in, her face alarmed. "Shhh, Gordito, *no lloras*! Don't cry anymore," she pleaded, gently taking the child from AJ, hugging him, muffling his cries against her shoulder as she murmured reassurances to him. When he finally quieted, she turned accusingly toward AJ.

"What did you do?" she accused.

AJ shook her head. "I heard him crying. I came into see what was wrong. You weren't here." She glanced at the rocker, at the window. "I rocked him to sleep, but there was this noise ..." Her voice trailed off. What would she tell Rosa? That *La Llorona* was not just a century-old legend? No.

Rosa shifted the baby and brushed her disheveled hair away from her face, nodding. "Yes. You were trying to comfort him. I am sorry." She hoisted Gordito, smiling a little. "He is a heavy boy. But I love him."

"Yes." AJ smiled and reached out to pat the baby's back. "He's definitely loveable."

"You've only known him a few days," Rosa said. "But you care for him?"

AJ raised an eyebrow. Did Rosa's question hold—something? A note of suspicion? Or interest? Or had memories of Gina and that damnable dream of the wailing woman made her unusually paranoid?

"Loving a baby is an easy thing," she said finally, and Rosa nodded sagely.

"Loving is easy," she answered cryptically. "Goodnight, AJ. I will watch Gordito until morning."

AJ started to protest, but decided not to. Rosa had every right to dismiss her from this room, after all. She made it back to her room and climbed back into bed before she realized the significance of the whole episode with Gordito. Whatever she heard—the sound she tried to dismiss as imaginary—had terrified Gordito, too. The eerie wail must have wakened him. He hadn't ever heard the legend, of course, and couldn't have understood it if he had. So—he'd reacted to a mother's agonized shriek of desperation? She shivered.

• • •

"Monterrey?" AJ didn't look across the table at Mike Towers as she sliced her egg into neat pieces. She couldn't afford to overreact to the unwelcome invitation to go with him to the popular, nearby business center. Invitation? He'd made it pretty clear he expected her to go. Sort of "payback," she knew, although he hadn't been that blunt, for the days she'd spent here at his estate in Nuevo Laredo.

"Yeah, sure." He grinned at her. "Hey, you couldn't have been there in years!" He drained his glass of orange juice, setting it down with a flourish. "Beautiful city. Great shopping. We'll have fun."

"Fun?" This time she did glance up from her food, but her apprehension must have been apparent.

He laughed, slapping the table heartily. "Lighten up, AJ. I just need someone to smile at some fat cats at lunch. And how can I go to the formal dinner afterwards if you don't come? I don't wanna be the only man there alone—everyone else will have a wife or girlfriend at the shindig."

"Well …"

"Now, come on, girl. You won't embarrass me by turning me down, will you?" The grin didn't fade, but his tone took on a warning note. "You'll be perfectly safe—your own room, and we're coming back tomorrow, because I have business in San Antonio."

She chewed her mouthful of food slowly to keep from having to answer right away. There really was only one answer, of course. She couldn't refuse to go. He would be annoyed, perhaps angry enough to send her packing. That would end the one small chance she had to rescue Rebel. Somehow she'd stay out of his bed. If need be, she could get on a bus or a plane. Tell him who she was. Tell him she'd see him in court. She'd lose Rebel that way, of course, but she would not degrade herself.

She swallowed, forced a smile. "Sure," she said lightly. "It does sound fun." She took a small sip of orange juice. The freshly squeezed liquid might as well have been water. "But I'm glad we'll be back so quickly." She might as well start setting her exit up. "I talked to Randy again."

"Randy—oh, yeah. The fiancé." Towers nodded scornfully. "So … does lover boy want you back?"

Careful. "Yes, he's wanted that." She played with her glass, pretending great interest in the way the liquid swirled around. "But, well, I told him I wasn't sure yet. I promised I'd let him know soon." She looked back at Mike. *Flirty. Not too provocative, though. Not with a night to spend in Monterrey.* "It just wouldn't be fair to anyone to keep things hanging like this."

"Sounds good to me, girl!" Towers barked, clearly pleased by her answer. "So, you throw some stuff in a bag—" He stopped, miffed. "You got good clothes?" he demanded.

She blinked. "Well, what do you mean by 'good'? I don't buy designer clothes, if that's what you mean." She smiled. "I couldn't exactly afford that on what I earned as a tour guide back home."

"Yeah, I guess not. I'd tell you to go buy something, but," he glanced at his watch, "the stores you'd need don't open till ten, and that's just too late."

Take someone else, AJ thought. How perfect if he changed his mind about taking her. She kept her thoughts to herself, though, not wanting to jeopardize her situation. If he really had business out of town—on the U.S. side, no less—then luck might finally be turning her way.

"Well, I just don't have any formal wear."

"You know what, I bet—" He put down his fork, pushed his chair back. "Rosa!" he shouted.

"Probably with the damn brat," he muttered, more to himself than AJ. "Rosa—oh, there you are!"

Rosa nodded at AJ before addressing her boss breathlessly. "*Si, Senor* Towers?"

"Speak English, girl," he growled, and Rosa flushed, but answered again. "Yes, Mr. Towers?"

"See if you can find Miss AJ something to wear. She needs something for lunch. And something for dinner—real elegant. Maybe some of Gina's stuff—"

AJ felt her face tighten and her stomach clenched. He wanted her to wear Gina's things? The bastard wanted her to dress in his dead wife's clothes?

Rosa shook her head. "No, Mr. Towers," she said, carefully respectful. "Miss AJ is much too tall. Mrs. Towers's clothes will not fit." She looked AJ over thoughtfully, then smiled. "I know! The clothes left from the fashion show!"

He looked at Rosa without comprehension. "What clothes?"

"You have forgotten. The show Mrs. Gina held to raise money for the children's home," Rosa reminded him. "You were away, I believe, so you might not know—"

He scoffed. "I know everything that's important. And you'd do well to remember that." He rubbed a hand over the back of the chair, considering. "That was a long time ago, though—"

"There were some very beautiful dresses," Rosa assured him. "I'm sure something will suit very well."

"But will it suit me?" AJ asked darkly, irked that she was being excluded from the conversation.

"You'd better hope so," Towers replied, winking. "'Cause otherwise you'll just have to find some other way to earn your keep."

Rosa's hand on her arm worked to silence her before she told Mike Towers where he could go. She'd do everything she could to bring him down in a day or two. Maybe tomorrow. She could put up with innuendo for one more day. And with his advances for one more night. Because she was sure he didn't really intend to leave her alone in her own room.

"Trust me," Rosa encouraged, motioning her to follow. "You will look ravishing."

"I want to leave within an hour," Towers called after them, and AJ tossed a smile over her shoulder.

"Ravishing in an hour?" she asked. "Luckily, I do trust you, Rosa." They were almost at the top of the stairs when AJ thought about one obvious fact that hadn't occurred to her earlier. Staying out of Mike Towers's bed had been easy enough with Chance around to save her. But tonight—she'd be alone with the man, 150 miles away from Chance. Suddenly, twenty-four hours was a long and dangerous time.

• • •

Monterrey, Mexico

Monterrey was vastly different from when she'd gone there as a youngster. The streets were busier and broader, the buildings higher and more impressive. Mike Towers had driven the 150 miles himself on the much-improved, divided highway, a sullen Jaime sitting in the back seat. But at least the bodyguard's presence served to keep Towers from pushing the conversation into uncomfortable channels.

They arrived in time for lunch in the regal surroundings of Los Reyes Hotel, and AJ silently thanked Rosa for choosing an elegant cream suit that let her feel on even footing with the well-dressed, bejeweled women from Monterrey's elite, along with a scattering of wealthy Texas families.

AJ frowned and shaded her forehead, looking out across Constitución Plaza. In the distance, mountains rose into the summer sky, helping trap the heat. She grimaced. Walking out here in the middle of the afternoon probably labeled her as a little strange, but the empty, elegant hotel room held no charm. She wandered aimlessly across the broad expanse, glad at least that Mike Towers wouldn't find her here. AJ knew women were much more involved in business than in the past, and there had been a scattering of influential women at the luncheon. But in the way of traditional Mexican power lunches, these men segregated themselves after the meal to talk business, while their pampered women headed for spas, boutiques, and other pursuits.

AJ hadn't minded at all when Mike told her he needed to discuss business with some of the other men at the luncheon, and asked if she minded being on her own for a few hours. He'd handed her a credit card and told her to knock herself out, drawing chuckles from some of the other men who had sent their women off to shop.

Several women invited her along, but AJ declined, claiming a nonexistent headache. Truthfully, she acknowledged to herself, she just had no interest in associating with any of these wealthy strangers. A few of the benches were in partial shade. Thankfully she walked over and sat down on the wrought iron, swinging her foot idly. A vendor passed, pausing to offer her ice cream, and from a little farther off, another vendor walked along shouting "*raspas*" at no one in particular. The idea of shaved ice tempted her. She patted her pocket, heard the jingle of coins, and stood to summon the vendor closer.

Just before she called out, though, she saw a man slouch across the plaza, a cap pulled low over his forehead. Disbelief shivered through her. She'd only seen the man once, but she knew where. The barn. The man that Chance denied knowing. Why was he here in Monterrey? Who was he?

The man paid the vendor and stood there briefly, raising the white paper cone to his lips and looking around the plaza. Shivers traced over her skin as he stared in her direction. She thought he might walk toward her, but instead, after a moment, he waved nonchalantly at the vendor and stalked away toward the back of the plaza, disappearing behind the fountain.

The vendor approached, pushing his unwieldy wooden cart ahead of him. On an impulse, AJ stood, waved the vendor off, and headed across the plaza in the direction the evil-faced stranger had just taken. She walked quickly and decisively, not sure exactly why she was following him, and pausing just for a second as she rounded the fountain, glancing around to see if she saw him. There were a number of passersby on the far side—more vendors, kids selling gum or washing cars, city residents hurrying about their business.

She didn't spot him at first. Then a few of the passersby shifted, moved, and there he was. Killer-faced, thin, and as solid as a steel rod. Bent over, talking into the open window of a late-model sedan. Talking to a man who looked very much like Chance Landin.

. . .

The evening's festivities were in slightly better taste than at the soiree at Mike Towers's, AJ thought wearily, leaning against a cool marble column in the back of a huge room. *Don* Antonio De Los Santos, a prominent Mexican banker and industrialist, owned an estate that covered a huge portion of an exclusive Monterrey neighborhood.

A live orchestra played and a brightly dressed crowed eddied and swirled around the room in dizzying waves. Exotic perfumes and colognes, some far too sweet and cloying, overwhelmed even the aroma of gourmet dishes lining an elegant buffet along one entire wall of the room.

At least Mike seemed to have closeted himself with other wheeler-dealers, she thought with intermingled relief and contempt. She wouldn't have to fend him off again for awhile. She'd come way too close to losing her temper and smacking him when he'd insisted on dancing with her, using their very public setting to hold her obscenely close and purr compliments in her ear. Tonight could be a problem.

AJ chewed her lip and breathed deeply, then swung her shoulders, trying to loosen the tension. If things worked out tonight, tomorrow might be the end—one way or the other. She simply couldn't wait much longer. Mike wasn't base enough, luckily, to actually force himself on a woman—at least, she didn't think he was. But innuendo was fast becoming demand, and sooner or later he'd tell her to give in or go home.

A couple strolled into the quiet, shadowed area behind the columns, intent on a few moments of privacy. They locked arms and lips, and with a small, grim smile, AJ realized she probably should move on. She glanced out at the crowded dance floor, wishing she could count on Chance's protection one final time.

The thought made her shiver a little. The man she'd followed spoke to someone who looked so much like Chance. But Chance was 150 miles away—wasn't he? And if not, what business did he have with the evil-faced man he'd denied knowing anything about?

"AJ, my dear!" Towers's voice halted her as she inched towards the far side of the room, intent on escaping into the bathroom down the hall.

Blue eyes bored into her. They glittered coldly, whether because of the bright light from the overhead chandeliers or her imagination. What had Gina ever seen in this man?

"You're not leaving, I hope?" he asked jovially, but she sensed anger beneath the suspicion. "Laredo's a long walk!"

"Yes, I know." She kept her tone light, strived not to sound too distant. Or too coquettish. "But you know." She shrugged. "Nature calls."

"Mikey, you can't argue with nature!" A Monterrey socialite, whose name AJ couldn't remember, latched onto Towers's arm possessively.

She tossed her head, dark hair swirling around her slender throat and bare shoulders. "I'll watch your man for you, *querida,* no?"

"Sure," AJ returned lightly, not worried over the venomous offer. "I'll only be a few minutes."

The woman urged Mike toward the bar. "Take your time," she called over her shoulder. "No putting off Mother Nature." She whispered something, and AJ heard Towers chuckle and wrap an arm around her shoulders.

Good, she thought again, but almost immediately felt a tiny surge of indignation puncture the relief as memories of Gina returned to haunt her. Did Gina face Mike's obvious interest in other women everywhere she went? Had she even gone out? Maybe he had left her at home more often than not, in spite of claiming not wanting to come here alone. She wished the few letters Gina had written had told more of her life. She would know better what she might face from Mike if she understood what Gina had endured. Mike hadn't bothered pretending to be faithful, or he wouldn't have his son with another woman hidden away in Gina's house. Women had been all over him at that first party, too— clearly he considered himself a player. Leaving his wife at home would have opened the field.

She shook off her dark thoughts and walked down the marble hall, her heels clicking on the hard surface. A man in a dark suit watched her and a cluster of women brushed past, jewels sparkling on ears, throats, and hands. She put a hand on the doorknob leading into the bathroom, then paused, feeling another chill. This didn't seem like the physical cold from the ballroom, though. It felt like death brushing past. Like the remnants of a tortured soul dissolving into the air around her.

Drawing a deep breath, she whirled around. The hall was empty.

"Damn!" she muttered, hugging herself. "I'm plain loony tonight!"

"Talking to yourself, Miss Owens?" A tall, gray-haired man smiled at her in bemusement. She recognized him from the luncheon as a member of the Monterrey city government, and flashed him an embarrassed smile.

"I guess I haven't gotten away from the legends as much as I thought. I must have been feeling *La Llorona* pass me by or something."

He laughed. "Ah, yes! The famous wailing woman of our people, no? And her endless search for the children she killed—in her futile attempt to trap a man."

She shook her head in protest. "I'm not sure I'd retell our legend quite that way."

"You can't excuse her actions," he argued in consternation.

She wanted to laugh at the irony of standing here, arguing ethics over a nonexistent wraith with a man who might easily be a billionaire. Still, she felt a strange urge to defend the imaginary woman.

"She was betrayed, as many women are."

"So you would excuse her drowning those precious little ones?"

"No. In modern times, no. But in her day … if she really thought they would perish from starvation and abandonment … I don't know."

He nodded. "We shall disagree politely, then." He turned to go, but paused. "You are all right, now?"

"Yes, of course," she assured him, smiling again. "Maybe I had a bit too much to drink—"

He snorted gently. "That, my dear, seems unlikely. I notice beautiful women, even when I shouldn't—and you seemed quite content to … how do you say it? Lurk in the shadows?"

"We're both getting a little too fanciful," AJ retorted, nodding at him. "*Con permiso*." This time, she reached resolutely for the doorknob, opened the door, and stepped into the bathroom, locking it behind her. Almost unwilling to touch any of the lavish trimmings, she opted to sink down for a moment on a brocade stool, kick off her silver heels, and flex her toes. The cool air felt good on the plants of her feet. A knock on the door reminded her that she had little respite, though, and she shoved her feet back into the shoes and stood, glancing at the mirror, then freezing in horror.

Her own face stared back at her—and behind her, the shadowy lines of a woman who looked much like Gina smiled a bloodless smile.

Choking back a tiny exclamation of shock and fear, she jerked the bolt back and rushed toward the ballroom, preferring the known menace of Mike Towers to the helpless feeling that she might be losing her mind.

•••

Chance drew a deep breath and sagged wearily against the rough wall behind him. The granite-textured cement still held the day's heat, although midnight had come and gone. Around him, the huge city had gone silent. Monterrey, cosmopolitan and modern, boasted its shares of night spots—clubs, bars, and all-night restaurants—but those held little interest. In fact, the city itself held little interest. He had only come to track Bone. *El Hueso*. Once AJ told him of Bone's appearance in the stable, he knew that he could find them. Money bought information, and Bone's reputation proved well known among a certain group of lowlifes.

Contempt twisted Chance's lips. The man might look like the diseased, discarded remains of some predator's dinner, but he was lower than the lowest scavenger. Undoubtedly his had been the hands that had destroyed those horses on Towers's orders. But he needed proof.

The fact that Bone showed interest in Chance's hints at a little "personal business" meant only that he was greedy. Until he could tie Bone to Towers, and to the deaths of those horses in Arizona, there was nothing to show officials. No way to prove his uncle's innocence. Towers had contacted Bone—Chance doubted he turned up in Nuevo Laredo for some other reason. How much danger were the new stallions in? Catching Bone in the act of attacking Towers's Thoroughbreds would only provide the proof he sought so desperately if he let the man get close enough to the horses to show clear intent to injure them.

He moved his shoulders against the wall, the pebbled surface acting as a soothing massage, although his shirt would undoubtedly be savaged—and more than a little grimy. Sighing, he pushed himself upright and glanced at the hotel with narrowed eyes.

Towers was there. With AJ. Bile threatened to choke him. He didn't understand the woman at all. She wasn't a tramp; he could tell. She wasn't a gold digger, either—yet she was in that damn hotel with a man who made his intentions more obvious by the minute. Her story about needing closure over her sister's death rang true—partially. Not completely, though. And her story about Rebel and the look-alike horse on the Texas side seemed absurd. For some reason, she'd brought a Thoroughbred with her from Philly to the border. Her trip would have been easier if she'd come alone; horses demanded food and care. This horse looked just like Rebel. He didn't seem to fit into any plan that made sense, though. Could AJ actually be out for some kind of revenge? Was she a physical danger to her sister's widower?

A police car crawled past, and he could see the officer on the passenger's side scrutinize him. Probably thought he was *un boracho*—an inebriated *turista* out too late. He dragged a hand through his hair and walked slowly toward his own hotel. Hoping that AJ was safe. Knowing he had no way to help her, even if she wasn't. A couple passed close by, arms around each other, giggling and whispering.

Damn. Everything turned his mind in AJ's direction—a futile path if he ever saw one. He could never have her, of course. Even if he weren't focused on Towers—even if he could help her with whatever problems tormented her. Because sooner or later, she would wonder about Gina. And she wouldn't be too happy to hear what so many would be quick to tell her. What he himself would have to say. And worse, what he had done that fateful night. The night he told Gina to leave if she was sure she wouldn't want to go back. The night he'd arranged for a car Gina could leave in.

The shriek of a fire engine racing by startled him so much that he stumbled a half-step. The huge red machine pulled up under the portico and fear for AJ raced through him.

No smoke billowed into the night air, but men in their protective gear were racing in, and some guests were coming out, alarmed and chattering. Frowning, he worked his way through some of them, moving toward the door, unsure why finding AJ mattered so much.

Another group of guests came out and Mike Towers, his white shirt half unbuttoned, swore at one of the hotel staffers, who apologized profusely for the inconvenience.

"Idiots!" he snapped. "A little smoke—you don't even know where it came from and you start knocking doors down—"

"The smoke seemed worst near your room," the man explained diffidently. "There must have been some kind of electrical short on your floor, and of course we could not risk your safety, Mr. Towers."

Chance gritted his teeth as he broke for the door, afraid that Mike would turn and see him. Behind him, though, Towers's voice went on lashing out at everyone around him. Mingling with the guests and staff milling around, Chance slipped through the lobby, scanning the crowd for AJ. She wasn't among the guests, though, and he definitely hadn't seen her escape from inside.

He rushed up the glossy steps, his shoes drumming as loudly as his heart. He knew the room numbers—Mike had left word where to reach him. He went by 216, paused at 218, and rapped softly on the door.

Smoke burned his nose and his eyes watered as he rapped again, more loudly. Could the fire have started here, in AJ's room? He glanced around, worried that Towers would find him outside her door. He doubted the man would believe he'd gotten the wrong room.

He lifted his hand to bang on the wood just as it cracked open.

"Chance?" Surprise colored AJ's hushed whisper, but she swung the door open, caught his arm, and jerked him inside, pushing the door closed behind her. "You're here?"

Then the green eyes so unlike Gina's darkened. "Why?"

He waved her question aside, catching her arms and holding her away to appraise any damage. She didn't look damaged. She looked suspicious, but also—maybe—relieved to see him.

"You didn't get out—"

She smiled a slow, smug smile. "No. Of course not."

He breathed in and coughed. "The smoke—"

"Worked pretty darned well, if I do say so myself!"

He gaped. "You … set the fire?"

"Well, not exactly." She shook out of his grip and motioned towards a towel. A travel iron lay on top of charred fabric.

"Actually, I only meant to make myself cough a little. Sound sick. Mike kept hammering on the door," she explained. "I never meant to cause a panic. There was more smoke than I expected, though, and the smoke alarm started going off. Then I guess someone in the hall rang the alarm out there. Technically, I didn't even cause all the excitement. But I was lucky … when the hotel staff came racing up, I convinced them Mike would be furious if he knew I'd been careless." She shrugged.

"They probably don't like Mike much, either. They told him there was a short in the next room. Promised not to tell him where the smoke started." She smiled again, still smugly. "A perfect plan. I told you, I can take care of myself."

He frowned, not at all sure he would draw the same conclusion. But just as quickly as she'd decided she didn't need him, she remembered he'd evaded her question.

"What are you doing here?" she demanded, and he sighed and ran a hand over his jaw.

"Watching Mike. And you."

She shook her head decisively and stared at him. "No," she said. "You're not here for that. I saw you earlier … talking to that man."

Play dumb, he told himself, cursing his stupidity. Why had he suggested Bone contact him in a public place? "Man?"

She dashed away his pretense of ignorance. "Yeah. The man from the barn you don't know. The one you spoke to in your car this afternoon."

He frowned. The woman was too damn smart for her own good. Persistent. And sexy as all get out. Some of the guests he'd seen outside wore their nightclothes; a few seemed to have dressed hastily. AJ, apparently confident enough in her ruse not to worry about either subterfuge or Towers, wore a slinky, curve-hugging nightgown in a dark emerald color that covered well enough— well enough to cause a whole lot of chaos to a man's systems. One system in particular. She had pulled on a gauzy robe, too, but had forgotten to tie the sash hanging loosely at her sides.

Annoyed at the immediate tightening in his groin and the urge to snatch her back into his arms, he took a deliberate step back. Didn't help, though—she still stood there, tousled and glowing with satisfaction.

"Damn!" he muttered, out loud this time, and her smugness turned into slight surprise.

She arched an eyebrow. "What's wrong?"

"You." The word slapped out like another oath, and he closed the distance between them with one half-lunging step.

"Dammit, AJ, come clean before I have to tell Mike you're his dead wife's sister!"

Shock and fear flitted across her face before anger sparked in her eyes and pulled her lips tight. "You wouldn't!" she cried, trying to jerk free from his grasp. He tightened his grip and kept her close.

"I'll do anything I have to," he snapped. "Anything."

She sagged slightly, her body going limp as if in defeat, and tears glinted briefly in her eyes. She blinked several times, hard, and drew in a long breath. He loosened his hold and stepped back.

"For God's sake, talk to me," he prodded.

"Mike's going to be banging on my door any minute," she pointed out, her voice calm again. "I gave a few bills to one of the bellboys hoping he could find a way to stall him, but there's no guarantee." She shrugged her shoulders, and the robe slipped halfway down her arms. She didn't seem to notice, though, just reached up, jerking a hand through her hair, and shoving at the constraining sleeve when it hampered her.

He drew in a shaky breath of his own that had nothing to do with anger or fear, and everything to do with the need to drag her the few steps back to the bed behind them. *Mike*, he snarled silently to himself. *Mike. Remember Mike.*

"That'll be a treat," he muttered. He waved a hand at her. "Any ideas? I'm not losing my job over—"

"Over what?" AJ demanded, with traces of her earlier anger. "You're the one who shouldn't be here, Chance. You're the one in my room—"

"And you're the one standing here with your clothes falling off! Damn it, AJ—you're killing me!"

She looked startled for a moment. Something like smug satisfaction touched her lips, turned them up in the slightest of smiles. The reaction wasn't what he expected. Not what he needed, when Mike might interrupt them, and any chance to save his uncle would be gone. Then she reached out and laid her hand on his cheek. Her touch warmed him. Trembled against his overheated skin, jolting him.

"We shouldn't have met in this lifetime, should we?" she murmured, and the smile faded. "I guess I'm not as good as I thought," she acknowledged. "I have no idea how to get out of this mess."

He glanced at the bed. "Any chance we can just stay here and think about it tomorrow?"

"Mike isn't strong enough to break the door down, but he could get a key with no problem at all. And I think climbing down the fire escape would probably make him wonder a little about me."

"But even if I can get out without being seen ... what do we do about Mike?"

She sighed. "I think I have to go next door and distract him. You leave."

"And you?"

She shrugged, this time hitching at the flimsy robe to keep from losing it altogether. She met his gaze unflinchingly. "Forget me, Chance. Just get out while you can. I'll take care of myself ... if I can."

"And if you can't?"

Her lips trembled slightly but her chin came up. "Goodnight, Chance," she said quietly, and walked to the door, pulling it open and peering out cautiously.

After a minute she turned and whispered, "Go! Now."

He saw no choice. Blood pounding in his head, he made his own quick survey and slipped out in the hall.

With Chance out of her room, AJ locked the door and searched hastily through her clothes, finding jeans and a loose sweatshirt and throwing them on. She drew in another deep breath to brace herself, but the remnants of smoke in the room made her cough.

She glanced around the room, spotted the singed fabric, and quickly took it and stuffed it in the wastebasket in the bathroom. Nothing else seemed out of place, although she hoped Mike wouldn't be in this room at all. Still, there was no point in being careless. Satisfied that the room wouldn't give her away, she went next door and rapped quietly.

Mike opened the door almost immediately, a grin splitting his face. "Well, well," he greeted her. "Come on in. Keep an old man company."

She managed a slight smile. "It's awfully late," she hedged. "I was just afraid you'd looked for me and didn't find me."

"Where were you?" He pulled the door open, and for a moment, AJ braced herself to be jerked into the room.

A couple came down the hall, talking about the false alarm with agitation. Tourists, apparently, as they spoke in English.

AJ nodded at them as they drew near, and Towers glowered but didn't reach for her wrist as she'd feared.

"So? Where did you disappear to?" he repeated as the couple nodded and passed. "Didn't find you downstairs. Damn idiots wouldn't let me come back for the longest time—"

"I'm sure they just wanted to be sure everyone was safe," AJ soothed. "I couldn't quit coughing. They had me see a doctor."

He looked at her suspiciously. "Doctor? What doctor? The hotel doctor?"

She shrugged. "I couldn't say. There were a lot of people. Someone said to get in line and see the doctor, so I did."

"Hmm. Better now?"

"A little nauseous." *Thinking about you.* "Still coughing a little now and then. But okay."

"Well, good." He looked her over from head to foot. "Sure don't look as good now as you did earlier," he said disapprovingly, and she realized he'd never seen her in the kind of clothes she usually wore.

She faked a frown, glancing down at the soft cotton shirt and worn denim. "My fiancé always liked me like this," she murmured. "Said I looked like a real homebody in my jeans and tees."

"Homebodies don't much interest me, to be honest. I like women who look like women." Towers took a step back, holding the door open wider. "Comin' in or not?"

She plucked at her jeans with nervous fingers, breathing a silent prayer that he wouldn't get ugly. Unmanageable. "Not, I think," she answered, after a moment. "You don't need me throwing up all over your bed." She managed a small chuckle. "I bet it'd take forever to get someone to clean up, after the night everyone's had."

Towers made a snort of assessment, but his eyes were ice cold. "Well, we did say separate rooms." His tone, like his eyes, sounded hard. Dangerous.

"Good night, Mike," she said, and he watched until she reached her own door and opened it.

"Be ready to leave at nine," he told her. "And don't forget our little deal."

"Deal?" she echoed, although she knew exactly what he meant.

"Yeah. The one where you decide whether or not your lover boy's worth going home to."

She couldn't think of anything to say, so she just nodded at Mike and went in to her own room, locking the door and fastening the security chain. Then she leaned against the door, trembling with relief. And revulsion.

• • •

Nuevo Laredo, Mexico

The trip back to Nuevo Laredo passed in a blur. As before, Jaime sat silently in the seat behind them, never speaking. She couldn't forget his presence, though, and again, considered it a mixed blessing. On the one hand, he smelled of beer and smoke, but on the other, he might make Mike more mindful of what he said. Mostly, Mike talked about the men he'd met with in Monterrey. She said little in return.

"You got a headache or something?" he demanded at one point, and she nodded and said that she did. Headache was hardly the word. Her head did hurt—but the threats closing in around her were the real problem. He'd start pushing her to sleep with him the minute they got back, probably. He'd been obvious enough about it last night.

For a moment she closed her eyes and thought about leaving Mike as soon as they reached the ranch. She'd brought Goof to Texas out of insanity, really—thinking somehow to smuggle him onto Towers's ranch to fool passersby until she could escape with Rebel.

She knew now that would never work. Even if she could get Goof himself across the river and on to Towers's ranch, Chance knew about him. Had enough of an eye to spot the differences between the two horses. And of course, one was a gelding, one a stallion. Anyone who worked with Rebel would notice the switch. Naively, she'd hoped just seeing the head over the stall door might be distraction enough.

She could leave Rebel and file legal papers. Fight for him. She doubted that would work. Towers had so much more money than she and her mother, and Texas was a community-property state. Towers could claim that Gina had left him the stallion. Rebel's papers were in her mother's name, but Gina and Towers had him at the time of her death. Apparently Chance thought the horse had belonged to Gina; others might have been led to believe so, too.

There would be no end of witnesses claiming the horse belonged to Towers. And even if she and her mother could win in court, Towers could simply keep the stallion in Mexico. The legal system was different, and Towers had money and influence on his side.

She sighed and Towers turned toward her.

"Am I borin' you with my little stories, AJ?"

"No." She smiled faintly, the throbbing in her temples increasing. "No, I just can't get the damned pain in my head to go away."

"I got a remedy for that, darlin'," he offered, reaching over to pat her thigh. She frowned and turned back to the window without answering.

"Well, now, where were we?" he said after a minute. "Oh, that man you were dancin' with last night—Armando Robles Castillo. He might be the next governor of the state."

Towers went on explaining how he, Castillo, and some others wanted to encourage trade from Monterrey and the rest of Mexico to use the one international bridge that bypassed Laredo, crossing from Nuevo Leon state rather than Tamaulipas state into Texas.

Although she really didn't care, AJ sat up straighter and asked occasional questions. Anything to keep him from the crude suggestions and leering, sideway glances. When they finally turned into the now familiar drive of Mike's property, relief washed over her.

Safe, she thought, though she knew that wasn't really true. Towers still wanted her. Rebel was no closer to home. But somehow none of that mattered. Chance would be back, too. And although he didn't trust her and might not be able to protect her from Towers, somehow she knew he wouldn't hurt her.

• • •

Chance let the nursery curtain fall as he saw the Escalade pull up in front of the house. Gordito gurgled a protest, reaching for the fabric and trying to pull himself free.

"Easy there, guy," Chance warned. "You're not Tarzan quite yet, and Rosa will have my hide if you hurt yourself!"

Behind him, the door closed softly, and he turned to find Rosa watching them with a slight smile that didn't touch her eyes.

"He's back," she announced. "With AJ."

Chance nodded. "I saw them." He set the baby down, and watched as the child scooted across the carpet towards Rosa, who scooped him up and hugged him.

"So. You have decided?"

He shook his head and scuffed his boot into the floor. "No. I haven't."

"But you know what you should do." She didn't ask, just stated it calmly, then walked over to him, laying a hand on his arm. "You know," she said again. "You knew the moment you realized that they were sisters."

Slowly, he nodded. "But it's not as easy as knowing. People will be hurt." He reached out to stroke a finger across Gordito's cheek. "You will be hurt."

"*No importa*. Some things cannot be helped. This cannot be helped." She blinked back tears and kissed the baby again.

"What if we're wrong, Rosa? We could be."

She shook her head, and Gordito clutched at the dark curls with a yelp of delight. "Ayyy! *Sueltame*—turn my hair loose, you silly boy!" She untangled the chubby hands from her hair and set the child down on the floor carefully.

"Mike hates Gordito. That is no way for a child to live, Chance. We both know that hate has no place in this baby's life."

He reached out a hand to brush one of her mussed locks back into place. "He has only known love so far though, Rosa. We don't know that Towers would do anything—why would he?"

She shrugged. "*¡Bastardo!*," she said bitterly, and Chance would have understood the word in any language. "He would do anything."

Her words cut him to the quick. A man who would do anything—and AJ had been alone last night. At his mercy, perhaps. He frowned. He couldn't dwell on what might have happened or not. AJ had known the danger and chosen to stay. Damn her! He tried to refocus on the woman standing there before him, her face full of fear for a child. For someone else's child.

"You'll lose him," he reminded her gently.

"And it will kill me," she whispered. "But I could not love Gordito more if he were truly mine. And no mother places her child in harm's way."

"Ah, but that's not true," he countered darkly. "Read the newspapers, *niña*. Remember the fables." He looked down as Gordito clutched his pant leg and hauled himself up, turning his face up to smile at them.

Rosa shrugged again, dismissively. "You would have me believe stories of *La Llorona*? No, I am no *niña*, no scared little girl who believes in legends. Women may give birth and not be mothers, just as not all fathers are truly fathers."

Chance smiled down at Gordito, then bent to pick him up. "True. But I wouldn't dismiss all legends so easily, *linda*. Because in my world, we have the boogeyman!" He growled the last words against the baby's cheek, and both Rosa and Gordito hooted with laughter.

"*Señor* Chance," a woman's voice called through the door, and he wrinkled his nose at Rosa and Gordito, recognizing the head housekeeper, María.

"The door's not locked," he called, and handed the child back to Rosa, stepping away from her. María gossiped and complained most of the day. He knew that few members of the household had any use for the middle-aged woman, but he had known her as long as he had known Towers. According to his uncle, María had kept the house in Arizona, too.

The door opened, and she came in, her thick face twisted in a suspiciously sweet smile.

"Mr. Mike would like to see you immediately," she announced, in a way that made Chance suspect Towers wanted to see him about some invention of hers. "He's very angry. I wouldn't make him wait."

"Thank you, María," he said, curtly and dismissively, not caring that her fake smile slid back into her usual venomous frown. "I'll go right away." He turned to Rosa and gave her a grin and a wink.

"No, no problem at all. The new maid must be doing her job well." He turned and headed towards the door, giving the scowling housekeeper a brief nod.

"Snake in the grass," he muttered under his breath as soon as he was out of earshot.

He found Towers in the study, turning the leather chair back and forth and staring absently at the far wall while he flipped a pen around in his hand.

"Close the door and sit down, Landin," he ordered when he spotted Chance.

So they weren't buddies any more. Okay. Probably someone—María—mentioned that he'd left right after Towers did. That was just a hunch, though, and so he sat down in the chair near the desk. "What's up?" he asked casually.

"Well, now, maybe you should tell me that," Towers suggested, stabbing at a notepad with his pen. "Funny how you don't follow orders too good. Makes a man wonder why."

"Seems to me my only orders when I signed on were to protect you and your interests, Mike." He shrugged slightly. "And that's exactly what I do."

"I told you to stay here," his boss muttered, and Chance nodded.

So someone did tell him. Fear tightened in his gut as he wondered if someone just mentioned he'd left, or if he'd been seen in Monterrey. God forbid he'd been seen with AJ. "You did tell me," he agreed, striving for patience. "But I can't protect you from 150 miles away. And I doubled the dog patrols and had someone checking the cameras for me. I called several times to touch base."

"And you can prove that, can't you, boy?" Towers made no attempt to mask his suspicion. "'Cause it's really easy to check on stuff like that. I'm not much with this modern stuff, but a moron can talk to the right people and look at logs."

"Hell, Mike, pick up the phone," Chance challenged, breathing a small prayer of thanksgiving that he'd actually taken steps to cover his tracks—thinking he was being needlessly cautious. Towers had never doubted him before, as far as he knew, at least not to the point of having him watched. Maria had certainly tried to cause problems for him before, but with little success. Still… He hesitated, gauging the man's reaction. Couldn't afford to blow his cover. Couldn't get himself fired—not with his uncle still rotting in a prison cell. Not with AJ still on the ranch.

"Why'd you tail me to Monterrey?" Towers demanded brusquely, not reaching for the phone.

"To make sure you were safe. I do not trust Jaime. Couldn't quit thinking that you only had his word for where that letter came from"

The dart hit the bulls-eye; he saw Towers's eyes widen slightly in surprise and then narrow. "Well, now, that's true enough," he conceded after a minute. But then he shook his head. "Not that I'm buyin' that, but it's a thought."

"Your choice to buy it or not, but Jaime's the only one who saw the kid—if there was a kid. And have there been any other threats since that one?"

Chance pushed himself out of his chair, and walked over to the door, then back, standing by the desk instead of sitting again. "Your trust could get you killed," he muttered. "I followed you to Monterrey hoping it wouldn't. I don't have anything on Jaime. But you know I don't trust the man. He gives me a bad feeling."

"Humph." Towers tossed the pen to the desk. "Seems like you'd need more than a bad feeling, being in charge of security."

"Sometimes gut instinct comes first," Chance retorted. "Sometimes there's nothing else to go on—and if you wait for hard facts, there's a drawn gun and a body lying in a pool of blood."

Towers blanched and rocked back in his chair. "Well, you'd need to prove it to me before I'd believe it about Jaime," he said finally. "But I'll keep my eyes open anyway."

"Can't argue with the wisdom of that."

Towers scooted his chair closer to the desk again. "Got to tell you, though—Jaime doesn't trust *you*. Had him watching the woman when I couldn't."

Chance's heart jolted, pounded. He tried to freeze his facial muscles into place so that he'd show no outrage. No fear. "The woman?" he asked carefully. "AJ?"

"Hell, yeah, AJ," Towers sputtered. "Know any other damn woman jerking me around by the dick? But I've just about had enough of that."

He kept the mask on, carefully kept his tone neutral. "Seems strange you'd need her watched in Monterrey. Who would she know there?"

Towers turned an icy stare his way. "I thought maybe you." He shrugged. "Lucky I was wrong. Just wanted to hit the stores, same as any damn woman. Wore her shoes out visiting shops. But something about that woman just don't sit right."

Relief flooded through him as he realized that Towers probably didn't know about his visit to her room. Still, he probed, trying to be sure. "Heard guests saying there was a fire upstairs," he said. "I saw you come out, but I didn't see Jaime."

"Nah." Mike shook his head and grinned. "Man after my own heart, Jaime is. Knew I'd be safe at the dinner and hotel—lots of big guns there, and they had their men with 'em. And since I had AJ where I could watch her myself—I told him to go get some ass." He winked. "Don't have to tell a real man that twice," he added.

Chance frowned. "Stupid, sending your only protection off like that," he muttered.

"Don't be callin' me stupid, Chance," Towers warned, the use of the first name tinged with sarcasm. "'Cause I ain't. For example—I think there's a little bit of a problem with you and my girl. And that don't sit too well with me."

The mask slipped and he just gaped. "Excuse me?"

Towers reached over to pick up his pen again, tossing it up and catching it, watching the pen instead of looking at Chance. "Well, you know, I don't buy this fiancé thing," he said eventually.

"There's a marriage license—" Chance lied, hoping that Mike hadn't already checked. What or who had made the bastard so suspicious, so close to ruining it all?

"Well, now, I'm not sayin' she wasn't gonna get hitched," he countered, finally looking back at Chance. "Pretty woman like her, sure she had some poor idiot panting after her. But she hit on me quick enough. Pretty clear what she wanted. Came over here with every intention of letting me lay her. And then what? She changes her mind?"

"Second thoughts," Chance suggested. "Maybe she really does think she can get back with her fiancé?"

Towers shook his head slowly. "I been thinkin' on this a lot," he said. "And a couple of other people had the same thought."

"And what thought is that?" Chance asked grimly, making a list of possible gossips and coming up with two. Jaime and María.

"Well, might not be your doin' exactly, but seems like the little filly might be findin' you more to her likin' than me."

"What bull!" Chance snapped. "I'm not in the habit of going after your women, Mike."

"No. Not in the habit." Towers stood up, stretching, and then leaned his hands on the desk, his eyes full of accusation.

"Don't think you've ever been stupid enough to do that. But I can't help thinkin' that the reason AJ keeps puttin' me off is 'cause she's hopin' for you."

Chance shook his head. "I pity you, then," he said with as much bravado as he could muster. "You've got pretty poor character judgment. Because I can tell you up front—she's got no interest in me." He paused, suddenly realizing he could jeopardize AJ even by denying her interest in him. At least in Towers's mind, the reason explained her actions to some extent. And since he himself wasn't sure of her real motive, the more Towers thought about her, the more likely he'd be to let his desire harden into suspicion. Into vengeance, if he realized she'd come here under false pretenses.

And if he found out that she was Gina's sister—then his own time here would be at an end. That couldn't happen. Not when he'd finally caught up with Bone and hinted that he needed a job done. He'd promised his aunt and uncle that he would find proof of Towers's guilt. That his uncle would be a free man again, and finally he was closer than he'd ever been.

"Look, I didn't mean to snap your head off," he offered in a conciliatory tone. "I just don't see AJ the way you do." He shook his head, and moved away from the desk. "She seems like—I don't know. A nice enough woman. She sure doesn't seem to be after me."

"'Nice enough woman,'" Towers snorted. "Like my wife the whore?" He slammed a fist down on his desk. "Ain't no nice enough woman, boy." He snickered.

"Then send her home," Chance suggested. His head throbbed. She wouldn't appreciate his intervention. She would be furious if Towers did chase her off. But the possibility that Towers could force himself on her sickened him. And infuriated him. He could only help her by getting her off the ranch.

But Towers just shook his head. "Hell, no," he said. "Ain't no way that woman leaves without givin' me what I want. Hell, she all but promised it when she came on to me that first night. And she owes me now."

He moved around the desk, walking up to Chance and laying one of his beefy hands on his arm. "Just watch her, Chance. Don't let me find you messin' with the one woman I'd hurt you over."

"Take your hand off me, Mike. If that's all, I need to check up with Santos and look in on the dogs. Would you like the logs?"

"No. We've said what had to be said," Towers said. He went back to his desk and sat down.

"I've got the governor's dinner in Austin on Friday," he said. "Can't miss it, and don't think I'll take little Miss Priss. The governor thinks I'm still mourning my dear departed wife." He leered. "He's on one of those stupid family values bandwagons— they all are, when it suits 'em. Probably leave tomorrow so I can take care of some business in San Antonio on the way up. But I'll be back Saturday. And then … AJ and me's gonna have a little talk."

Chance managed to nod nonchalantly, to speak past the anger tightening his throat muscles. "You're the boss. But we should get together and talk about some security issues before then."

"Maybe." Towers reached to pull the phone closer. "I don't much worry on the Texas side, not once I'm away from my place. Once I head up north, nothing will happen. The governor's bash will be plenty safe." He paused, squinted a little in thought.

"'Course, it might be good if you were back in Laredo. I've got Jaime and the boys here, and no one's runnin' the show there. Besides," his tone dropped a note, "that way there's no doubt AJ'll get you outta her head, if that's the problem."

Chance pulled the door open. "Like I said, I'll do what you tell me. But I'd agree that the Laredo side's safer than here. I'll be pretty useless sitting in a room in Laredo if someone pumps you full of lead on this side. Might keep that in mind." Before Towers could infuriate him any further, he stepped out in the hall and closed the door behind them.

As he closed the door, realization struck. Mike thought AJ had gone shopping. He knew that she hadn't. She'd been in the plaza when she saw him with Bone, and she told him she hadn't bought a thing—that she hadn't wanted to owe Mike a penny. But clearly, Jaime had lied—and told Mike she'd spent the afternoon shopping. Why? Jaime had no reason to cover for AJ—so had he been covering for his own carelessness? More than ever, the bodyguard's behavior seemed totally off.

And as he wondered about Jaime, he wondered again how the hell he could save AJ, a baby, and his uncle, if he couldn't save himself. (To address your suggestions about making Jaime a more important character)

Chapter Twelve

AJ twisted her hair into a knot and pinned it in place, hoping that she could find some relief from the searing temperature. As cool as it was in the house, a step or two out into the yard and she'd be drenched with sweat and cursing the heat.

Not that she was sure she'd leave her room. Somewhere out there, Mike waited. He might be going about his business, but he'd pop out of nowhere if he saw her. And Chance would be around, too, with looks laced with a mixture of concern, suspicion, and—what? Heck, even María, the sour-faced housekeeper, seemed to be frowning her way more often than not.

"Does wonders for the ego," she mused out loud. "Not a friendly face in the place."

The gurgle of laughter behind her belied that assessment. Gordito came toddling in, all laughter and gladness. She'd been amazed to return from her short trip to Monterrey and find that he'd started trying to walk. She grinned and snatched him up just before he fell, kissing him loudly on the cheek and then laughing out loud when he tried to mimic her and blew a wet, noisy kiss on her cheek.

"You're a breath of fresh air," she told him, hugging him gently. "You probably shouldn't be here, though. Your mom will be worried about you."

She smoothed the baby's fine tangle of blond hair and pressed a kiss to the top of his head. "You sure don't favor your mom," she murmured against the scalp. "Not even your dad, really. But genetics are funny that way."

Gordito twined a chubby hand in her dyed hair and jerked experimentally.

"Owww! Hey, I have enough that it hurts when you pull it!" she scolded, carefully untwining his fingers. "Gina would have loved you. You know, your eyes are just about as blue as hers." She buried her face momentarily in the toddler's chest, breathing in his essence, thinking of Gina.

Gina, whose last letter—one of only three she'd written during her marriage—told of a miscarriage. AJ's chest hurt, and she could still see the tear-stained page. Still remember how she'd cursed her sister for not leaving and just coming home, sure from the absence of information about Mike Towers that the desperate pain over losing a baby was unimportant to the man who'd isolated her from her family.

"Dear Lord, how she must have suffered," AJ whispered against the baby's shirt, and managed a smile when he tugged her head back up. She kissed his cheek. "But you're just priceless, aren't you? Let's get you back to your room before anyone worries."

Rosa met her just outside the door, her face pulled into a frown. "This boy! He cannot be kept in one place!"

"He's a smart little guy," AJ agreed, handing him over after a final hug. "Fast, too!"

Rosa grinned. "And never tired. But eventually—he will get his nap!"

Alone again, AJ went back inside her room and walked to the window, looking down on the yard outside. Far off, she saw movement; when she squinted, she could see it was Chance, walking alone near the barns. He disappeared, and she leaned her forehead wearily against the glass. Just the brief image of him made her stomach clench, her breath catch a little in her throat. Did he wonder if she'd slept with Towers? She'd have to face him again to find out.

She straightened. What he thought couldn't matter. Not when Rebel was on this property, and the subject of insurance fraud had come so easily to his mind when he'd found her with Goof. Not when she'd seen that horrible man hanging around the stable and talking to him in Monterrey.

Damn you, Chance, she thought. *Damn you to hell. Why couldn't we … just be? Why do you have to work for Mike, be loyal to him?*

She paced a narrow circle near the foot of her bed, caught up in the futility of her situation. Monterrey had shown her clearly that Mike's patience was at an end, and he'd expect her to deliver on the promises he'd assumed accepting his invitation implied

She clapped her hands together as she paced, trying to get rid of the nervous energy threatening to make her scream.

"He won't rape me," she told herself softly. "He won't." She said it again, weighing it. Wondering if that were true, here where the circumstances would be seen as suspicious on her part. She'd accepted a strange man's invitation to spend "a while" at his ranch in a foreign place. An invitation that came with the implied understanding that she wouldn't come and go, but stay there as tradition dictated. Even her friends would claim that was inviting disaster.

The door opened suddenly, startling her.

"María," she murmured. "I didn't hear you knock."

The woman shrugged. "Perhaps *la senorita* was lost in her thoughts of her man."

AJ lifted a brow at the woman, not masking her annoyance. "My thoughts are not much your business, though, are they?" she demanded. "Even if I was thinking of Mike—"

María snorted her contempt. "I said your man, not *el jefe.*" The dark eyes glittered with malice. "He should not have come here. He is not one of us."

"Mike?" AJ asked, not sure she followed the woman's train of thought.

"No. Again." María walked over to the dresser, smoothed an embroidered doily, and caught AJ's gaze in the ornately framed mirror. "Your man. Chance."

Fear tightened her chest, and she muffled a quickly drawn breath of surprise at this woman's attack. She'd never been friendly, but until today, she had also never seemed a threat. She couldn't decide what to say, but María went on anyway, her eyes merciless.

"Any fool could see that it is him you want, and not the boss. *El jefe* is a fool if he does not see it himself. He should not have brought Chance Landin here. Jaime takes care of him. There is no need for Chance."

So. María's problem had to do with prejudice. Or something deeper that she felt for the disreputable *guardaespaldas*? AJ walked over to the closet and made a show of searching for something, collecting her thoughts. Had María seen something, overheard something?

Apparently the older woman hadn't finished. She picked up a blown-glass partridge from the dresser, waving it in the air. Light speared through the translucent blue and green figurine, spattering a wall with color. The housekeeper ignored the show of colors, again closing their distance and wielding the bird more like a weapon than an adornment.

"The boss always pays us too little attention," she hissed. "Jaime is a better man than Chance Landin has ever been. Yet he brings the man here to sleep with his woman. Again. Different women, but the same man made a fool of him with both."

Frustrated, AJ drew herself up straight, then snatched the bird from the woman's hands. She walked over to the dresser, deliberately set the bird in place, and then confronted the woman again.

"¿María, *de que hablas*? What are you talking about? Chance and I—"

María snorted. "No. The boss has not given you a chance, or you would have been in his bed." She walked to the door, rested a hand on it. "We both know that. But I know he brought *la señora* Gina here to keep her away from Chance."

AJ's breath caught. Her heart thudded, too slowly and painfully against her chest, and her fingers dug into the denim of her jeans. Gina? María was saying that Chance had wanted Gina?

María eased the door open, her face stone-hard, her expression chilling. "He never said. But he brought Chance only when he could no longer *ponerle cuernos*—make him a fool." Then she chuckled, an unnerving guttural noise full of ill will. "For the good it did. She died with another lover anyway."

The door closed softly behind her, leaving AJ clutching the dresser in stunned silence.

• • •

A slight noise in the room woke her, but even in her grogginess, AJ went still, clutching the linens in her fists and twisting them to help her remain silent and motionless.

Had Towers returned from San Antonio and crept into her room, planning on assaulting her before she realized what was happening? Or had she merely imagined a presence in the room? Awake now, she heard nothing.

Slowly she sat up, holding the sheet and thin bedspread close as if they could protect her from whatever unseen dangers lurked.

Just as she sat, a lamp on the far dresser went on, and with a click, dimmed to its lowest setting.

"You?" She dropped the linens and clambered out of bed, her face flushing with anger. "What the *hell* are you doing sneaking into my bedroom at—at—"

"It's a little after one," Chance supplied, voice low. "I had to be sure María wasn't lurking around anywhere. She seems to watch everyone." Then, in a lower voice, "For God's sake, put something on!"

His hoarse plea reminded her that she wore her shortest, skimpiest nightgown. For an insane moment, she wanted to refuse, to face him wearing virtually nothing, relishing the obvious attraction he felt toward her. But just as quickly, common sense and indignation swamped her, and she groped for her robe without turning away from him, knowing she always left it hanging on the corner of the bedpost.

She shrugged into it and belted it without speaking, then glared across the barely lit room at him.

"You haven't explained how you had the nerve to come slithering into my room—"

"Keep your voice down," Chance muttered. "You're squeaking again."

Squeaking? Unbidden, the memory of the first time he'd accused her of squeaking rushed back. He'd said that she didn't squeak around Towers.

Before she could say anything else, though, he closed the distance between them. Dressed in gray and black, he seemed just another shadow in the room, one that moved as the moonlight pushed through the window, aiding the lamp in dispelling a bit of the darkness. His stealth was unsettling, but she resisted moving away from him.

She wasn't afraid of him. Was she?

When he raised a hand, though, she flinched. Then she saw that he was holding an envelope, and felt silly at how intimidating she found him in the small space they shared.

"So, are you going to tell me why you're here?" she prodded.

"Go look out in the hallway," he ordered, not quite whispering. "If nobody's around, lock the door."

She did as he said. "Why didn't you just lock the door while you were sneaking in?"

She heard impatience when he answered. "If you woke up screaming or something because I startled you, I thought whoever came to see why should find the door unlocked. I hadn't really thought of what I'd say, but luckily—I didn't startle you enough to cause problems."

She hated how much sense he made, so she tried to find holes in his reasoning. "And how do you know someone won't try the door after I lock it, genius?"

"Because if María saw me come in, she'd hang around to see how long I was in here. You'll catch her in the hall if she's there. Glance out."

AJ opened the door, ready to tell anyone eavesdropping that she'd been startled by a noise. The hall was silent. Empty.

Relieved, she closed and bolted the door as he'd asked.

"What if someone besides María followed you?" she demanded, irritated that he rarely lost a discussion.

"No one's here at night besides María and Rosita. Rosita's no danger."

"She—" AJ bit back the accusation that the maid was clearly in love with him. It was none of her business, and Rosa certainly didn't have to answer to him.

"Was your sister's best friend," Chance said matter-of-factly.

The words hit her with physical force, making her knees go weak and slamming her backwards against the wall.

"What—I don't—"

"Come sit down," he ordered, waving at the bed. "We need to talk. What I need to say can't wait."

"No." AJ shook her head. "You have nothing to say to me about my sister. You—you sick bastard! If you're going to tell me you had an affair with her, don't. I knew Gina. She never would have cheated. She loved Mike!"

Not at the end. Her last letter was testimony to her desperation. Loyalty to her sister kept her from admitting the little she knew of Gina's final weeks. Still, according to María, Chance Landin had tried to seduce his boss's wife—

"Do you ever check your facts?" he retorted coldly. Then he shrugged. "I guess that's hard to do when you're pretending to be someone else."

"This isn't getting us anywhere," AJ pointed out and walked over to sit where he had indicated. He didn't sit, just moved around to lean against the dresser so that he could face her. He propped his hip on the edge and rubbed a hand roughly over his face.

"You should understand something, AJ. I didn't know Gina well. Most of what I heard came from Rosita, Mike, and María. The times I met her were when I was acting as Mike's head of security, and one of the people he accused of wanting him dead was your sister."

"Gina loved him," she repeated, then drew a deep breath. "Okay, I know they ran into problems before … before she died. She hardly kept in touch with us. It's almost like she wasn't allowed to. But Gina would never have hurt anyone, and you"—her voice shook with anger and disgust—"you were the one trying to sleep with your boss's wife. With my sister!"

"Who fed you that line of bull, AJ? Because it's crap. I had no interest in Gina, except to protect Mike. And since she was his wife, I felt I had to look out for her interests, too—as much as I could."

"María said—"

His expletive filled the room. "Seriously? You're that bad a judge of character?" He shook his head. "She's the one who started getting Mike to pay attention to Gina again—in a bad way. From what I heard from people I trust, like Rosita—she acted with special *gusto* when she saw a chance to attack *la gringa*."

In spite of herself, she believed what he said. María's clear dislike of Chance seemed based on his origin as much as the fact that her allegiance was blatantly pointed in Jaime's direction.

"So," she forced herself to ask, "you and Gina weren't involved? You didn't want her for yourself?"

'He pushed himself upright. "Your sister was a beautiful woman, but I never—never—am interested in someone else's woman." He walked over to the window and moved the lacy curtain aside before turning back. "My ex-wife was one of those women like Gina. Being married didn't mean anything to her, either. I have no use for cheaters—in marriage or anything else."

She stood, too, facing him angrily. "Gina wasn't a cheater. Men noticed her. She didn't encourage them. She didn't use men. If anything, Mike Towers used her." Chance didn't argue with her, just stood there, too close, looking agitated, the envelope still in one hand.

Finally he shrugged and walked to the door, cracked it open, and glanced out. When he closed it, he locked it again.

"How well did you know Gina?" he asked, finally. "You never came to visit."

The old pain of their estrangement crept back. All the wasted time, short as it had been.

"She was my sister, Chance. I knew everything about her." She fell silent a minute, wishing she didn't feel so drawn to be honest with the enigmatic, scowling man in front of her. Wishing she didn't want to trust him with her secrets when he could destroy her so easily.

"Look, she and I had a falling out when she met Mike. I thought she was being stupid—that she shouldn't have fallen for a man from out of town, with too much money, and who was so much older than she was. She disagreed, claimed she loved him. And don't you dare even suggest it was about the money!"

"Shhh. Calm down, AJ. I didn't come here to pick a fight." He jerked a hand through his hair and inhaled sharply. "There's so much we need to talk about, and I can't—cooped up here like this." He paused, and even with the clear frustration in his voice, he smiled. "In that gown, you're just too big a distraction without a little more distance between us."

"Humph. Not a problem for me, Chance." She walked to the door and opened it. "And there's an easy answer. Leave."

He didn't though, just walked up to her and poked his head outside once more, then turned in the narrow door frame and laid a hand on her arm.

She didn't draw away, tried not to let him feel how quickly her pretended ease slipped into jumbled feelings—none of them easy or welcome.

"Mike won't come back before that damn conference ends, unless María calls him. I don't think anyone else is a problem. So we've got ... what, four days? He might be back late on Friday, although he might stay over and come back Saturday. We'll go somewhere tomorrow, if we can do something about María. You need to hear what I know about Gina—"

He cut off her protest before she could start.

"And I'll listen to you, too. I promise. But tomorrow. Tonight ..." The word slid out on a sigh. "There's something I want you to know tonight."

He eased out the door. "But I'm warning you, once I tell you—you can ruin lives. I hope you won't. Meet me in the nursery in about ten minutes."

He closed the door as he moved away.

• • •

The nursery? In the dead of night? Her stomach clenched and she took several deep breaths as she slipped out of the gown and changed into a T-shirt and sweats. Why on earth would he suggest the baby's room—Gordito's room—as a meeting place?

She thought suddenly that she seldom saw María up here, and most certainly never with the baby. Could it be that María resented Rosa's little one? Or the position it might give Rosa if Towers recapitulated and recognized the son he appeared to ignore altogether? Maybe some of María's bitterness stemmed from fears that she could lose her status as housekeeper to the younger woman. (The explanation requested about how Rosa could affect Maria's status through the baby)

She glanced at the desk clock, its gold frame glowing softly. She hadn't taken ten minutes, but she wanted to hear whatever Chance was selling now. She only hoped she could control her temper and not wake the baby if he attacked Gina.

She checked the hall, glad no one else seemed to keep these insane hours, and padded barefoot down the hall to the nursery.

Electric candles glowed on the baby's massive dresser and the room was tastefully decorated, but too elegant and formal to meet an exuberant child's needs. Not a dragon, horse, or toy car in sight. Her lips twitched in amusement. She hadn't been a child in a while. Maybe kids didn't play with anything that mundane anymore.

Drawn to the crib, she smiled down silently at the sleeping child, resisting the urge to touch him gently.

But as suddenly as tenderness overcame her, something dark and sinister swept over her, and she clutched the railing of the crib, dizzy. The feeling of being watched—or hunted—raised the hairs on her arms, and she jerked away from the crib, one hand going to her mouth to silence a gasp of fear.

`And Chance came through the door sideways, apparently seeing her, as he locked the door before he faced her. "My God," he muttered. "You look like you saw *La Llorona*. Or maybe—like you're her."

"There's something evil in this room," AJ muttered, rubbing her hands over her arms. "I'm freezing. Won't the baby—" She stopped then. "Do you know I don't even know Gordito's real name? What kind of a life does the kid live, anyway?"

Chance looked around the luxuriously furnished room and lifted a shoulder. "Some would say he lives just fine."

"And you, Chance? What would you say?"

"All the money in the world isn't worth a damn without love." He walked over to the baby's crib and smiled faintly. "He's much sweeter asleep."

"So—is he named after his dad? After Mike?"

Chance shot her a sideways glance, then leaned his own hand on the crib, unaffected by whatever strange sensation had overwhelmed her just seconds ago. "No. Gordito's name is Alejandro Robert."

AJ's mouth opened and she gulped, trying to drag air into her lungs.

He pressed the paper closer and added, "Stanford."

She took the paper with hands that shook and managed to unfold it. Then she stared at the space listing her sister as the mother of the baby, Alejandro Robert Stanford. No name was listed for the father.

"She lost her baby. She told me—" Tears streamed down AJ's face. "She—why would she lie?"

He took the birth certificate back, folding it carefully and putting it in his pocket, then rubbing a hand over his face and sighing.

"We can't talk here," he whispered. Gently he took her arm and led her to the wooden rocking chair across the room from the baby's crib.

He folded her into the chair, then went to the crib and pulled a crocheted afghan from the foot of the bed and draped it around her shoulders.

She couldn't stop the silent flow of tears as he knelt in front of her, taking both her hands in his and squeezing.

"I'm sorry it's such a shock," he murmured. "I couldn't wait any longer to tell you, though. We're both running out of time, AJ."

His words were a dull hum in her ears. Running out of time for what? But she couldn't talk.

"I have to go. If María doesn't see me making rounds, she'll start paying attention." He brushed ineffectually at her tears. "AJ, stay here with Gordito if you want, but you have to pull yourself together. You can't spend the whole day with him. María and the others can't know anything's different. We can't risk them getting in touch with Mike before we have a chance to talk."

This time, most of what he said registered, and she nodded slightly to let him know that.

He blotted her cheeks with his hands once again, and she sensed his hesitation. Then he leaned forward and kissed her forehead.

"Try to get some sleep."

She watched as he pushed himself up. As he reached the door, she realized that he'd just given her Gina's son. A living, loving remnant of her sister.

"Thank you," she whispered through the lump still clogging her throat. She didn't know if he heard her, but the door closed softly and he was gone. Leaving her alone with Gina's son. With her nephew.

Chapter Thirteen

Sandpaper eyes, stubble, and a vague but constant feeling of dread accompanied Chance through the empty house. He paused in the kitchen to make a quick cup of instant coffee and gulped it down, ignoring the burn. "With any luck, I'll get out of here before I have to see that woman's face," he muttered.

"*Señor* Chance," María purred behind him, and he tried to cover his words by fanning his hand in front of his mouth.

"Damn coffee burned me," he said, hoping she hadn't heard him clearly.

The housekeeper's eyes glittered with her dislike.

"*Hay que tener más cuidado*," she said sweetly. "You—"

"Should be more careful," he finished for her. "You're right." He shot a quick smile at her over his shoulder. "How are you today, María?"

"Humph. I am as I always am." She moved around him and took the coffee pot. "There was real coffee," she pointed out. "*Señor* Mike likes my coffee."

She took the pot over to the table and set it on a mat, poured herself a cup of coffee, and sat down.

"Would you like breakfast?" she asked without looking back at him.

"No, thanks. I want to make my rounds and check in with Mike to see if he needs anything."

"He will be away for all of this week?"

Chance leaned against the counter as he sipped the remainder of the coffee more carefully. "Those were his plans when he left," he said. "I haven't heard anything different, and I know he'd like to be there to see the governor on Friday."

He dug his phone out of his pocket and walked over to look out the window as if he'd forgotten María altogether. He hit Towers's button, and after a few minutes, his boss came on, groggy and annoyed.

"What the hell you want, Landin?" Mike demanded. "Don't have to be up for an hour or two yet. Something wrong down there?"

"No, Mike. Sorry I woke you up. Just wanted to touch base on a couple of things. You told me to keep AJ here on the ranch?"

"AJ? Oh … uh yeah."

He heard the muffled complaint of a woman and Mike's rude order to "just shut up," and felt sick. How could AJ risk herself for a horse? Or even for her sister? Gina was dead, for heaven's sake.

"What's the deal with the filly? She bolt or something? Maybe shack up with that supposed fiancé of hers?"

"No, she's here. I don't talk to her much, but she asked if I knew when you'd be back. Said she really didn't have any reason to stay if you weren't here, but that you'd told her not to be coming and going, so she'd stayed."

"Well, now, sounds like she's come around!" Towers fell silent for a minute. "But I can't come back till Saturday. You have any idea how important the governor's deal is on Friday? He might announce his run for presidency. And Thursday—tomorrow—there's a huge luncheon to plan strategies for some of the candidates. I heard I'm gonna get a position on one of the finance committees." Again the silence, followed by a heavy sigh. "Try to cheer her up, Landin. But not too much, if you get my meaning."

"She was talking about wanting to eat out and do a little shopping. I wondered if you'd like me to drop her off in Laredo, then pick her up and take her back when she's ready."

"Take her, but try to keep an eye on her. Don't know why she wants to leave the ranch anyway."

"Might be better," Chance suggested. *How much can I push this thing? Gordito—but María's such a worthless snake.* "Thing is, she discovered the baby. Plays with him a lot. Harmless, but she might get really attached to Gordito—"

"She'd better not. Might have to pay Rosita off just to leave with the baby unless I need him for something. I don't want women who want babies. Gina wasn't smart enough to listen. Too much a whore to have my brat anyway."

Towers's callous words sent a chill through him. Had he missed the man's dislike for AJ's sister so badly? Mike told him the day he started working that Gina had cheated on him. More than once. Sudden doubt niggled. But he ignored it and plowed on. "I'll take her back across for the day, then, Mike. Solve a lot of problems with one stone, so to speak. But I wanted to clear it with you, because I need my job." He turned around as he said that, fixing María with a hard stare that made her look away briefly.

"And your life," Mike retorted, chuckling. "Just kiddin', Landin. But keep your hands clean."

He disconnected and Chance put his phone down on the counter and folded his arms. "María, I'm going into Laredo. AJ wants to go shopping, and Mike wants her happy. But I was thinking—you never have a day off. Are you sure you wouldn't like to go with her?"

María sniffed. "I need nothing from your country or your stores. I go there with *Don* Mike because he pays me well to take care of his home affairs. But I will not go there with that—"

He shrugged. "Your call," he told her, and exited the kitchen, whistling.

•••

She shouldn't be here. Chance and Rosa had both insisted she shouldn't change her routine. She couldn't, not if Robbie would suffer. Robbie. A real nickname. She raised the baby's chubby hand high enough to press a kiss on the back. He stirred slightly, but didn't wake. She smiled. She'd held him for hours, watching him sleep and wake, feeling more like his mother than the aunt he didn't know he had.

Her smile faded and her mouth tightened as questions stormed in. She must have been shocked into a numb mindlessness when Chance showed her the birth certificate. He'd known? He'd known and hadn't told her! Why? She paced a short path near the crib, rubbing her arms as she felt chilled air raise goose bumps again. What the hell was wrong with her, imagining evil lurking in this beautifully appointed room? With goodness itself sleeping paces away in that crib.

Robbie hiccupped and she took a step toward him, but he rolled over, pulled his blanket off, and nestled his face into its softness, clearly not ready to face the morning. (kept the blanket—he's almost a year old)

"Neither am I, little man," she murmured, feeling the sting of tears and blinking hard. Why hadn't Gina told her about Robbie? Or at least told their mom. A tear escaped as she thought of her hard-working, often solitary mother. A grandmother! She could have Gina's son if—if Mike Towers could be convinced. She wouldn't demand money. She could support him well enough. But why wasn't Mike Towers listed as Robbie's father? Screw Chance Landin with his secrets and his claims that Gina had been unfaithful. Nothing—no one—could have driven her sister to cheat. They'd had many a fight as teenagers over whether or not you could cheat if you were cheated on. Gina never bought into that mentality, as she herself once had.

"AJ," Rosa whispered behind her and she jerked toward the door. "You must leave. Chance has found a way to talk to you. Go."

"But Robbie—"

"Will be here all day. Please. Go!"

AJ hesitated, reluctant to listen to Rosa. But she'd clearly been putting the baby first since Gina's death. Causing the nanny problems wouldn't help anyone, least of all the baby.

"Can I talk to you later, Rosa?" she asked quietly.

Rosa nodded. "We'll find a time and place. I don't trust María when the boss isn't here. Now please, go!"

AJ hurried down the hall and into her room, pushing the door shut with her foot as she stripped off her T-shirt and hurled it toward the bed.

Then she heard someone suck in air and swear softly. Chance Landin stood by her bed, staring at her, his mouth slightly open.

Shock stunned her momentarily, followed quickly by embarrassment and then rage.

"You—you pervert!" She advanced on him in a fury, her hands balled into fists, and slugged him in the chest. "You sneak into my room, hide—"

"I didn't sneak in." He caught her hands as she moved to hit him again, holding them away and half turning. "You're kind of naked, AJ. Please stop … jiggling all over the place."

Jiggling? Jiggling? A different kind of outrage froze her instantly. She was fit, toned from working out and from her days of throwing hay bales around. She did not jiggle.

She jerked her hands free and reclaimed the T-shirt, shoving it on.

"So exactly what are you doing here?" she demanded. "I hardly expected to find you hiding in a closet or—"

"I didn't sneak in and I wasn't hiding." He spoke slowly and calmly, as if he doubted her intelligence. "Rosa said she'd tell you I needed to see you."

Rosa. Right. She had said that, hadn't she?

AJ's anger faded, but the slight embarrassment remained. She could only imagine what she'd looked like, exposed from the waist up, launching herself at him, flailing around—and jiggling? Color rose in her cheeks even though she told herself to get over it. Maybe she had jiggled.

"She did tell me," AJ admitted. "But can we talk here? María—"

"Get dressed." He shook his head once, hard, when she started to say something. "After I leave. We're going to Laredo for the day. I'll pick you up in the kitchen in fifteen minutes."

He didn't look back at her as he hurried out, not even checking the hall for passersby before exiting the room.

AJ walked over and locked the door before casting the T-shirt off again and flinging it on the bed. Fifteen minutes? Not much time to get ready. She threw make-up into a small case and headed for what she hoped would be a five-minute shower.

Chapter Fourteen

Chance glanced at his watch. He had no idea if AJ was ready, but his sweep of the grounds had run late. He broke into a jog, startling the stocky man walking sedately behind him.

"*¡Epa, compadre!*" the man complained. "I am not young like you!" In spite of grumbling, though, he too broke into a jog, steadying the holstered pistol at his side.

"Aw, come on, Santos! You need the exercise and I'm late." They reached the kitchen door and Chance pulled it open for the older, heavier man, who gasped for air as he clattered into the kitchen. Across the room, María fixed both of them with one of her unflinching stares.

"Hey, María. You know Santos, yes? Helps me with security and the dogs when Mike needs me elsewhere?"

"We know each other." María turned away with a slight sniff and went back to going through a pile of pinto beans, looking for small rocks that might have made it into the batch.

Good. She doesn't like Santos the way she does Jaime. He allowed himself to wonder if Jaime and María were lovers. Jaime scored a fair number of women—good-looking women—simply because Towers kept his pockets full. At least, so Mike had led him to believe. Chance tamped down his resentment and patted the pocket where he'd tucked a couple of hundred-dollar bills. People—men or women—had to live and they couldn't always choose the cleanest path.

"Let's look at the monitors in Mike's office," Chance said, ushering him into the spacious room and closing the door quietly.

"Have you heard from the boss?" he asked and Santos shook his head.

"Me? No." He rubbed a hand through hair that brushed his shirt collar. "The boss doesn't know I'm alive, most of the time." He sighed. "The last time he knew was when that witch," he waved in the direction of the kitchen, "caught me sleeping in the office when you and the boss had gone across. Took a picture of me with her phone and *por poco*—well, she nearly got me fired."

Perfect. "Yeah, I sort of remember." He gave the man his most genial smile. "Came down on me—said why did I keep someone who couldn't do the job?"

Santos shuffled his feet in the carpet and glanced away. "Sorry," he muttered.

Chance clapped the man on the arm. "Water under the bridge. Besides, María sticks knives in everyone's back."

"*Seguro que si*—for sure!"

"Have to tell you, Santos, I'm a little worried. I told the boss that Ms. Owens—you've met Ms. Owens?" Chance went on when the man nodded. "Well, she wants to go into Laredo. The boss sort of abandoned her here and told her to stay put. But he wants her to be happy and he told me to take her across, let her spend some money—"

"Do what *las mujeres* do," Santos finished, nodding sagely. "Women need their little excursions. Of course."

"Look, Santos, Towers told me to take her across, but María hates her—hell, she hates me, too. Last time we happened to wind up across together, she had the boss ready to shoot us both."

"He could do that, too, and get away with it," Santos muttered, "long as he did it here."

"Well, it won't come to that. But just in case you think María's stirring up trouble somehow—I don't know—calling Mike with lies, or anything obvious—let me know, would you?"

"You want me to stay in the house?"

"Yeah. Huerta's got the outside and dogs. Stay here, watch the video. She probably wouldn't call on a house line, but walk around the house now and then." He shot the guard a smile. "Drink a lot of water. She hangs out in the kitchen a lot—hatches her plots there."

"My pleasure," Santos agreed easily, nodding.

"Just stay awake," Chance warned, grinning to take any threat out of the words. He slid the folded bills out of his pocket. He'd decided on two hundred instead of three hundred, not wanting to raise suspicions.

"This is just because I know I can trust you, and because—hell, hassle with Mike is never worth it. So if María starts—"

"You'll be the first to know," Santos assured him, beaming. He reached out and pumped Chance's hand. "You're a good friend, Chance."

He smiled and clapped Santos on the shoulder just as he heard an impatient knock on the door, followed by AJ's voice. "Chance? María said you were in here?"

"On my way, AJ," he assured her, and pulled the door open.

She stood there, dampness darkening her hair, somehow making a sailor top and a pair of jeans look incredibly stylish. And deliciously sinful. The memory of her half-naked, coming at him in a fury more arousing than intimidating, crashed back.

"Let's get out of Dodge," he muttered, moving toward the door and brushing past her. Hoping she hadn't noticed the effect his recent memory of her had on him.

•••

He pushed through the door, his arm actually brushing her, expecting her to follow him. She ignored the brief flare of warmth where their skin touched, that tiny current of physical shock, because she wanted to know what she'd seen in his face before he ducked away.

The glance he shot her seemed full of—apology? If so, for what? Desire? Had he been remembering their encounter a short while ago?

The glare of the sun, already blinding and hot, made her blink away the images of his face and focus on this unplanned excursion. She hadn't asked why they were leaving. She'd planned on spending as much of the day as she could with Robbie. Just the thought of him made her smile.

"Happy to escape for a while?" Chance asked as he opened the door for her to his Jeep.

"Yes," she admitted, climbing in, "but … "

He closed the door and went around, swinging up. "You're worried about Rebel and Robbie," he finished for her. "Not to insult you or anything, but both of them were fine before you came and nothing has changed that endangers them in any way." He seemed to rethink that. "Well, we do need to talk, especially about Robbie. That could change before we're ready. You have to be more careful, AJ. Not to show interest in him—not more than usual."

"He's my nephew!"

"Which is exactly why you're going to be careful. Until you leave with him."

Leave with him? Her heart pounded. She'd thought fleetingly of the possibility in the early morning hours, watching him sleep. But—how? You didn't just pick up a child and walk out with him. A man like Mike Towers could make it impossible.

She drew a deep breath and pressed her eyes tightly closed for a moment, mentally counting backwards from ten to one. Patience. And quiet. She always thought better with silence around her.

So she said nothing else, just watched Laredo flash by, not questioning Chance. She'd deal with it all when she knew what "it" was.

Traffic eased as they reached the outskirts, and she realized he was taking her to see Goof. She'd been worried about the gelding, and had managed to sneak brief phone conversations with Ed, but she couldn't wait to throw her arms around Goof's neck and hug him. At the same time, she knew she'd have to give Chance some deeper answers than she had before.

She didn't know if she could. He'd told her about Robbie. But could she trust his plans for Rebel?

She didn't hear herself sigh, but Chance looked across at her and gave her a brief smile. "My thoughts exactly," he offered. He pulled up to the trailer and killed the engine. They both just sat there a moment. "Did you bring your key?"

She fished briefly through her bag and extracted it after a momentary panic.

"Let's go. We've got a lot of ground to cover today," he told her.

Again, Ed appeared out of nowhere, smiling broadly and holding out a hand as he greeted AJ.

"Nice to see you, Joanie. It's been longer than I thought—but don't you worry. I care for that horse like he's worth a million dollars!"

The irony wasn't lost on Chance, whose lips twitched slightly as he held out a hand to the caretaker. "Chance Landin," he introduced himself. "Sorry that we haven't had a chance to come by."

"Before you leave, Ed, I want to pay you for another week or so and be sure Goof has enough food," AJ said, and he nodded.

"Sure thing, miss. No one trying to win me away at my age, so this job suits me just fine."

"Give me the key, AJ," Chance ordered, holding out his hand as Ed wandered away. "Or should I call you Joanie?"

AJ raised an eyebrow. "Give you my key?"

He reached out and snatched it. "Seems to me turning on the air would be smart," he explained. "But my guess is you won't go near the trailer till you've seen your danged horse."

She laughed. "You're catching on, Chance. Turn on both units, or we'll boil." She didn't wait to see if he could manage the sometimes tricky door in her eagerness to see Rebel's brother.

He lifted his head when she popped into the small shed and let loose a plaintive burst of snorts and nickers that filled her with guilt over abandoning him for so long.

"You're an overgrown mutt," she scolded, stepping into the stall and letting him press his head into her chest and puff happy little breaths across her face. "Just a puppy who didn't stop growing."

"I can't get over how much he and Rebel look alike," Chance observed, coming in and patting the gelding's neck. "So, are you going to be honest today?"

AJ sighed and gently pushed Goof's head away. "Depends on the questions, Chance. And on one other thing."

"Which is?"

"Whether or not you do the same."

• • •

The units humming in the windows of the old trailer hadn't helped yet. Humid, musty air encased them and AJ absently pulled at her blouse, feeling it cling to her damp skin.

"Look, we could find somewhere else," Chance suggested. "Although I don't think we'll be here long."

"You said we have a lot to do," AJ noted, tossing her bag on the sofa. "What? And how did you decide to spring me, anyway?"

"We can't afford to have María call and find some reason to drag Mike back. She'd already started with her innuendo and insults when I got down to the kitchen. I don't know if she knew how long you'd been in Robbie's room. I called Mike in front of her and asked permission to bring you over for a day of shopping."

She snorted. "What am I supposed to buy?"

"We'll worry about that later. Do you need breakfast?"

"No."

Chance leaned against the bar dividing the kitchen and living area. "So tell me the real story, AJ. Tell me how you planned on getting Rebel back. Tell me why you brought Goof." He paused and she thought his eyes looked darker and his face angrier.

"Tell me why you thought the only way to get your horse back would be to sleep with your sister's husband."

Chapter Fifteen

The questions weren't unexpected. But they hurt anyway.

She swallowed and turned away for a minute, deciding what and how much to explain. Anger and pride urged her to tell him to go to hell and walk out of the trailer. But she couldn't do that. He could keep her away from Robbie and Rebel.

Her heart whispered, *Chance won't do that. He's a good man.*

Logic reminded her that she'd been burned several times in her life by good men. And that Gina died under Mike Towers's care. And Chance Landin's watch. She stiffened and faced him, waving at one of the couches. "Sit down. I'm going to tell you about Rebel and Goof—but then it's your turn."

Chance glanced at the couch. "I'm fine standing. Not a sitter. Why not start with how you didn't know about Robbie? Why you didn't come to Gina's burial?"

The words slammed into her and she couldn't breathe. Then the welcome anger she'd contained for months stormed back.

"That sounds more like something you should explain to me, Chance Landin! Head of security? The one who held her a virtual prisoner? Because I don't believe that she wouldn't have come home to us if she could have!"

Raw fury propelled her over to where he stood, straightening as she approached. Without thinking, she stabbed a finger into his chest as she snarled, "Maybe you can explain why Mom didn't find out about her death for three weeks after the fact? Why she was told services had been held, but that Towers would ship Gina's ashes if she wanted them?"

He hadn't known. She could see the shock freeze his face. He completely ignored the thrust of her finger into his chest. And knowing that he hadn't been a participant at least in the final outrages committed against Gina suddenly meant the world.

"You didn't know," she breathed, and sagged against him as the rage and resentment dissipated, leaving her unable to stand.

• • •

He hadn't known. He heard her say the words and recognized the truth in them. Easy barbs came to mind—above his pay grade, not his job, the relationship between a married couple wasn't his business.

He couldn't excuse himself. He should have known. She fell forward, her anger abruptly gone, and he wrapped his arms around her and held her.

"I'm so sorry," he whispered into her hair. "Mike told me he called you the night of the accident, and again when the funeral arrangements were made." His arms tightened around her slightly, the warmth and hardness comforting, a granite pillar heated by sun. She let her own arms slide around his torso, keeping him close until she could regain her own strength.

"Gina and Mike both told me there was a sister. She told me you all had problems after she married." He eased her slightly away and tilted her chin. "You need to know two things, AJ. If I had known you hadn't been told, I would have found a way. I had your mother's number, if not yours."

"And the other?" she prompted, when he just stared down at her, features tormented.

"I knew she and Mike weren't happy. Mike told me she'd been unfaithful." He silenced her by laying a finger across his lips. "He denies that Robbie is his son. I never have decided what I think. But I suppose he planned on using Robbie to keep Gina under control. As greedy as the man is, he probably wouldn't have agreed to a divorce. (Addresses the question about why Towers' kept possession of Gordito) But no matter what—if I had ever seen abuse—if I had seen him hit her, or if Gina had told me he wouldn't let her call home—anything like that—I wouldn't have put up with it. Please understand that. Believe me."

She reached up and patted his cheek, and he hoped she couldn't feel the shiver of heat her touch generated. Where had the simple desire to comfort and reassure her gone?

She stepped back and he suspected she'd felt the change between them. The charge, small but electric. Distance was good.

"I believe you," she sighed. "It just doesn't help. It doesn't change what happened."

She went over and sat down on the couch. "I'd offer you something to drink, but I doubt anything in the refrigerator would still be good. Not sure the tea I made is still drinkable."

He checked his watch and swore softly. He'd probably covered his tracks with Mike even though María tried to cause problems. But they hadn't dealt with the real issues yet. The problems were thorny as hell—and he didn't have a solution. He thought of how easily he'd followed her here the first time. The mess she'd made going through the files in the stable office. He smiled. As bad as she was at being furtive, he doubted her plans for rescuing Rebel were solid.

"What's funny?" she demanded, catching him grinning at her.

"Sorry, nothing. Look, why don't we get an early lunch somewhere and bring something to drink back. We'll talk—fast," he warned, "and then we need to make stops at a mall and—well, there's someone I need you to meet."

"If Mike gave us permission to be here, then why are we hiding?"

"He doesn't know we're here in the middle of nowhere—and he can't. He's not spying, but it wouldn't take that. Just a friend of a friend who knows me saying he saw us together at some secluded trailer. Besides, he'd have a whole different view of us spending the day together or spending the night together. Farfetched as it seems, we just need to hurry. And you have to buy something, because he assumed you were upset that you haven't been shopping or going out anywhere pretty much since you met him."

"Food would be nice," she agreed, after a minute, "but you go. I need to hang with Goof as long as I can."

She seemed to see his concern, because she waved off any protest. "I'm hardly in a position to flee, Chance," she said, and he saw tears well up in her eyes. "You control the two most important things in my life right now."

He didn't want to see her cry and he couldn't hold her again. He had to be able to watch out—now, not just for his interests, but for hers as well. As he shrugged and left, he knew that his interests could no longer come first—even though his aunt and uncle's lives depended on him.

•••

Chance seemed to take forever and AJ fought off her worries time and time again. She jogged Goof around for a while, then went to work scrubbing the table, counter, and sink in the old trailer clean.

Outside dogs barked and the barely cooled air grew colder around her. AJ ran her hands over goose-bumped skin, then covered her mouth to stop the scream trying to tear its way out of her throat.

A heartbeat! She'd heard a heartbeat, loud and frantic, in this tomb-like place. A touch, feather light, brushed across on her back and she locked her knees to keep from falling. No one—no one—ever did that to her except Gina.

I've lost it. This is impossible. I didn't sleep much last night.

Casting away the fear, she bolted out the door into the sunshine and sanity.

The dogs weren't barking now and Ed bent near a struggling garden, poking at the soil. She took a few hesitant steps toward him. Absorbed in his task, he never glanced her way.

Low and faint, she heard the plaintive wail she'd heard when she took Goof down to the river while considering her rescue plan.

Wind.

Leaves on the nearby foliage hung limply as the dogs began barking again.

Ed straightened with a groan, a hand going to his waist. He twisted, apparently trying to loosen the kinks from his yard work, and finally spotted her.

"Well, Miss Joanie! What brings you back out into the heat?" He squinted at her. "You look—I don't know. Afraid?"

The plaintive wail grew slightly stronger and she jerked her head in the direction of the river. "Do you hear it?"

"What?" He cocked his head. "You mean that noise coming off the river?" He chuckled. "You can't think it's our old *Llorona*, can you?"

"No," she lied, but waved her hand. "But there's no wind—"

"It's buffered here by all the stuff that rows along the river, and it eddies and dies real fast in this heat. Least, that's what I've been told," he assured her, smiling.

He made sense. There could be no *Llorona* wandering the riverbank. Gina's spirit didn't pursue her, seeking Robbie. Pleading with her to care for her lost son. AJ managed to smile back, but gestured at the dogs. "They kept barking—"

He snorted. "Worthless, the lot of 'em, but their families love them. They got no pastime but to bark."

Chance pulled up just then, and slid out, loaded down with fast food bags.

"Hey," he greeted them. "We were about to have lunch. Why don't you join us, Ed?"

"Oh, I couldn't do that," the handyman demurred. "I'm hot and sweaty—"

"At least come get a plate," AJ insisted, not welcoming going back into the trailer. Chance would be there, but that was almost as dangerous as the terrifying feelings playing with her mind.

Ed gave in to their insistence with some embarrassment, but left happily with a plate of chicken and trimmings and bottles of lemonade that he assured them his wife would appreciate. Before he went, AJ fished in her purse and presented him with a check to cover his past expenses plus another two weeks, aware that her savings from her Philadelphia job were virtually nonexistent.

She served herself and sat in the corner of the couch, balancing the food and soda, and waited to start eating until Chance sat down, too.

She bit into a piece of chicken, but her appetite seemed to have fled. She wanted to question Chance about Gina, about the pregnancy her sister told her had ended—but all she could think about were the times she'd felt a ghostly presence in her room, or Robbie's nursery—or along the river. Chance would think she was certifiably insane, but she needed to ask. Standing, she put her plate down on the table and sat down again, twining her hands.

"Chance, while you were gone—I felt something. And I've felt it before this—this presence. Remember when you showed me Mike's stables across—we heard something."

"A coyote," Chance nodded.

"No," AJ repeated. "Whatever we heard wasn't a coyote."

He sighed and stood up, putting his plate on the table, too, staring down at her. "What then, AJ? A ghost?" He shook his head. "I don't believe that. Neither do you. Not really."

"But," AJ insisted, stubbornly, slowly, thinking out what she needed to explain, "what if there's—something? *La Llorona* lost her children—"

"No. She killed her children. It isn't the same thing."

AJ sprang up, agitated, knowing that she sounded crazy, but needing him to listen. For her sanity's sake. "Look, why did she kill them?"

"Vengeance," he said immediately.

"Not in the version I heard. She was destitute—a rich man left her penniless and without any means to care for her kids. One was only a baby. She couldn't stand to let them suffer slow, cruel deaths—"

"Dammit, stop, AJ! This is crazy talk, and we've got so many real problems—"

"Gina lost her baby," AJ went on, refusing to be silenced, pacing the tiny area in a frenzy. "Not a miscarriage, the way she told me, but through death—" She had reached the counter, but whirled, walking up to him, and catching his arms. "Gina used to sneak up on me when we were little and trace a cross on my back. She never stopped doing it. While you were gone, I heard Gina's heartbeat in this room. The air conditioner barely works, but everything turned cold. And I felt her fingers make the cross on my back."

He lifted his arms, cupping her cheeks gently. "Your heart is broken over Gina. You're clinging to the pain and the sorrow," he said gently.

She felt the slow burn of tears trickling down her cheeks, and the slight friction of his fingers blot them away, and wished she could pull him close. That holding him would somehow unlock answers she might never have.

But holding him wasn't an option when nothing was resolved. She pulled away and began gathering the mostly uneaten food and putting it back in bags. "I felt something in my room. And in Monterrey. And the night you told me about Robbie—so did he. He cried when I heard that wail. I'm not crazy, Chance."

She didn't look at him, and he didn't answer, but she heard his sigh.

"What now?"

"Staying here isn't working for us. Guess we can talk driving back into Laredo. Maybe hit a store and you can buy something—anything. Maybe get make-up or something—hell, I don't know what you need."

"That shouldn't take long. I don't really want anything."

"I have the card Mike gave me for expenses. You need to put a couple of items on it. Look, Mike's—controlling and he's—paranoid. He told me to take you shopping." He took the bags from her and passed over her purse. "He's the kind of man who will check his card to see where you were, when."

AJ opened the passenger door and stowed the bags of food on the floor behind her seat. "Yet you weren't worried about how he treated Gina?" she asked neutrally, not wanting to annoy him.

He closed her door and went around to climb in. "No." They passed Ed gathering mail from a cluster of boxes, and Chance honked while AJ waved.

Finally, with a glance around as he merged with traffic coming in off the interstate, "You need to understand, AJ. Besides not knowing your sister well, I told you I was married before, remember?" he asked. "Thought I was madly in love and didn't want to let her go. I would check and see where she was. Drove by sometimes to look for her car." He shot her a sideways glance. "I wasn't abusive. I never considered myself a stalker, though she claimed in court that I was. Look, I don't want to justify what I did or didn't do because I'd seen it all before. Because I'd done some of it."

He didn't say anything else and she shifted to watch him. "So … who asked for the divorce?"

She didn't think he was going to answer at first. "I did," he said eventually. "The second time I came home and found her with someone. Someone different."

"I'm sorry."

"I'm not. Just bitter, and that's stupid. She didn't love me. Thinking back—" He let go briefly of the wheel and held his palms out. "I'm not sure I loved her the way I should have."

He must have seen her surprise, because he laughed and immediately caught the steering wheel, lowering the knee he'd used to steady it. "Don't tell me you've never used your knees for props," he said, and made a show of stretching his leg as much as he could. "Knees are handy."

And if you follow a leg from the knee up to the thigh ... She shivered a little, aware that her overactive imagination couldn't have had worse timing. It didn't matter anyway. Days from now, she planned to be home with Rebel. And Robbie.

As long as he talked, she didn't have to. "So, what attracted her to you in the first place? If you weren't in love?"

His fingers tapped on the wheel as he maneuvered the narrower streets in central Laredo, sometimes peering at the street signs as if he hadn't been on these roads very often. "I'd say she was pretty, but so many women are." He shot her another sideways look, along with a smile. "Really, it wasn't Linda's looks, though. She—she seemed so fragile. So broken, when I met her. She'd been in a horrible situation. It started with taking her out to eat or just walking with her while she talked." He flipped on his turn signal and maneuvered through a turn. "Just grew from there," he concluded, and pulled up in front of a simple frame house with a sagging chain-link fence.

"I guess I'm not buying designer shoes here." AJ grinned as they got out. "Where are we?"

He hesitated, his demeanor suddenly serious. And a little grim. "My aunt Emily's house. She's my aunt by marriage. Come meet her and then we need to do some actual problem solving."

AJ nodded and let him open the gate for her, glancing around the yard. "Dobermans?"

He laughed at that. "No. But look out for her cat, Duchess. The beast can't get enough attention."

"Aunt Emily?" He called out as he reached over AJ's shoulder to knock on the door. "Emily, it's me, Chance!"

AJ heard steps on the wooden floor inside, then the screen door opened and a thin, middle-aged woman emerged, wrapping her arms around Chance's middle and breaking into tears.

He soothed her as he might a child, holding her and rocking her gently, drying her tears. AJ watched in silence, thinking that more often than not, this was the Chance she'd seen. Loving and gentle. Could he have stood by and watched Gina kill herself that night she fled Towers estate in someone else's car?

"I'm sorry," the woman mumbled, flushing with embarrassment as she moved away from Chance. "I … I haven't seen him in so long." She patted Chance's arm. "He comes when he can."

"Emily, meet AJ Owens. She's my friend." He looked at her as if he wasn't sure that's what she was. After dabbing at her pale cheeks with the backs of her hands, the woman embraced AJ briefly.

"Come in, please." She opened the door and waved at the sofa and armchairs taking up most of the living room. There were pictures on the wall, mostly of a middle-aged man with a kind face. There were also photos of two beautiful horses with tightly braided manes and the English-type tack of show jumpers.

"Sit down, y'all," she encouraged, clucking and walking over to move a sleepy calico cat from the middle of the sofa. "You'd think only she lived here," Emily clucked. "What can I bring you to drink? Did you eat?"

AJ smiled. "Yes. I'm fine, thanks."

Chance refused anything, and his aunt wandered off carrying the cat. "She usually locks her up when she has visitors," he explained. "I keep telling her she doesn't have to." He leaned close to her. "AJ, don't bring up Robbie. Or children. She lost a baby, and sometimes … well, she still hurts."

Emily came back, bringing a glass of tea and setting it down on an end table, then folding herself into a chair. "So, what brings you here with this pretty woman, Chance?"

Chance smiled at his aunt. "I've wanted to visit, I just couldn't get away. You know how demanding Mike Towers is, Emily."

Her face darkened when she heard Towers's name. "That—that beast," she muttered. "You should quit."

"You know I can't," he answered softly.

"Give it up." She looked down, then back at Chance, tears streaming down her face again. "You've done what you could."

He crossed the floor, kneeling in front of her and shaking his head. "Never. I will not give up. I'll get my uncle out. I'll prove Uncle Robert didn't kill the horses," he told her, his voice soft but fierce.

"You might lose too much. Robert and I have already lost everything."

AJ's heart squeezed at the pain in the woman's voice, even as surprise jolted her. Chance was trying to prove his uncle's innocence? Had she understood the undercurrent—that he was after Towers?

Suddenly Emily went still, then clutched feverishly at Chance's shoulders, her fingers digging into his shoulders, her eyes wild.

"Do you hear it, *hijo*? Listen!"

"Emily, we've talked—you're hearing the wind through cane. We're two blocks from the river. You can't—"

But she shoved against him, lunging past, almost knocking him over.

"You hear, don't you, AJ?" Emily grasped her wrist, her fingernails digging in to the skin. "You hear her—*La Llorona*?"

The wailing woman. Faint but distinct, then rising before dying away. Yes, she heard. But across the room, Chance was shaking his head furiously at her, warning her in every way he could not to agree. Warning her to lie to this poor woman, who took her other wrist too, and whispered, "She took him, you know. Our little Beto." She laughed wildly. "Roberto, but we called him Beto, you know. Such a good little boy—do you hear her?"

Dear God, what answer will help her more?

"*Mi hijito*! My baby boy!" Emily keened, then cast away AJ's wrists as if they burned. "Why won't you help me? Why won't anyone help me?"

She fled. AJ took a step after her, but Chance cut her off. "She'll be okay. She's been much better, but sometimes it still gets her."

"Beto—Roberto—"

"Miscarriage after my uncle went to prison. It was an unexpected pregnancy, at her age and—well, she couldn't hold on to the baby. Almost destroyed her."

"And your uncle?"

"He's in prison in New Mexico. When Emily came back, her mother was still alive, but she passed away early this year."

"Poor woman."

"AJ, we don't have much time. If anything happens, and Mike comes back—tomorrow, you and Rosa are getting Robbie out."

"What?"

"You saw how he lives, AJ. Besides, if Mike ever discovers you're Gina's sister—"

"Okay, so we get him out."

"And bring him here."

"Here?" The word croaked out. "After—"

"She'll be okay. And Rosa and you will be here."

"Why not a hotel?"

"You'd have to register. Rosa and you will be safer here. No one knows who I am or who Emily is."

That made sense. But—

She took a deep breath. "And then I go back for Rebel?"

Chance's face hardened. "You don't get Rebel, AJ. Robbie's the best I can do."

Chapter Sixteen

It was like he'd punched her in the gut. He saw the shock in her face. She tried to step toward him, but her legs shook and she sagged backward, a chair arm breaking her fall. He held his breath, expecting her to fling herself at him, shrieking and flailing.

Instead she sat there like a stone for several long seconds, with an expression he couldn't decipher. Then she straightened and looked around.

"Go say goodbye to your aunt." It was an order, not a suggestion. He stared at her for a moment, then shrugged slightly and did as she said.

When he came out of his aunt's room, AJ was outside in the sun, bending over the side of the truck and staring down into the bed.

You could literally cook eggs in this heat. He'd seen it done on the hood of cars on news programs. He wondered why the burn didn't bother her. Didn't speak well for the conversations they still needed to have.

He clicked the lock open but didn't open her door, going to his own side and turning the air conditioning on. "Get in, AJ," he called, as he did the same.

He waited until they were heading back toward San Bernardo Avenue before he broached the subject again.

"Look, AJ, I know I took you by surprise, but you know you can't get him out."

"He's ours. My mom and I own him. We have the papers. We can prove it."

"But Mike *has* him. Possession—"

"Isn't nine-tenths of any damn law! Mike stole him!"

"Did he?" Chance challenged. "Because that's not what I heard. Not even from you, at first."

He crossed San Bernardo, with its crush of traffic, and headed toward the stop sign on the access road.

"Where are we going?" AJ demanded.

"Shopping."

"No."

"But—"

"Say we fought. Say I didn't feel well and wanted to get out of the heat. Tell him to go to hell and to take you with him! I want to go home—no, not home! Just back. To my nephew—and to Rebel."

He turned sharply onto the access road and headed toward the bridge. No point in trying to reason with her while she tried on clothing anyway, he admitted to himself. But María would notice. An old truck lumbered across in front of him and he swore violently and jerked the steering wheel to avoid a collision.

"Look, AJ—we can get Robbie out. We put him in the car and take him for his next round of shots. We can say he isn't eating well and we don't want to take chances with him while Mike's gone. There are easy explanations for escaping with Robbie. But Rebel—you know we can't do that."

"I came here for him," AJ said, not looking his way. "And I won't leave here without him."

"And you would do that how?" he asked. "Mike has a horse trailer. But no matter what I did, you'd be stopped before you got to the bridge."

"Maybe I wouldn't," she argued. "Maybe I could get to the bridge. If I got to the U.S., I'll go to court. Even if I didn't, there are honest courts here. I could find someone—"

"You're assuming Mike wouldn't do something as spiteful as having Rebel shot to death in his trailer. Just to make a point."

She went white and hunched forward, clutching her stomach, as if sickened by his words.

He reached over to pat her arm, but she moved away.

"Tell me more about your uncle and Emily."

Another order, but she had a right to know. Because of his uncle, he couldn't let her have Rebel. Maybe down the road, but not now. He turned onto the narrow road that paralleled the river as it meandered toward the outskirts of Nuevo Laredo. Lush vegetation flanked the road on both sides, creating a curtain that shielded cars from viewers along the river or those on other, more major roads. Not far down the road, a small cross with roses dotted the empty landscape. He hoped AJ didn't ask. She didn't, and he thought she must have known instinctively whose life and death the small monument marked.

Gina had died when her speeding car flipped, of course, but he'd always considered this the perfect place for an ambush. He'd warned Mike, who had ignored his suggestions to have the foliage trimmed, but he felt the danger again now. He hoped AJ did—maybe she'd admit he was right. There'd be no chance to save the big red horse crawling down this road in a trailer. Even if she went to the authorities and they decided to confront Mike, Rebel's safety couldn't be guaranteed. And AJ—he shuddered with revulsion thinking about what could happen to her.

"Your uncle," she reminded him, insistent, but not as harsh.

"He had a good reputation as a trainer, but he moved around a lot, followed show circuits—sort of floated. That is, until he met Emily."

He smiled with genuine fondness. "You could see it the night they met each other at a potluck dinner for someone's birthday. They married almost immediately, but Emily didn't feel comfortable traveling. They didn't want to be apart. And then my uncle met Mike Towers."

"In New Mexico? I thought he was a Texan?"

"He's a bastard who moved around making money off everyone he found. His first wife was a Mexican national. She left him a fortune, although there was some funny business to keep it in the stepson's name. Strangely enough, the stepson hasn't been seen or heard from in years."

"So how did he get to New Mexico?"

"Second wife. Married him and made him a partner in her real estate business. She left him after less than a year, but he kept the company in the settlement. There were rumors she was so afraid of him she preferred to just start over somewhere else."

"And you knew this when you found out he'd married Gina? Yet you believed every terrible thing he said about her?"

Damn! Won't she stop already? He shifted in his seat and looked out again at the moving vegetation. They were so near the river, and it was clearly breezier here than it had been in central Laredo.

Abruptly he felt uneasy, almost sure that men would jump out on either side of the truck and open fire. Or a demented woman would run in front of the truck, wailing for her lost children. He could feel his heart accelerate and cursed himself silently. His aunt's desperate sorrow and AJ's grief were soaking into him, making him—

Something large splattered against the windshield.

He jumped. Beside him, AJ couldn't bite back her little "iiig!" of alarm.

They exchanged glances and AJ finally smiled. "Stupid butterfly."

"That's harsh," he protested, turning into the drive up to the house. "But yeah—stupid butterfly."

He parked the truck, but let it idle. "AJ, careful with María. You came back because you didn't feel well, or—"

"That won't work," she said immediately. "Because I'm not going to stay in the house all day. I might swim." She opened her door, but tossed over her shoulder, "And I am going to see Rebel."

He sighed and slid out, ready to call off the dogs if they were loose. Then he followed a few steps behind her as they went in out of the blistering heat.

He still hadn't figured out how she thought she could escape with Rebel. He couldn't let her try, though.

He had one last chance to prove that Mike Towers trafficked in insurance fraud, that he framed innocent people for heinous crimes. And to do it, he needed AJ to take Robbie and go. She'd have to be safely across when he outed her—when he told Mike Towers that Gina's sister had come for her horse.

. . .

María was in the living room dusting and fussing with the embroidered runners covering many of the furnishings when they went in.

AJ knew María held her in great contempt, but she still gave her a fleeting smile.

"Back so soon?" the woman asked, her voice too sweet. "And with not a bag to show for being gone most of the day?"

AJ shrugged. "Nothing suited me." Then she turned up her smile, matching María's false demeanor. "Besides, I wanted to get Mike's opinion on the dress I really want. Wouldn't want to get something too sexy—or not sexy enough."

María glowered and turned away, setting a candle down on a table so hard that it rattled the glass top.

Beside her, Chance grinned and mouthed something— "*Touché*," she thought he said. She acknowledged his praise with a nod, then remembered they had issues to settle. She walked over to the stairs, turning to address both of them.

"I'm lying down for a while. The heat gave me an awful headache. I hate to ask, María, but do you think someone could bring me a pitcher of ice water? I just need to go lie down."

Chance looked puzzled at that, but she didn't care. María hated her and probably wouldn't take the water—she'd send Rosa. And Rosa would walk in that door holding the pitcher in one hand and Robbie in the other.

She smiled all the way up the stairs and down the hall to her room. So Chance thought she couldn't be smooth and sneaky? She'd show him—no, no she wouldn't. She'd talk to him one last time about Rebel, and if he didn't give in and help her, she'd just do what she'd come to do anyway. Robbie would be safely out of the way and—and Chance would be here to face Mike Towers's rage. Alone.

Fear for Chance gripped her. In the short time they'd known each other, he'd become important. Someone looking out for her. Someone at cross-purposes, maybe. But a man she could want. A man whom she could—she bit back the word. She couldn't love him.

"*Señorita* AJ?" Rosa called softly, and AJ went over to open the door, smiling. She was right, and immediately pulled Robbie out of Rosa's arms, hugging and kissing him as she shut the door.

"Sorry to make you bring water—"

"Don't be silly," Rosa said matter-of-factly. "I'm a servant."

"Not mine," AJ muttered. "But I'm glad you came instead of María."

"I think that was the plan, no?" Rosa winked. "Were you really going to lie down?"

AJ kissed Robbie's tummy, hands, and toes and settled him on the carpet. "No, actually," she admitted. She looked at Rosa, wondering what, if anything, she knew of Chance's plans for Robbie. This woman had apparently been Gina's last friend. Piercing pain cut through her and she reached for the baby again, but he gurgled merrily and crawled away, leaving her to focus on Rosa.

"Rosa, has Chance—?"

"Wait," she whispered, and went to peer out the door. "I have seen María listen at doors," she explained.

"We must talk about tomorrow," she acknowledged. "But first—AJ, I want you to know I came to love Gina. I … don't have family now, and she was like a sister."

"Thank you." AJ blinked hard. "I'm glad you had her, and that she had you. Rosa … how bad was it for Gina?"

Rosa sighed and walked over to the window, pulling the curtain aside. She peered out and spoke quietly. "Gina seemed happy when I met her. So pretty, always laughing—so alive."

Then she faced AJ again, her face hardening. "There is no man as evil as Mike Towers. When he had guests, he would show off your sister like—like a Hollywood starlet. Bring her out in beautiful clothes, covered in jewels." She smiled slightly, remembering. "Gina won over many of her husband's friends. But then …

"He always had affairs, but he hid them from her at first. Then—" Rosa shrugged. "He would have women at his home, here or in Laredo. He seemed to encourage the men he invited over to make passes at her, and then he would insult her and accuse of being unfaithful."

"She never let me know anything," AJ whispered, tortured. "Could she have?"

Rosa shook her head. "At first, I know she could have. Even later, I would have done anything she asked to help her. I think she thought she could change him. But once Mike brought Rebel over here—and then Gina found out she was pregnant—I think he threatened her. She never said so, but I think she was afraid of losing everything if she did anything he didn't want her to."

She glanced at her watch. "I cannot stay much longer, and I need to take Robbie." She came across the room and embraced AJ. "Have faith, AJ. Trust me. And trust Chance." She picked Robbie up from where he sat playing with the handles on one of the dresser drawers, and held him up. AJ brushed a kiss on his cheek, fear gripping her at the thought of losing him now that she'd found him.

"Bye, Gordito," she whispered, and he patted her, then gave her a sloppy kiss before yawning and tugging Rosa's hair.

"Dinner," Rosa translated, then repeated, "Have trust."

"I'm trying. I just keep thinking Chance could have done more."

Rosa spun around, but AJ held up a hand. "We can argue later. We don't need María outside the door."

"Hard to believe tomorrow's my last day here," Rosa murmured, and then, when AJ raised an eyebrow, "I won't be able to come back without Robbie."

"I hadn't thought of that," AJ admitted, ashamed that she hadn't. Rosa reached for the doorknob, and AJ remembered the question she'd asked herself so often.

"Rosa, you're college-educated, a U.S. citizen. Why have you stayed with Mike?"

Rosa snorted in disgust. "For the very worst reason in the world," she answered. "No, I have never been his lover, as I'm sure you thought. I am his daughter."

Chapter Seventeen

"What?" AJ breathed, stunned.

Rosa shifted Robbie more comfortably on her hip and brushed at her hair. "Yes. It comes as a shock, no?" She managed a half shrug. "Almost nobody knows. But I cannot talk now. Robbie needs to eat, and I must go down to the kitchen to help María before she looks for me here."

She opened the door and called over her shoulder, "I'll bring you supper in a bit. Be sick."

And she was gone. AJ sat down on the edge of her bed. The words rang in her ears, and she had to swallow past a lump in her throat. Rosa's declaration explained everything. Or nothing. What web of deception had Gina fallen into? What had she walked into herself?

Her phone buzzed, announcing a text message. She glanced at it, then re-read it carefully. *Meet me in the barn at 9.*

Chance. Her head throbbed dully. She was one more nervous shock away from a full-blown, bang-your-head-on-the-wall migraine. The phone buzzed again. *Try to bump into Santos. He'll have the dogs tonight. Tell him you needed air. In case María sees you.*

She slid off her shoes and reclined on the bed, staring at the ceiling. Tomorrow, Chance wanted her to leave Towers's place. She'd get Robbie away. But Rebel—her stomach clenched.

She wouldn't leave Rebel. And Mike was due back the day after tomorrow. Not much time to convince Chance to help her. Then he'd be screwed, too, as far as working for Towers.

But he couldn't refuse. She wouldn't let him.

Someone moving about in the dim room woke her. For a moment, she didn't move at all, letting feelings penetrate her sleep-dulled senses. No unnatural chill; no feeling that Gina's presence inhabited the room with her. AJ propped herself up on an elbow and saw Rosa setting a platter of fruit on a portable table.

" Rosa!" AJ protested, embarrassed. "Since when do you bring my dinner?" The irony stormed back—Mike Towers's daughter? Waiting on her? Not irony, she realized. Injustice.

"Part of the plan, remember?" Rosa answered with her customary good cheer.

"But—"

"Robbie's asleep. I managed to slip him out this afternoon for awhile—introduced him to the joys of a swimming pool. Veeerrry carefully," she assured AJ.

"I hope this is enough. I thought María might be more convinced you didn't feel well if I didn't bring anything heavy."

"Too much food," AJ murmured, surveying the heap of cantaloupe, watermelon, strawberries, and grapes, and a mountain of salad greens in another bowl, with two different bottles of salad dressing.

Rosa pulled the chair from the dresser over. "Thought I'd help you." She grinned.

AJ sat down on the edge of the bed, and hunger stirred. Neither she nor Chance had eaten much of their impromptu brunch. Why couldn't she think of anything—anyone—other than the man who represented a far worse danger than Mike Towers?

"You must be thinking about Chance," Rosa decided, chasing a grape around her plate with a plastic fork, then picking it up with her fingers. "You sighed."

"Did I? I didn't realize. Never mind Chance." She ate a bite of watermelon. "Rosa, can I ask you about—"

"About being *la hija del patron*? The boss's daughter?" She ate a forkful of cantaloupe, then shrugged. "I suppose so. There's not much to know, really."

"Have you always been with him? Why are you working—"

Rosa stood up, pushing aside her unfinished fruit. "No, I did not spend my childhood with him. I confronted him when I was seventeen and taking college classes along with my high school classes."

"Confronted?"

Rosa smiled. "You and I think a lot alike, AJ. Meeting him was … essential. I dressed in my shortest skirt and lowest-cut blouse and showed up at his house in New Mexico, pretending I wanted a job."

AJ raised her eyebrows. "But—how—why?"

Rosa flushed with anger, her answer blunt. "I am the product of rape," she said. "My mother—I am told that I look just like she did as a teenager. She did not have many advantages, and when she was working as kitchen help during one of his parties …"

Her voice trailed off and in spite of the matter-of-fact tone she used, pain and anger tormented her face. "My mother never asked him for anything. She didn't press charges, although he wasn't nearly as strong or well known then. But at least she put his name on the birth certificate or I would not have known."

"When you spoke to him, that first time—"

"He decided he would rape me, too, when I refused his kind offer of fifty dollars."

AJ flinched. Towers had made it clear that he expected sex from her, but he'd never tried to force himself on her. Resentment flared. Did he think he could pick and choose his victims by their apparent circumstance in life? She felt sick. "How did you stop him?"

"I had a knife. And a copy of the birth certificate," Rosa said calmly.

"You've worked here for so long."

Rosa walked back over to the window, looking out as she had earlier, then turned around, facing AJ, her arms crossed tightly over her chest.

"AJ, I planned on killing him when I started. I had this big idea of revenge, gaining vengeance and peace. Then Gina came here, and as I saw her struggle to change him, as I saw her sweetness and determination at the beginning—I don't know. I knew my mother couldn't gain anything from me going to prison for killing another human being. She died three years ago, right around the time I met Gina. I kept planning on leaving, but he pays me well, my college was paid. No one knows. Gina did, and now I have told you—but I have not even told Chance. I am ashamed not that he is my father—I could not help that. I am ashamed that I have stayed here. But I told myself at the right time, I would do something. And then—" Her face lost its darkness. "Then there was Gordito. And I am happy you have come, but sad that soon I will lose him, too."

Tears threatened. "Rosa, if you help take Robbie out of here—"

She shook her head, anticipating. "I cannot come back. But I don't need to. I would never leave Robbie alone here. But I will never come back. Towers doesn't consider me his daughter. He would hate nothing worse than if my existence became public. He knows that I have given a copy of my birth certificate to family members. I never told him who, but the threat of being exposed has kept him in line."

"But if he isn't Robbie's father—" Just saying the words felt like a betrayal. Gina would never have betrayed her husband. Not even a monster like Mike Towers.

"I wish I knew what Mike's game is with Robbie. He has told us all, even during the earliest weeks of Gina's pregnancy, that he was not the father. Gina told me that he was, that she had never been with another man after she met Mike."

"She wouldn't have been," AJ agreed, "but why wouldn't he recognize Robbie?"

Rosa snorted. "He used the pregnancy, and then the baby, to keep Gina from leaving him for months. I don't know who left his name off the birth certificate—him or Gina. But I think it was to have more hold over her, and to deny Robbie anything as he grew older. He would tell Gina in front of María and me that he would never legally divorce her because she would not get a penny of his money."

Oh, Gina! And my pride kept me from even wondering why you didn't write more often, before that last letter. How could I not have known you were hiding something?

Tears seeped out of her eyes and ran down her cheeks. Rosa came over, picking up a napkin from her side of the table and handing it to her.

AJ dabbed her cheeks and stood up. "I guess Towers used Rebel as a weapon, too," she mused. "Before Gina had Robbie to worry about, he probably kept her from contacting us or leaving us because she wouldn't have gone home without Rebel." New tears stung, but she refused to give in to her gut-wrenching sorrow. "And all the while, Chance stood by and did nothing! Nothing!"

"How dare you?" Rosa's voice shook with rage. "Listen to me, AJ. I did not know of Rebel until Chance found out who you were. I liked you before I knew, and I like you now. I loved Gina. But don't you dare blame Chance for any of this!"

"He's the head of security—"

Rosa gripped one of AJ's arms and shook it. "He's a man whose family was destroyed by Mike Towers. Like mine. Like yours. He came here as I did, to avenge his uncle's destruction. He didn't owe any of us anything, but he gave more than was safe. He gave me friendship. He loves Robbie like a son. And he helped Gina when he could, though he believed her to be a cheat and user like his ex-wife."

She let go of AJ's arm. "As much as I like you, AJ, I will tell you that you are a fool if you do not look at Chance Landin and see a real man. A man whom most women would give their hearts to for far less than what he's done for you!"

AJ closed her eyes and nodded. "I won't question him again in front of you, Rosa. He has done a lot. But—"

"Would it help you to know that he could have lost everything the last time he helped Gina? He could have been kicked off Towers's properties. Mike could have had him killed. I still do not know how he convinced Mike that he had no part—"

Dread replaced the sorrow, but she hoped Rosa would tell her. "What? What did he do, Rosa?"

"One of Mike's accountants took an interest in Gina. Not physical. He wanted to help her because he knew she wasn't happy, that she was virtually a prisoner here. He asked Chance not to tell Mike, to clear the way for him to get her out of the place, and to keep Robbie safe until she could get an attorney and come back for him."

Rosa paused, letting her words sink in. "Chance helped Gina get out the night she left. He put the dogs up and changed some of the guards' patrols. He kept Mike busy in his study with a made-up threat. But then Gina died in the crash."

● ● ●

Neither of them bothered trying to stem the tears the memory induced and they exchanged brief hugs. Then Rosa drew away. "I sometimes think he didn't move against Chance because—I'm sorry, AJ, but—"

"He got rid of Gina without paying a penny," AJ finished, flatly. Rosa didn't answer; she didn't need to.

"Who was driving?" AJ whispered, after a minute.

"The police said that she was—that she was driving full out."

"Do you think … " AJ scrubbed her bare arms, trying to get the question out. "Do you think she planned on crashing? Since I heard the news, I—I just knew that she'd taken her own life. That's one reason I wanted Mike to—to pay somehow."

Rosa shook her head slowly. "I don't believe she did. She told me that she was not *La Llorona*, that she would live on the street rather than give up Robbie."

"She had us. She would never have been without what she needed."

"She knew," Rosa said gently. "She blamed herself for the fight you two had, and said she wished she'd listened to you. She was planning on taking Robbie to you and your mother. I have to go." She patted AJ as she started picking up the leftover food. "Trust Chance. He's our best hope."

She reached the door, then turned back, a look of sudden recognition in her face. "AJ, I just remembered. When I was going through Gina's things, I found one of those large mailing envelopes. It had a paper with your address inside it. So I mailed it to the address in Philadelphia I found a few days before Chance told me who you really were. Keep your eyes open, when you get back."

She slipped out of the room and the roller coaster of emotions climbed back in. Gina had tried to reach out. She had lost Gina, but not her sister's love.

She glanced at the clock on the dresser. She'd napped longer than she realized. Time to get ready to meet Chance. To hear him tell his version of Gina's last hours. To thank him for what he had done, and try to ignore what he might not have done. And to make it perfectly clear that she wouldn't leave without Rebel. No matter the risk. Risks be damned—she'd take her nephew and her horse home.

· · ·

Chance walked along the fence of bougainvillea, its rustle no different than on any other summer evening, when only a slight breeze moved the air at all. This evening, though, the creaking and scratching of leaves and branches raised the hair on his forearms and the back of his neck. And that brought AJ to mind—face white, green eyes wide, insisting that she'd heard and felt something otherworldly. Messages from a dead sister, manifesting themselves in touches and moans. Masquerading as a demented wraith from centuries of storytelling. *La Llorona.*

He didn't believe in ghosts. He clucked at the pair of Dobermans accompanying him and cut across the yard toward the stable. AJ wouldn't have come yet, but he'd look at the appointment book again. Go through—what? He'd found nothing in the almost three years he'd worked for Mike Towers. No proof that Mike had paid to have Bone destroy those magnificent animals. The insurance company had whined, but hadn't really investigated thoroughly. Kind of like the way Alydar's wealthy owner had not suffered consequences for his stallion's death. He sighed and reached for his phone.

"Santos," he said, when the man answered, "will you come get the dogs? Look, Ms. AJ asked me if she could visit the horses. She's thinking she might leave soon, with Mike sort of disappearing and all."

The man agreed, and in a minute or two appeared from his post.

The man whistled the dogs over, lifting a hand and immediately retracing his steps, keeping the guard dogs close. Chance nodded in unseen approval. Too bad all of Towers's employees weren't so agreeable.

Chance looked around one more time. Nothing unusual, but the anxiety clenching his gut and increasing his pulse warned him of some unknown menace. He didn't believe in ghosts, but he believed in feelings like the one gripping him.

He'd had the same feeling on the night Gina died. He'd handed her the keys upstairs, on his way down to engage Mike. "He'll be safe," he'd said, and she'd nodded, knowing he meant Robbie.

Gina had gone back to hug Robbie and Rosa one last time. He'd gone downstairs, passing Lenny, the accountant, on his way out the door, pretending that he was merely finished for the day.

And then he cornered Mike in the study, doing everything possible to make a new threat seem real. They were still together when Jaime called his boss, telling him that Gina had been in a car crash.

Chance ducked into the stallion barn and headed toward the office, ignoring Rebel's snort and *Incendido's* usual frenzied behavior. Halfway down the aisle, the suspicion hit him.

What if Gina's death had been murder?

He swallowed hard. Impossible. Mike hadn't had time to act. Police at the scene said that Gina was flying, even though she hadn't driven in—he couldn't remember her leaving the Nuevo Laredo ranch. He'd seldom seen her drive even in Laredo.

He slammed the wall nearest him. The plan had come together so easily, with Lenny and Gina begging him for help. He hadn't really known Lenny, an affable, unmarried man who served as a liaison between Mike's accountants in two countries. Mike had accused Lenny of being "after" Gina, but hadn't kept him away. The accountant had even met with Mike right before the escape attempt.

So convenient. Mike had raised hell but not done any of the things Chance expected. Suddenly, it all seemed clear. Lenny had been another of Mike's unknowing victims. Chance had bought into the lover accusation so easily. Hell, Mike even insisted Robbie was the accountant's kid, after Gina and Lenny died. AJ had berated him for not doing more. Suddenly, he saw his actions through her eyes.

He walked into the office and sank into the chair, swamped by guilt and despair. He couldn't forget the way she'd looked when he told her she couldn't have Rebel back. He'd appeal to her tonight.

Without Rebel, he didn't have a shot at proving Towers wanted the horse killed for insurance reasons.

If he even survived getting Robbie across. He'd have to go into town on some visible and verifiable errand, letting AJ and Rosa spirit the baby across the bridge. He couldn't be in a position where he seemed to have known. Towers might not buy that again, but if he could make it all seem plausible enough, he could go to the police station. He would report a threat on Mike Towers to them. That would create a paper trail. Although what if someone called and told Mike? They all knew him, and if they thought he might reward them for the tip—

He sensed movement and looked up. AJ leaned against the doorjamb.

"You're early," he said.

She shrugged and pushed off the frame, coming into the office She ignored the chairs, propping herself on the corner of the desk and swinging her leg back and forth.

He wished she'd stop.

"Rosa verified what we're doing with Robbie."

"I can't think of a safer way, AJ. We can't wait and risk Mike coming back early. You can't take much with Robbie. Rosa was going to try to fit as much as she could in one bag, and I'll try to put another one in the trunk. But if they check the car at the bridge, I don't want it to look like you're moving him from one country to the other." He paused. "Where's his birth certificate?"

"Hidden. But I won't forget it."

He nodded, but couldn't look away from her leg, still swinging like a rhythmic pendulum. The urge to reach out and capture her ankle, stopping the hypnotic movement, was overwhelming, so he stood up and moved to shut the door she'd left open.

"So, did she fill you in well enough? As long as you get to the border, everything will be fine, so I'm really not worried."

"But … when Mike finds out, you'll have problems?"

He rubbed his face and nodded. "Yes," he admitted slowly "I'm hoping that I can deal with them, though, as long as I'm not here when you leave."

"You're banking on a lot going your way," she pointed out tartly.

"I'm open to other choices. Do you want to fight Mike for custody? Because I'm willing to bet he'd claim he's Robbie's daddy if he had to, to spite you. He'd claim Gina didn't list him because she was cheating on him and wanted to cut him out of the picture."

"If he could prove paternity," AJ retorted, and realized what she'd said when Chance's eyebrows raised.

"Even Rosa doesn't believe Gina cheated," AJ muttered. 'It's just—"

"I know. Look, once you're on the U.S. side, just go to Emily's. Wait there to hear from me. Don't call the ranch."

"How long do we wait?"

"Two or three days." He didn't think AJ got the finality of leaving the ranch. "Because if I don't call you by then, I'm sure I'll make the news. Dead."

Chapter Eighteen

Dead? She hadn't considered how different Chance's position was from hers. As long as Mike didn't come back from Austin early, she didn't foresee any problems other than convincing Chance to give her Rebel back. Putting Robbie in a car and leaving him on the Laredo side was nothing major. No one was here who would stop them. With any luck, if María were somewhere other than the front rooms that looked out over the driveway, they might get away without being missed for hours.

But Chance's job as head of security was to keep the baby from leaving. Towers would know that he hadn't done that.

She closed her eyes briefly. *Please, God. Not this man. Not for Robbie and me.*

Aloud, she tried to press home her need to get Rebel out, too. "I'm only going to have a day or two after I get Rosa and Robbie settled at your aunt's. When Mike comes back, he won't let me near this place. You see why you can't keep Rebel, right, Chance?"

He shook his head. "AJ, be fair. You're getting Robbie. You have to understand about needing to take him out first."

"Of course."

"I'm trying to manufacture an excuse Towers will believe. If I manage, everything will be fine. And if I don't … well, there's just no point borrowing trouble."

Silence fell between them, broken only by the sounds of the horses in their stalls outside.

He finally broke the silence. "So, why did you really bring Goof, AJ?"

"Decoy," she admitted. "And company. Let's go visit Rebel."

She led the way, hugging the horse's chestnut head as he greeted her. "He's almost as big a baby as his brother." She leaned against the gate, laughing when Rebel blew wisps of her hair around. "He's a big ham. You should have seen him with a blanket of flowers on his neck."

"Must have been quite a thrill. How were you getting Goof here, AJ?"

"At first, I thought maybe I'd be lucky and that Rebel would be on the Texas side."

"I'm not sure you could have gotten a strange horse there, either," Chance pointed out. "So how were you going to do it?"

She colored, and turned back to fidget with Rebel's forelock, while he stood there as docilely as a pony. "Ride Goof across the river, sneak him into Rebel's stall, and ride Rebel back across." She glanced at him. "The Goof part's gone, but it's still what I plan to do."

He gaped at her. "You're kidding, right?"

"No!" She looked away. "Okay, we've established I'm not a CIA operative. Not all my plans make sense maybe, but when I met my ex-husband—"

"You hid that pretty well." Chance laughed shortly. "Why should it surprise me? Guess we're all married here—or divorced, anyway."

"Why would I have told you?" AJ demanded. "None of your business. And I certainly couldn't have told Mike."

"Certainly not." He leaned on the gate with her, their shoulders touching in the narrow opening. "And the fiancé you kept mentioning to Mike and me—real? I mean, I know you're not engaged now, but was there someone?"

"Of course not. My ex cured me of thinking men can be faithful, or even useful. I met him when I was a teaching assistant in the college English department. So weird—he's from Laredo. He and a friend used to smuggle horses back and forth across the river. He said it wasn't a bad business, although not as popular as his father told him it was."

"Yeah. I imagine drugs are more profitable and plentiful than horses," he acknowledged. "Rebel might not cross the water. It's low right now, but there's a deep middle channel here."

"I know. I read some of the geological reports. And I see the news. Immigrants are pouring across this year because the water level's so low. The river's broad there, so the flow isn't as strong in a lot of places. And Rebel loves swimming. We built him up again after his injury using hydrotherapy."

"Well thought out," he said, nodding slightly. "But—no."

"No, you don't think it will work, or—"

"No, you can't do it, AJ." He turned, shifting her with him. They stood inches apart and AJ could feel the heat from their bodies searing the air around them.

"AJ, you'll have Robbie. If Mike decides to claim paternity, you might have to fight, but I'm sure, in spite of his money, you'd have legal standing. I mean, he didn't even want Gordito for a year. He kept him hidden away. Rosa would testify to that." He put his hands on her cheeks, stilling her when she would have shaken her head in frustration.

"I will do everything humanly possible to get Rebel back to you somehow. But if I let you take him now, there's no way to dupe Towers. No way to draw Bone in and try to catch him." His hands fell away and he finished, "No way to rescue my uncle. Or help Emily. I can't let Rebel go, AJ. Not only that—once I know you're out of reach, I'm telling Mike who you are. I think he'll want to be sure you won't move against him to recover Rebel. But he's too greedy not to try to turn a profit. He'll call Bone. I really think that he will—if I get out of the mess when Robbie disappears." He moved a step or two away. "AJ, I'm not going to see you after tonight, at least—not until—maybe someday." He forced a stiff smile. "But I'll always hope that someday comes, AJ. You're … something else."

"Tomorrow?"

"I'll be gone around eight thirty. You and Rosa need to leave around nine." He shrugged. "I'll stow a few things in the trunk. But you can't come back, AJ."

"Mike won't be back—"

"Unless something gets screwed up. AJ, listen to me. Don't risk coming back."

She wouldn't lie to him by agreeing. But she had to let him know, just in case something got screwed up, how much he'd come to mean to her. Her protector, her nephew's angel, her sister's reluctant hero. The first man she wished she could take a chance on.

"Goodbye, AJ," he finished and turned away.

She caught his arm before he could leave, pulling him around. "Chance, thank you," she whispered. "For Gina, for Robbie—for everything." She reached up to kiss his cheek, but he turned, his lips meeting hers. Her hands traced over his face, twining in his hair, and he deepened the kiss, his mouth teasing hers open, one arm bracing her shoulders, the other hand sliding down over the curve of her bottom, then cupping her and lifting her against him.

She moaned and ran her teeth gently over his neck, protesting with an inarticulate moan as he moved away.

"Anybody could walk in here," he pointed out.

"The office—"

"Has cameras. We're so close, AJ. If we get out of this—" He leaned in and kissed her again, gently this time, and grinned. "If we get out of this, we'll get a room."

She giggled, in spite of an urge to break into tears. She didn't argue, though she wanted to rip off his clothes, risk everything. But she behaved, in spite of the heat burning through her, in spite of the dampness and ache between her legs.

"Goodbye, AJ," Chance whispered, and placed one last, lingering kiss on her mouth.

"Get up to the house so I can tell Santos to let the dogs loose," he ordered, back to being head of security. "Everything needs to look normal tonight." He headed toward the door and paused. "Ten minutes with Rebel," he told her and she heard a catch in his voice. "That's all I can give you." He looked at her one last time, and his eyes glistened, but he walked away.

She glanced at the stall door. Rebel watched her, head alert, ears pricked.

She ignored him, in spite of his plaintive nicker, and went back to the house, Chance's stricken face haunting her, tears streaming down her own face. Knowing that tomorrow, she would see him one last time.

She knew he thought he could keep Rebel safe, but she knew he couldn't. She could imagine Mike Towers's rage when he found out who she was. She didn't doubt Towers had killed those horses, not Chance's uncle.

But she couldn't sacrifice Rebel. Chance wasn't stupid. He'd have to leave once she'd taken Rebel and gone.

• • •

The traffic crawling across International Bridge One wasn't particularly heavy for a week day morning. She hated that she was driving Gina's car, one that apparently hadn't been used since long before her death. She almost felt Gina's presence in the sedan, with the rosary hanging from the rearview mirror and a unicorn-shaped air freshener dangling from one of the knobs on the panel.

The light leading to the inspection booth went green and the car crept forward. Tiny beads of perspiration dotted her hairline, something she hoped could be blamed on the heat. She stopped and opened the window as the officer peered in, and she and Rosa gave their citizenship papers. The Customs officer leaned in a little to look at Robbie, sleeping soundly in his carrier. A second officer circled the car with one of the drug-sniffing dogs. The dog made a precursory circle and then the officer moved away to the vehicle behind them, and the woman who had asked their citizenship nodded, wished them a good day, and stepped back as they drove away.

AJ wanted to let out a victory shriek, or throw herself across the seat and hug Rosa. She didn't, aware that cameras were on almost every post, and that the odyssey wasn't over yet. As soon as they turned onto Convent Avenue, though, heading away from downtown Laredo, she let out a heartfelt "Yes!" and Rosa crossed herself and closed her eyes in prayer.

"Do we need to stop anywhere?" AJ asked and Rosa shook her head. "I have food, diapers, and clothes enough for today—for a couple of days. We're going to have to let Emily and Robbie get comfortable."

"How well do you know Emily?" AJ pressed, still concerned about Emily's reaction. "She ... she seems to have emotional issues."

"Chance said that she'll be okay. We'll deal with problems when they happen," Rosa answered. They drove in silence, AJ cautious as she drove through the town she had been born in, but had been away from, for so long.

"Can't believe how much this town has grown," she told Rosa. "Very different from the East. Philadelphia's so much bigger, but Mom's stable is down in Florida. She's on the outskirts of Ocala, which is much smaller."

Rosa smiled and nodded, but didn't comment. Then she looked across at AJ and sighed. "It feels weird, knowing I've put revenge aside for good, now."

"Because of me," AJ said. *Something else I didn't think about.*

"No, it was just time," Rosa murmured. "I realized I couldn't kill someone. Killing Mike would have served no purpose."

Robbie stirred in the back, opening his eyes wide when he found himself somewhere new. Rosa laughed and twisted to caress his cheek, and AJ risked a quick glance in the mirror, her heart bursting with happiness. And love. Gina's son—her nephew—was on his way home.

"Do you think we should call him Alex instead of Robbie?" AJ asked, as she pulled up outside Emily's fence. "Because the baby she lost, they'd been going to name him Robert—to call him Beto, but since they're both Roberts—"

Rosa chewed her lip as she climbed out, then shook her head. "No. Robbie would be confused. When the time comes, I'm sure she'll understand that you must take him."

Emily came out just then, her face joyful. "Chance called me earlier," she said, hugging both women and taking Robbie away from Rosa. "He told me you'd stay for a bit. Come on in." She ignored them and went in, carrying Robbie tenderly.

AJ and Rosa exchanged glances, and AJ shrugged. "Let's hope this doesn't get out of hand." She sighed. "Guess we can carry the rest of the stuff."

The next two hours passed in a blur. Watching Robbie explore new surroundings filled AJ with joy. When he spotted Emily's cat Duchess on top of a bookshelf, he managed to pull himself up and take a hesitant step forward before he sat down with a thud.

Too bad Chance isn't here. AJ stood and stretched, then smiled at the other women. "Time to go," she said.

"Okay, dear. When are you coming back?"

"Tomorrow." After that, Mike Towers would be back. And anything not accomplished would be over. Forever.

"What?" Rosa jumped up. "That's not … you're not supposed to leave, AJ."

Emily got up to rescue a porcelain swan from Robbie's grasp. "Bring Chance next time," she encouraged. Robbie suddenly crawled toward the kitchen with a burst of new energy, and Emily hurried after him.

"AJ, you know Chance told you to stay. When María realizes Robbie and I are gone, she'll call Mike. You know that! Mike could be back in three or four hours, or he could hire a plane and be back even faster. You can't go."

"I have to, Rosa."

"Does Chance know you're going back?"

AJ didn't answer. "Look, Rosa, I left a couple of things there I need to pick up. I'll be back."

"You're going after the horse."

"Yes."

"You are being so stupid!" Rosa's voice shook with fury. "Listen to me, AJ Owens. You have a duty to your sister's child. You cannot have everything. And if you get Chance killed—because you could—not to mention yourself, if Mike Towers finds out who you are and that you took Gordito—if you get Chance killed, I will curse you every day of my life!"

"Give Robbie a kiss for me, Rosa," AJ whispered and left.

Chapter Nineteen

Chance leaned against the porch rail, taking in the manicured lawn and missing AJ. And Robbie and Rosa. The morning had seemed to go well. He'd gotten texts from Rosa and his aunt, telling him that everything had gone as planned. AJ was the only one who hadn't reached out.

He sighed and sat down on the porch swing for a moment, leaning his head back against the edge of the seat. Memories of AJ pressed in. He'd told her he didn't believe in ghosts, but she might be the woman who haunted him always. He closed his eyes, remembering the unexpected kiss that went from innocent to soul shattering in a heartbeat. If they never saw each other again—he wished he'd ignored all the danger. Swept her up and carried her into the office or an empty stall. He'd go crazy imagining.

Annoyed, he got back up and headed down to the stable on a whim. If the police verified to Mike that he'd been away from the ranch when Rosa and AJ took Robbie and fled, maybe—maybe—he'd get by with one last deception.

But he couldn't get Rebel out. Mike would never buy that. Maybe he shouldn't tell Mike who AJ was. He'd thought it would speed the process up, if Mike thought he might lose Rebel eventually. From now on, he couldn't leave Rebel unwatched. He wondered how far Santos could be trusted for some extra money. Extra eyes on the horse to keep him safe.

He inspected the railings above Rebel's stall, reassuring himself that the cameras were set. Mike could disable them, but he might not think of that, assuming he could just wipe them clean. And the cameras would play on the monitor but save video to his laptop.

His phone buzzed. He glanced at it, then swore violently and hurled it against the wall across the aisle, watching it fall apart.

With fingers that shook with nerves and rage, he picked up the pieces, reassembling them and breathing a sigh of relief when it worked.

Then he headed toward the house to pick up the pieces after María confronted AJ.

Clearly traffic had been light, because Gina's sedan pulled into its usual parking space before he made it all the way to the house. He slowed, not wanting to appear out of breath or panicked when he intercepted AJ. *Don't let María find her before I do … don't.*

But when he hurried through the kitchen, he could hear María's harsh voice interrogating AJ.

"Look, María, I don't answer to you," AJ replied, a haughty tone in her voice that wouldn't placate the older woman at all. "I told you, Rosa was worried about Robbie. She's with him at a clinic. I would have told Chance, but I couldn't find him."

Good. She'd remembered his alibi and held to it.

"*¿Qué pasa?*" he asked, joining them.

"*Ella se robo el niño,*" María accused. "*Ella y Rosa.*"

"I told you—I told her," AJ said, focusing on Chance. "Rosa took Robbie to his pediatrician in Laredo We didn't steal him, for heaven's sake. The doctor here was out, and Robbie had a fever. Rosa was worried, with Mike gone." She glanced at her watch. "I need to go pick him up when she calls me."

"Did Rosa think it was serious?"

"He just wasn't himself," AJ explained, hoping she wasn't overacting. She shrugged. "Anyway, I don't know much about kids."

"María, doesn't seem to me like there's a problem here," Chance said. "AJ, I spent the morning at the police station. Mike received another threat on his life." He looked at her. "You left the ranch not long after we got it. I'm sure you had nothing to do with it, but—" He shrugged. "Would you step into the study and look at the message someone put in the mailbox for Mike?"

"Of all the—" AJ glared at him, then at María. "I don't know which of you two is stupider. To accuse me—"

He frowned. They couldn't afford drama right now. She must have picked up on his tenseness, because she fell silent and walked to the study wordlessly.

"María, I've told you before. You'd better be careful with AJ. Mike wouldn't like to come home and find you'd pissed her off to the point she left." He stalked away, hoping she'd picked up on the warning. He didn't go immediately to the study, though, walking around, checking window latches, peering into the fireplace as if he thought someone had managed to conceal a weapon there, and hoping he wasn't as bad an actor as AJ seemed to be.

When he finally entered the study and shut the door, she flung herself at him, wrapping her arms around his neck and kissing him on the cheek.

"I am so sorry," she apologized. "You knew I would come, though."

Yeah. Yeah, he had. But she shouldn't have.

His phone buzzed and he pulled it out. "Santos, what … " He read the line of text and stared at it numbly.

"Santos just overheard two of the guards talking. Mike's on his way back to the Nuevo Laredo airport in a private plane."

"What?" AJ gasped.

The door opened without warning and AJ jumped. Chance looked across the room at María, who stood there gloating.

"You and Rosa should have been careful last night," she said contemptuously. "No wonder you're trash. That's all your sister was, Joanie. *Don* Mike says he doesn't know how he missed it."

"Where are Rebel's papers, AJ?" Chance hissed.

"At the trailer, in a metal box. Mom has copies—"

He didn't listen to her, just glanced at the monitor on the desk. "Shit!" he cursed. "AJ, Mike just turned in. Get down to the stable, put a bridle on Rebel, and have him ready to run."

She hesitated. "You?"

"I'm right behind you. Go!"

•••

AJ's heart slammed against the wall of her chest. Any minute she expected to be attacked by the guard dogs or cut down by gunshots. She could hear Chance running behind her, and knew he was protecting her. Still. She burst through the stable, grabbed Rebel's bridle, and tried to put it on with shaking fingers.

The stallion fought the bit as usual and flung his head back, rolled his eyes. "Come on, boy," she whispered, and got the bit in and the headstall over his ears. She led him out and Chance practically flung her up, then vaulted up himself.

"Go!" he shouted in her ear, balancing as the stallion danced and sidestepped under the unexpected weight of a second rider. She squeezed Rebel and he spurted out of the barn and thundered down the path that headed toward the riverbank.

"Aim for the trees so they can't follow us in the car," Chance shouted, just as the sharp report of a rifle shot split the air. Rebel shied slightly and AJ slipped crazily, Chance almost falling, too.

Panicked by the shot, Rebel plunged into the trees, throwing his head up and slowing when branches hit him in the face, then thundering forward when AJ shouted, pushing him on.

In the distance, the sound of a helicopter starting up made them both swear and yell Rebel's name. Another shot sounded and AJ risked a glance behind. She'd expected Jaime or the other guards, but a maniacal Mike Towers raced after them on a big pinto, raising his rifle to take another shot.

"Go, Rebel!" she shrieked.

"The helicopter's registered in the States," Chance shouted over the din. "Whoever's in it won't stop at the river."

Rebel plunged on through the tall cane and undergrowth, panicked and unmanageable. The foliage ended on a clear strip of riverbank, and he lunged into the water without hesitation, flinging his head but not veering sharply enough.

Another shot rang out and terror gripped AJ. He'd hit Chance or Rebel if he kept shooting.

Incredibly, over the rotors growing closer and the echo of the gunshot, she heard it—the distinctive, high-pitched wail. She glanced back again as Mike's horse hit the water. The pinto threw its head up and plunged sideways. Mike had thrown on a saddle. He slipped and his rifle fell away, but he stayed upright. Cursing and slashing the horse with the reins, he drew a pistol from his waistband. The helicopter came over the trees.

"Damn! Bone's in the chopper and he can shoot," Chance muttered. "Come on, Rebel," he pleaded, although AJ knew Rebel couldn't move any faster. She felt it when he started swimming, slowing to almost a stop, then found his footing as they neared the other side and broke into a gallop again, his breathing unnaturally loud.

The wail behind them rose, and as Rebel clambered out on the far bank, Jaime fired at them, missing. The bullet kicked up mud near Rebel's foot.

AJ cast a worried glance back. The pinto stumbled and balked, again nearly throwing Mike.

Suddenly Mike seemed to convulse, twisting in the saddle and flailing at the air.

New rotors sounded, moving toward the river from the south, and a Border Patrol helicopter appeared.

"Thank God," Chance whispered in her ear, as Towers's chopper turned and headed back.

AJ noticed it, turning, but couldn't tear her eyes from where the pinto took a huge leap forward. As if bound by an invisible rope, Towers toppled backward into the river. He struggled briefly, then disappeared. The wail rose, becoming almost a piercing sound, then faded, and the vegetation along the riverbank went still.

Shivers shook AJ. *Gina*? *La Llorona*? She didn't know. But she wept for them both.

Off in the distance, sirens sounded, but closer to home, three men on horseback rode out of the bushes.

For a moment, terror clawed at AJ. Rebel was spent. The horses were sturdy, clearly not able to take on a Thoroughbred on any other day. But now, they'd stay with him easily if he tried to run again. The men had guns. Then the green uniforms registered.

One of the men nodded at them.

"U.S. Border Patrol," he said needlessly. "FBI Agent Jaime Bustos told us you needed assistance."

Chapter Twenty

"This is just the strangest thing," Ed marveled, looking from Rebel, in his brother's stall, to Goof, wandering loose around the shed under AJ's watchful eye. "They look like twins." He squinted at the two horses. "Now which one was on the news again?"

She smiled and pointed to Rebel, and laughed when Goof wandered up and butted Ed so hard he almost knocked him down.

"You took care of the jealous one," she told him. She re-fastened Goof's lead.

"Thanks again, Ed. If you don't mind, I'll stay in the trailer. My friend's coming for the horses tomorrow."

"It's been a real nice job. Thanks," Ed said, and they shook hands.

She walked back to the trailer. A clean cloth covered the table and she'd put clean linens on the bed. Hard to believe that the chaos from their escape hadn't died down.

Proving ownership of Rebel hadn't been difficult and he'd been cleared to go home to Florida.

AJ and her mother had temporary custody of Robbie, with adoption papers to follow.

But she and Rosa had almost come to blows over Mike Towers's money. Neither of them wanted it.

"His money is filthy!" Rosa protested, when Chance and she insisted that Rosa lay claim to the Towers's fortune. "My mother is gone, and—and what would I do with money?"

While she eventually agreed that she might be able to use it to undo some of the damage Towers had done, she and Chance turned the tables on AJ, insisting that she should consider Robbie's future and find out if he was Mike's son or not.

AJ sighed. She hadn't agreed yet. But Rosa had thrown in the most persuasive argument yet.

"AJ, you got it all back, except Gina," Rosa pointed out. "Chance lost everything. His job, and his chance to help his uncle and aunt. We might be able to help him with legal fees—or something—down the road."

"Or something?" AJ prodded and Rosa laughed.

"Hire him," she suggested. "He loves horses and he loves Robbie. Why not make an offer?"

Maybe because she hadn't seen him in a week.

While lawyers worked on her problems, he'd been called in by one agency after another to make statements about Towers, his death, his holdings—one complication after another.

A shiver shook her, not from anything unnatural now, but because she worried. Those who had been loyal to Mike, or who thought Chance might know something that could hurt them, might come after him, even here.

She swallowed hard. Rosa and Robbie had flown to Ocala, leaving Emily distraught, but no worse than before. Rebel and Goof would head home in the morning. Now, the only loose thread was Chance.

• • •

Chance finally knocked on the door, then came in, looking thin and pale, still too big for the small confines of the trailer.

She thought seeing him again would be easy, but she couldn't speak past the lump in her throat.

He stared at her silently, too, then caught her in his arms, hugging her so close that she could feel his heart thudding against her chest.

She trembled against him and waited for him to kiss her, but he moved away slightly and brushed at her sweat-dampened hair with a gentle hand.

"The tablecloth's a nice touch," he said, weariness in his voice. "But you probably need a good air conditioner more."

Really? After all we went through? Panic needled her.

"You look tired," she told him, not wanting to make small talk, but not sure how to move forward.

"Yeah, I am." He managed a smile. "When do you leave, AJ?"

She stared at him. "Briana picks up the horses tomorrow. Robbie and Rosa should be home in an hour or two. I—" She stopped. "It's hard to find words, Chance. Everything that happened—what didn't happen. Remember the night before it all crashed down?"

She didn't want him to stand there and watch her with those defeated brown eyes. She closed the distance between them and clasped his face. "I thought … I thought there'd be something for us after all the dust cleared."

He removed her hands gently, pressing a kiss into each palm.

"AJ, the dust hasn't cleared yet. Not for me. I'm not dragging you through this. An FBI agent spoke to me yesterday. They were looking at Mike Towers for murder and for theft—not for insurance fraud." He traced a finger from her chin down her neck and she shivered.

"None of that matters," she insisted. "Chance, why would you do all you did—just to walk away?"

"I keep thinking about something you said, AJ." His voice was hoarse and full of pain. "You were right. I didn't do enough for Gina." He shook his head when she started to argue. "I never even thought that he lied about Gina cheating. All I could think of was how I felt when I found Linda with someone else. I knew there were rumors that he'd killed his first wife and his stepson, yet I never thought Gina didn't just flip the car because she was speeding."

"Gina would say you'd done everything for her that you could," AJ protested. "She wasn't demanding. And you protected the one thing that mattered the most to her—Robbie."

She pressed close again, this time wrapping her arms around his waist and clinging. She took a shuddering breath and leaned her head into his chest. "I want a chance—we owe each other that."

He tilted her face up and looked down at her. "We don't owe each other anything. But I guess if you think you want a 'chance'—" Something of the old sparkle touched his eyes. His lips touched hers and he gathered her close.

"You don't owe me anything," she agreed, loosening her grip to look up at him. "But if nothing else, I owe you big time."

She knew the minute she said it he'd take it wrong. He froze, looking down at her almost in disbelief. Then he stepped away. "Do you know what Linda told me the last time we had sex?" he asked tonelessly. "She told me she'd owed me."

"I didn't mean—"

"No. But I need to see if I can salvage anything, AJ. Right now I can't afford to owe anything. And I don't want anyone staying in my life to pay some debt they don't owe." He fished in his pocket and withdrew a small, beaded bundle, then folded it gently in her palm and closed her fist. Gina's rosary. Then he leaned forward and brushed her lips with a kiss so slight she sensed it more than felt it. He turned at the door. "Maybe. If the dust ever does settle," he said in a voice just slightly louder than a whisper. And left her alone in the trailer.

• • •

Ocala, Florida

Going through the small package of Gina's belongings was torture, but she was glad that it had been forwarded from Philadelphia. AJ sat on the floor, propped against the bed she'd slept in before she left home, and pulled out items one by one. A journal with a few entries, all bright optimism that ended abruptly with a scribbled note.

"AJ, I miss you. Don't forget your baby sister."

Robbie's ultrasounds. Tears streamed down AJ's cheeks. She wished Gina had been there, showing her, making her look time after time.

She put them away carefully. There were only two or three items left in the manila envelope, so she turned it upside down and shook. A couple of scraps fell out, along with a snapshot, which landed upside down.

AJ turned it over and clapped her hand over her mouth as she gagged. Bile rose in her throat and she battled it. When she could, she lifted the print again, breathing deeply. A blood bay horse lay in a twisted, bloodied heap on a stall floor. With fingers that shook, AJ opened one of the scraps of paper, but it was blank. She reached for the other.

"Bone. He told me Bone could do the same thing to Rebel that he did to Bold Attempt. I'm so sorry, AJ."

The tears started again. First for Gina, haunted by her mistakes and fears, willing to suffer eternally to protect others—first her horse, then her own son. But as the significance of the picture pierced her, she wept for Chance, for the family he thought he'd failed, and the future he didn't know he deserved.

Chapter Twenty-One

Rosa threw a pillow at AJ, who batted it away impatiently. "Now what?" she demanded.

"You don't remember, do you? Remember when I warned you I'd hate you forever if you killed Chance? How do you know you're not killing him? You act like he never existed."

AJ frowned. "Leave it alone. He's the one who opted out, Rosa. You know I wanted him to stay."

"I guess I do," she said, after a minute. "I'm taking my baby brother to the petting zoo at the mall and feeding him ice cream until he pukes." She shot an angelic smile at AJ. "Then I'm bringing him home, because I'm not the parent."

"Have fun," AJ said absently, looking back at the pedigree she'd been studying. Her mom couldn't decide what bookings to accept for Rebel, or even if she wanted to try to bring him back for one more season on the track. Rebel and Robbie—good medicine for her mother. And for her, she acknowledged, smiling, and tossing the pedigree aside.

She'd headed for the stairs to shower and change when the doorbell rang. "Surprised they didn't wait five minutes and expect me to come out naked," she muttered, and pulled the door open.

Chance stood there, a bouquet of flowers in one hand and a newspaper in the other. He handed the paper to her first. An Arizona newspaper, showing a picture of a beaming middle-aged man hugging him. *"Trainer Cleared of Insurance Fraud."*

"Chance! That's wonderful!"

"These are for you, from Robert and Emily," he said, holding out the bouquet. She took it and moved aside.

"Come in, Chance."

He did, looking around. "Robbie?"

"Eating ice cream and puking, if Rosa has her way."

He smiled briefly, but grew serious again, watching her as she pulled a glass from a cabinet and set the bouquet in it.

"AJ … remember when you said you owed me?"

"Yes." She stiffened. "Why?"

"Well, if you owed me for Robbie and Rebel, I guess I owe you for Robert and Emily—so we're even."

"Chance—"

"The dust has finally settled," he added. "If it still matters."

She took a deep breath and reached out to trace his lips with a finger. He shivered.

"It still matters," she whispered. "It always will."

More from This Author
(From *His Temporary Wife* by Leslie P. García)

Esmeralda Salinas leaned forward over the wheel of the rented pickup and peered at the road ahead. It disappeared between two sheer cuts, dotted on both sides with scrub cedar and large rocks that looked likely to fall onto the road at any minute.

In spite of the cold air blasting out of the air conditioning vents, blowing loose tendrils of hair around her forehead, beads of sweat trickled down her cheeks.

"And I thought I could drive anywhere!" she muttered and glanced momentarily into the rearview mirror, checking the horse trailer behind her, carrying all she had of her past. She couldn't see her Appaloosa mare, Domatrix, of course, but the late-model trailer seemed to be riding well and taking the curves.

She glanced at her dash and gulped air. Three, maybe four minutes more of the treacherous Hill Country back road and she'd come out on the state blacktop taking her into tiny Truth, Texas. Taking her home—if you could call a town you'd never been in, home.

Her tension eased when she turned gently onto the asphalt. She could have gone a longer way around and spared herself a lot of stress and worry for the mare's safety, but she had been in the Hill Country years ago and hadn't thought the "hills" were particularly frightening. A boyfriend had been driving then, and she couldn't say she remembered the narrow roads, the twists or much of anything.

With relief she reached out and turned on the radio, immediately picking up a country station out of San Antonio. The station reached most of central Texas and had been her favorite back in Rose Creek.

She knew the song immediately and joined in, reveling in the music. A car on the other side of the two-lane road passed and the driver waved. She waved back, something she'd done routinely since she got off the interstate. Seemed all the drivers were friendly, even more than they'd been in Rose Creek. Maybe she could truly find a home here.

The next song blasted out, a song that had been huge for the singer Cody Benton. "Afraid for You" had rocketed up the charts to number one, and Cody was tagged as country music's next goddess. But she'd died in a drug-induced stupor, right here in Truth. Esme slowed as she coasted over a hill and passed the sign welcoming her to town. Goose bumps peppered her arms as she noticed the large billboard "In Memory of Cody Benton," and her anger pricked. She didn't remember Cody being born here or living here for much of her short life. Couldn't the town find a more tasteful salute to the woman than claiming her memory?

Still, Cody had brought Esme here in a way, so maybe she shouldn't be so judgmental. She bit her lip. She'd planned on leaving Rose Creek for some time, planned on going somewhere bigger, with women who didn't know and fear her, and men who didn't look at her with way too much interest. She'd made some poor personal choices over the years and just knew it was time to go. She'd been surprised and touched that her formal rival, Luz Wilkinson—Luz Estes now, she reminded herself, glad that it didn't hurt at all—held a small party the night before she left. Even the town veterinarian came, a clear sign of forgiveness for her trying to snag the doctor's husband for her own.

She'd chosen to come here to Truth because she'd heard her aunt was here now, and because of a late-night interview she'd seen with Cody Benton shortly before the singer's death. Cody had been vamping with the host, who'd asked her why she was spending so much time in a "one-horse town."

Cody had laughed and answered that she owned two horses herself, so that problem was solved. And then she'd winked, "If your life's been a lie, maybe you should try a little truth."

Whether or not the line had been rehearsed, Esmeralda couldn't forget it. And when she decided for sure to leave Rose Creek, she headed northwest without a moment of indecision.

Esmeralda saw her destination ahead on the right and slowed almost subconsciously. So here she was, about to drop in on the aunt she hardly knew. Tina Cervantes, her mother's sister, had visited three or four times over twenty-odd years. Once she'd gone to college, Esmeralda hadn't seen her aunt again. She could count on both hands the times they'd spoken on the phone, too. Tina had called to wish her a happy birthday about four months ago, not really near her birthday. Esmeralda didn't tell her she was two months late; she just relished the brief contact with the woman she always thought would have been a better mother than her own had been.

And now here she was, jobless and homeless, hoping to find the roots she'd struggled to cut when she'd left home back in Laredo, fleeing from cold parents and an abusive brother, heading up the I-35 corridor until she settled in Rose Creek. Gregarious and independent, Tina always insisted that Esmeralda should visit. Once, long ago, she'd offered her house, "any time, just come on over." Tina was living in Chicago then, with a man she'd never mentioned before, and Esmeralda would never have considered going. Besides, she'd been perfectly happy in Rose Creek with its proximity to San Antonio, and its easy driving distance to Laredo for those infrequent visits to her parents.

She turned carefully onto the side street running along the weathered-wood look exterior of Tía's. The neon sign outside the club was unlit, but pictured a smiling woman surrounded by an explosion of stars.

Somehow the sign sent confidence surging through her. If Tina billed herself as the town's "aunt," or *tía*, then surely she'd be delighted to have her only real niece turn up out of the blue. Right?

Apparently the business catered to an evening crowd; only two cars were in the parking lot and their proximity to the side door suggested employees, not clients. Esmeralda parked carefully, taking up a lot of space, but being sure delivery trucks or anyone cutting through the large parking lot could maneuver around the trailer. She disliked leaving the mare unattended, but couldn't see driving out to the farm where she'd found a stall for rent until she'd spoken to her aunt.

When she opened the side window, Domatrix immediately stuck her velvety nose in the opening and nickered plaintively.

"Five minutes," Esme promised. "I'll get you out of here before you know it!" Gently pushing the mare's nose back in, she fastened the panel, drew a deep breath, and headed off to find her aunt.

The front door was locked. She should have just tried the back. Esme glanced around. Across the street, a restaurant had customers going in and coming out. Probably the social hub of the town, she decided. The three—three!—bars in Truth undoubtedly catered to the cowboy and tourist crowd that wouldn't be in town until nightfall. Next to the restaurant, a neat, cheeky little salon sported a sign claiming to offer "Truth In Beauty." She smiled and retraced her steps, seeing a large pickup, dark and gleaming, slide into a nearby space.

The back door opened, letting her into a brightly lit food-preparation area. She could smell oregano-spiced *menudo* simmering on a stove and hear the sound of someone humming from somewhere unseen.

"Hello? Tina? Anyone home?" Esmeralda called, reluctant to go any deeper into this unknown place and startle someone, or set off an alarm. She moved a step or two farther along the island,

and stopped short, her attention snared by the mirrored back of the door separating—she supposed—the club area from the kitchen. She brushed at the strands of hair that had come loose during the drive—light auburn hair made darker by the dampness from heat and drive-induced stress. Her breath caught suddenly in her throat as a figure loomed behind her, light glinting off almost-black hair, brown eyes spearing her own in the mirror—a formidable, unexpected stranger.

But surely this person wouldn't have just walked in if he didn't have that right. Apprehension dissipated with the logic, and she turned and held out a hand, hoping it wasn't as damp as her hair.

"Hello. I'm Esmeralda Salinas, Tina's niece." His brows went up slightly, as if her introduction surprised him. Did he know her aunt, then? He didn't look like a delivery man, in his Western shirt, creased pants, and polished boots.

Her parents had called Tina some awful names, in Spanish and English. The kindest thing Esme could remember hearing from her mother was that Tina "liked men." Could this man be her partner? The names, and the possibility of a man or men in her aunt's life, didn't bother her. Lord knew she'd been pegged, usually by other women, as everything from a tramp to a whore. None of the labels were true, but she never disclaimed them—gossips wouldn't change their minds and she didn't care. But her aunt might not appreciate her deciding to just drop by and say hello, taking her up on that long-standing invitation to come any time.

Esme ignored the misgivings. If her aunt didn't have room or time for her, she'd hang around a day or two and move on. She had a degree, a few dollars in the bank, and absolute confidence in her own abilities.

The man still hadn't answered. She arched her own brow. "And you are?" she prompted, with a tinge of sarcasm.

His head moved back slightly, almost as if he weren't used to being challenged. Then he smiled and took her hand. "Rafael Benton."

Her hand tingled under the firm pressure of his, but she ignored it. She'd come to Truth to find herself again, not a man. She'd committed a professional blunder back in Rose Creek, toying with a six-year-old's emotions because she wanted the little girl's father. One could argue that she hadn't done any real harm, but she expected more from herself. Always.

He released her hand and took a step back, but she could swear he was looking at her left hand.

Did he wonder if she was married? Was he thinking about striking up a conversation? Finding a way to ask her out? He'd better not be involved with her aunt, then. She'd been burned more than once thinking a man was free. Or giving herself free rein to pursue men who weren't available, figuring it didn't matter to her if their own women couldn't keep them from straying. Never again, she vowed.

He didn't toss her compliments or suggestive lines, though, just peered past her at the door. "You caught me by surprise. Tía never mentioned having a niece." He seemed to think that would hurt her feelings, judging from momentary awkwardness in his quick glance her way. "Not that we've spoken often."

The humming stopped and Esmeralda heard something fall, followed by a brief curse in Spanish. Then a woman emerged, her apron spattered, but her thin face changing from annoyed to pleased as she greeted Rafael.

"Rafa! How are you?" Then dark eyes turned her way and Esmeralda sensed immediate suspicion.

"Yes? May I help you?" she demanded, wiping her hands on the sides of her apron.

"I'm Esmeralda—Esme Salinas. Tina's niece."

"Her niece—oh." At least this woman, who clearly worked for her aunt, didn't seem surprised that Tina had a niece. Startled, maybe, but not surprised. She walked over to offer her hand to Esmeralda, giving her a polite nod. "I'm Angelica Morales, but your aunt calls me Angel." A slight smile lightened her expression. "Tía says a place like this in a town like Truth needs every angel it can get."

"She isn't wrong about that," Rafael Benton muttered and both women shot him a glance. He shrugged and added, "You should know, the place I live is called Witches Haven by the locals."

"Rafa," Angel scolded, her face troubled. "Why would you even repeat such gossip? Hasn't there been enough trouble in this town without helping it along?"

His lips tightened and his chin tilted, making him look angry and a little intimidating. "The trouble isn't with a house on a hill, Angel. We both know that witches had nothing to do with this town's personal slide into hell."

The bitterness and darkness of his words bothered Esmeralda more than they should. "Well, it was nice to meet both of you," she said robotically. "I'll come see Tina later. Do you think she will be in later, Ms. Morales?"

"Tía comes in every day. Mostly." She glanced at a decorative clock on the wall. "About an hour, I imagine. She always comes in to check before we open at four. You can wait—"

"No, thank you. I have a horse with me, and I need to get her unloaded. I'll drop by in a while." She nodded briefly and left.

She had her hand on the doorknob when she heard Rafael's voice, low and fierce, as he whispered to Angel, "I'll kill her.

For more from Leslie P. García, check out:

Unattainable

Praise for *Unattainable:*

"Kudos, Leslie P. Garcia, on writing an excellent and emotional debut. I would recommend this book to everyone who loves a strong heroine who will keep you cheering for her throughout the entire book."—Harlequin Junkie

Wildflower Redemption

Praise for Wildflower Redemption:

"I honestly cried while reading some scenes in this story. Both Luz and Aaron as well as Chloe have suffered enough for a lifetime and deserve happiness, but until they both learn to trust they will not be able to get past mistakes, misunderstandings, and manipulations . . . If you want a sweet, heart-breaking and second chances love story, don't miss *Wildflower Redemption*."—Harlequin Junkies

"Ms. Garcia takes readers through some highs and lows with this dramatic romance."—Julie Caicco, *InD'Tale Magazine*

In the mood for more Crimson Romance?
Check out *On His Watch* by Susanne Matthews at
CrimsonRomance.com.